MW01165985

You're reading a writer who loves literary fiction. If you enjoy reading about people in overseas settings, consider signing up for my newsletter. In addition to updates, you'll also receive a free copy of the award-winning Love Comes Later about an unusual love triangle. I got the idea for the story from living in Doha, Qatar, a small country on the tip of the Arabian Peninsula.

http://mohadoha.com/newsletter/

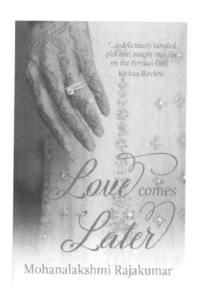

"...a deliciously tangled plot and insight into life on the Persian Gulf."
Kirkus Review

Love comes *Later*

Mohanalakshmi Rajakumar

About the Author

Mohanalakshmi Rajakumar is a South Asian American who has lived in Qatar since 2005. Moving to the Arabian Desert was fortuitous in many ways since this is where she met her husband, had two sons, and became a writer. After she joined the e-book revolution, Mohana dreams in plotlines. Learn more about her work on her website at www.mohadoha.com or follow her latest on Twitter: @moha_doha.

Also by Mohanalakshmi Rajakumar
Fiction
The Opposite of Hate
An Unlikely Goddess
The Dohmestics (please enjoy the free excerpt included at the end of this book)
Love Comes Later
Saving Peace
Coloured and Other Stories

Nonfiction
From Dunes to Dior
So You Want to Sell a Million Copies
Mommy but Still Me

Receive a free copy of the short story collection, *Coloured and Other Stories*, by signing up for her newsletter: http://www.mohadoha.com/newsletter.

At the end of this novel you will find a free preview of the award winning contemporary romance, *Love Comes Later*, which is also set in the Arabian Gulf.

Pearls of the Past

Mohanalakshmi Rajakumar

Pearls of the Past
Copyright © **2017 Mohanalakshmi Rajakumar**

This is a work of fiction. Any similarity between the characters and situations within its pages and places or persons, living or dead, is unintentional and co-incidental.

Family Tree

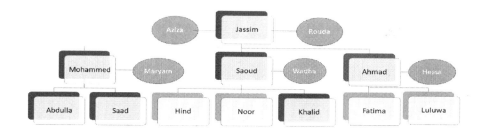

Prologue

Khaldoon, trapped in the body of a cat, shied away from the salt water spray kicked up by the humans' machinery. His feline snarl was far less impressive than the dagger-like teeth he revealed when in his true form, a jinni of fire who would not be cowed by humans or their devices. This feeble display, shaking his head once, then twice, was all he could manage to show his annoyance at the interruption to his feasting. Despite his best efforts, the pinging sound in his head would not be shaken loose. A wayward insect had maybe mistaken his flesh-pink ear's upward tilt for a flower. The mosquito, or fly, or whatever it was, burrowed further into his ear. The jinni cursed his current form. Four decades embodied as a cat in the damp mildew of an Indian port felt more like a punishment than a blessing. For a jinni created from fire to hang around water was torture. But he had his debt to pay. And even the jinn were bound by the laws of honor. The small ping grew to a thunderous roar. He pawed his left ear, then his right, on the side where a round, perspiring face shone in the overhead light spilling from the tower crane.

"Pull them in!" The dock supervisor's jaw clenched and unclenched as the gears creaked into motion. Clad all in black, his body melded with the darkness, his head like a floating exclamation mark as his agitation took him dancing back and forth across the dock in an awkward jig. His lackeys, wearing black thigh-high waders, rushed to the dock's edge to secure the moorings for the exploration ship. Five crewmembers on the boat, clad in matching shorts and t-shirts, scurried like ants to berth the ship. Only one person remained seated, on the edge of a metal bench, catching her breath, a slim-hipped diver in a wetsuit.

"Find anything today?" the supervisor asked in a sing-song voice, fingers pressing together.

"Nothing," the diver muttered, pulling off her mask. She rubbed at red-veined brown eyes, full lips twisting in a grimace. "There's nothing to find. That boat is long gone."

"The thermal scans show something is there," the man in black insisted. "Try again."

"I've hit my maximum hours," she said, pulling her feet out of her flippers. She rolled her head once, then twice, before standing to stretch. "Wait for the next shift."

The humans on the dock carried on, oblivious to the jinni's growing agony. They scuttled around, tapping handheld electronic devices and grunting to each other in the Indian dialect that was now as familiar to him as the language of his own kind. He gave a yowl when the next ping in his ear came so strongly that it reverberated through his skull. Spots radiated before his eyes. Nothing in this earthly world could cause him that much pain.

"Shut that cat up," the supervisor shouted in Hindi.

The jinni swished his cat's tail, his attention shifting to the approach of thick-soled boots. He leapt to one side with the grace of his adopted species. A boot missed its target. The man flailed to regain his balance.

"Leave that poor cat alone," the diver called out sharply.

"Get rid of it," the supervisor said, steadying himself on a stack of oblong boxes. "Mangy cat; it's been hanging around here for years."

"This is its home," the diver said, hands on her hips.

"What? Oh, forget about the cat." The supervisor approached her slowly, holding out his hands.

The jinni slunk into the shadows cast by the stacked boxes. The diver was right. He had made this his home so he could watch over moments like this. The ping in his ear told him Benita was still down there. Trapped beneath the murky depths, she waited on the boat the humans were so desperate to find. Little did any of them know that Khaldoon's constant fiery heat, central to his nature as a fire jinni, clouded the thermal signatures on their sensitive instruments.

"There's something down there now," the supervisor said. He tapped his device, turning the glowing surface toward her. "See? See?"

"Learn how to dive," the diver retorted, "and find it yourself. Because this has been two weeks of solid searching in incredibly rough open water. At least half your guys are sick each trip. Trust me, there's nothing down there but trash and polluted fish." She hoisted herself out of the boat and onto the dock, flip-flops slapping on the pavement. Her towel-enclosed form struck the formerly industrious ants motionless. They cast their eyes downward. A few of them elbowed each other like teenagers. As her figure receded, the pinging faded and stopped.

The jinni gave a sigh of relief. So Benita thought she could reveal herself—and the resting place of Al Muhanna—to the diver through the rough, turbulent waves. He padded his way back to his unfinished meal. She didn't know that he was here, his constant presence thwarting her efforts to be found. He gnawed the flesh from the bones. Another diver sent home. And so the secret remained safe. This was why he remained on this reeking, moldy platform, decade after decade. To secure the vessel. A service rendered in exchange for the human saving his life. As long as Benita existed, the jinni's fate was tied to hers. With each decade, his hope of ever finding freedom from this animal form waned. The spirit world knew what would happen if he abandoned his post. Carnage and destruction in the place he knew as Bombay. That much, no one would mind greatly. They were content to let the humans live their ephemeral lives according to their nonsensical ways. But a jinni without honor? He squeezed into a discarded crate, resting his head on his paws. There would be no place to roam, on this earth or in the parallel world, for such a creature. He closed his eyes, craving the blissful oblivion of sleep, his only respite from this tiresome earthly form.

Chapter One

Not many men would knock on the door of an apartment they owned, but then Abdulla's situation was far from typical. "Oh." He stepped back as a woman led a large white poodle by the leash. An apartment tower didn't seem like the ideal place for a pet. *Expats loved dogs, like their children* he reminded himself of the crowded London parks. The expat tenants in this tower changed at such a pace he couldn't keep track of who lived where. His reflection in the burnished elevator door showed him what she saw, an unsmiling local man in traditional dress, a head taller. "Have a good day." She gave a quick nod, avoided meeting his gaze and rushed into the elevator, keeping the dog tight against her leg.

The door to his unit was ajar, the bolt was pulled back, leaving the door unlocked. "I'm coming in," he said from force of habit. Men always announced themselves. "This isn't safe," he chided, releasing the bolt and shutting the door firmly behind him.

"Oh, I was waiting for the water guy. Such a pain to hop up every time someone wants to come in." His fiancée waved from a bar stool on the other side of the kitchen, wide brown eyes popping up above the laptop screen. With her manicured eyebrows, yards of dark hair, and caramel skin, she could have passed for a local, rather than the Indian woman his family grappled to accept. In a ribbed, grey tank top over black sweatpants, she was the antithesis of the well-heeled women sipping their coffees in the cafés below. "Besides, safest country in the world." Newspapers, pens and pages of notes littered the countertop like all of his brother's homework assignments gathered together in an avalanche. "If you don't count the traffic accidents, that is."

"People should." The somber note in his voice seized her full attention.

"Oh God, I'm sorry." Sangita clasped her palms over the moon shaped face he loved. "That's what happens when you spend hours staring at the screen. You forget how to talk to people."

He crossed the marble hallway and pressed a kiss to her forehead. "She's been gone for years now, *Allah yerhamha*." The death of his first wife, in a fatal collision, had unmoored him from the conventional life his family had planned for him. "Got your million followers and bestselling book deal?"

Sangita leaned up, her lips like the wings of a butterfly against his cheek. Proximity to her was heady, like the feeling people got on drugs, an influence he wasn't sure he could control. Or wanted to. His phone beeped—a reminder of his first appointment. James had arrived and was ready for meetings. No time for the luxury of distractions. Abdulla retreated to the kitchen for some water.

"Fifty thousand followers on Twitter, thank you very much." She swiveled the screen to show him.

He gave a low whistle. "If I were this fridge, I'd be mad at you." Inside sat a pack of soda, two KitKat bars, and otherwise empty white shelves. "You're not in college anymore."

Sangita shrugged. "Last time I bought bananas they went black before I could even eat one. That's what comes of no preservatives in your food. Waste."

He shut the fridge and leaned against the counter. "You like chemicals with your fruit. That's what you're saying?"

She rolled her eyes at him, pretending to shoot him with her thumb and forefinger.

She's still learning. These and other basic facts were still new to her, having moved to his country only a few months ago. To him, they were as were familiar as the air. Produce without additives or preservatives expire quickly. One of those invisible truths you breathed in without question. "Looks like the time Saad pulled an all-nighter for the Science Fair." Abdulla nudged aside a stack of binders.

"Those are the prospective franchises." Sangita pointed at the heap of folders with her pencil like a magic wand.

"Hm. And you think we should go with ..." He flipped through a few folders, recalling a similar stack in his bedroom at his father's house.

"I don't know." She ran her fingers through her hair, letting loose a cascade down her back. "I sent you a list of questions; that's always a good starting point. I studied literature, remember? I could ask Ravi to take a look. He's working with my dad on some business thing with ships in India—"

"No." The word came out more sharply than he intended. Sangita's brother, like Sangita herself, was someone he'd discovered during that impromptu trip to London last year. Another landmine in the field of subjects they skirted while planning their future together. Abdulla had gone to London intending to call off his engagement to his cousin Hind, Sangita's college roommate, only to find Hind falling, for a time, in love with Ravi. Sangita spoke to Ravi when Abdulla wasn't around, which, with the time difference, couldn't be that often. Not that he wanted to keep her from her only sibling. But the name still sent pinpricks of irritation all over Abdulla.

"They said they're fine with doing something after the wedding. Maybe in New York?" She gathered up a handful of Arabic flashcards strewn across the counter.

Abdulla took a deep breath. Another concession she was making for him. The men's part of a wedding in the Gulf lasted a few hours at most while people exchanged greetings. He didn't think he could be nose to nose with her brother—not yet.

"Under Your Abaya?" The words came out before he fully understood what he was reading. "That's the name of your Twitter account?" No wonder she had so many followers. The black robe-like *abaya* covered up what women from the Gulf wore underneath. Expats were obsessed with discovering the true lives of these women. "You'll be wearing one too," he pointed out. "Until Luluwa gets married."

"I get it. The foreigner denigrating everyone's good name." Sangita snatched the laptop around so that it faced her again.

Abdulla winced. "It doesn't bother me. It's the family."

"I know that. Or I wouldn't be here." She squeezed his hand on the counter. "That's a working title. Meant metaphorically. You like the layout of the website?"

He came around to the other side of the bar, resting his arms on the countertop and looking for something to praise. "Minimalist design. Makes it easy to find what you're looking for."

"Right? See, here's the tag cloud, and you can search by the most popular terms."

Culture. Gender. Women.

Feminazi. The word popped into his head before he could shake it out. "Anonymous," he said. "Write what you want, but keep it— "

"Unattributed; I know." She chewed at the end of her pencil like a kid working on a tough exam.

Abdulla's phone buzzed with a text from James. *Ready when you are. Thanks for the nice digs!* "I'll see you this afternoon," he said. "If we wrap up early, let's try that new sushi place."

"Yes," Sangita said. "I'll be, you know, presentable." She waved her hands over the tank top.

"You're perfect as you are." He allowed himself a kiss, a real one, lips pressed to hers, as they might do in the more liberal families.

"Promise?" She laid her head against his neck, her chin catching his collar.

"Yes. See, if you wore makeup, then this *thobe* would be ruined." He gestured to the starched expanse of his long white gown, the everyday clothing of men in the Gulf.

"I would wear makeup, if we saw each other at normal hours." She pretended to poke at him with a pencil. "The sun's been up for, say, two hours?"

"Doesn't look like you've been to bed," he said.

"I get more done through the night."

"The life of entrepreneurs." He caught both her wrists together in one hand. "Yes, I much prefer this to fake eyelashes."

"Those are coming." She twisted free to pull a newspaper off a stack of glossy wedding magazines. "Delivered yesterday by your mom's driver. Don't you worry; they'll have me all trussed up for the wedding."

"As long as they come off."

Sangita waved goodbye from the laptop. "Those and a lot of other things."

His heart skipped a beat like a teenager's, and he felt thankful for the distance "Behave."

* * *

Mornings in the Arabian Gulf were as interchangeable as the pieces of the checkers game his kid brother loved, each one as shiny as the one before. Sun glazed the water along the Corniche so that it shimmered in his peripheral vision. Forty years ago, dhows littered the horizon as men went out to dive for pearls. Now their grandsons sped along a six-lane highway to spend their days encased in glass towers. *Refrigerators in the desert.*

"Too early for so much melancholy," Sangita said, her voice resonating from the car's speakers. She yawned into the phone.

"Did I say that out loud?" Abdulla laughed. "How much did you hear?" Despite having left the apartment a scant twenty minutes ago, he'd called her on the pretext of wanting to talk about possible dinner options, unable to say he just loved the sound of her voice. *Was this love, wanting to be with someone every second?*

"All of it. The generational change, the ennui of the new generation—"

"Okay, okay!" He chuckled while waiting at the light to turn left into the city's business district, leaving the manmade shoreline behind him. "I get it, Madam Interviewer. It's not my fault I get confessional with you."

"All I asked is, how much longer until you get there?"

He laughed again. The guy in the BMW SUV to the right gave Abdulla a stare over the rim of his sunglasses. *What are you so happy about in this bumper-to-bumper rush hour?* His closely trimmed beard and centered *agal* left no room for humor. Abdulla was the first to look away, clearing his throat and sitting up straighter.

"After all, I'm the one stuck inside all day, in the apartment you shared with your first wife."

She's tired. "How could I forget? You remind me every day," he said, without further reflection. "What's next on the blog?" He said it quickly, hoping to jar her back into a good mood. In the yawning silence he clenched the steering wheel, wishing he was as good at funny comebacks as his fiancée.

"I'm looking into these *boyas*. Apparently they wear their *abayas* like *thobes,* with collars and everything."

Abdulla squinted at the horizon where heat shimmered along the asphalt like drops of water. "The girls who pretend they're boys? Who told you about that?" She had an uncanny ability to find the smallest facets of the fringe elements in their culture and tease them out.

"I saw some, last time Luluwa took me to the mall. She said they're pretty common, particularly at the national university— "

"This is all under the alias?" Abdulla said, to reassure himself as much as anything.

"Call me later," she replied, her words clipped, the playful undertone replaced by a more mechanical one. "On your way back." She hung up before he could say another word. Sangita still didn't use "home" to describe the apartment they would soon share as newlyweds.

Abdulla raced ahead and cut in front of the BMW to make a right turn. The other driver honked but continued straight.

"Her choice," his mother always said in the circular discussion about his impending marriage to a foreigner. "Her choice to come here, where she knows no one but you."

The engine idled while he waited in the curved driveway for the valet to take his car. Ten years ago this hotel had been the lone block on this side of the road. Now the Hilton flanked it and the Mövenpick Suites glinted across the street. Someone had parked a blue Maserati out front. His SUV would not make the lineup of luxury cars placed at angles in the entryway.

"Welcome back to the Four Seasons," a dark-skinned man said, wiping at his gleaming forehead. Humidity laced the air, though it was not yet nine.

Abdulla grabbed his leather carryall, a leftover from university days in the UK, and pushed thoughts of Sangita aside. He swept past the valet and two other men in embroidered tops and tan slacks, who nodded their hellos. He went through the metal detector in the lobby, a new security feature that seemed outlandish in their historically safe emirate, but was introduced after a spate of terrorist acts in nearby Kuwait and Saudi Arabia. The security screening, marble foyer and uniformed Asian hotel staff were all signs of modernization, each of them a reminder of how far the city had come from the sleepy desert town of his childhood. He passed the cascading floral arrangement placed to woo guests the minute they set foot in the lobby. Meeting in luxury hotels was *de rigueur* for business in the Gulf region.

The screening, however, was pointless, since the man in the black suit conducting it kept his smile trained on Abdulla, rather than turning his eyes to the screen. "If you wanted to blow something up, you'd have done it by now," Sangita had said when they came to the hotel's Italian place for dinner. This was the kind of irony that leapt out at her as a new arrival—he merely accepted it as old hat. There she was, like a grain of sand, refusing to be pushed out of his mind despite his efforts to focus on the morning's work. He had to give this project his all, for both their sakes.

He would make it up to her for having to spend another long day alone by taking her to dinner and a movie. She loved to see what parts the movie censor chose to cut, rather than being irritated by the jumps like those for whom life in the Arabian Gulf was not a novelty.

"Good morning, sir," called the young Filipina woman behind the check-in desk. "Welcome to the Four Seasons."

Abdulla nodded in her direction. If you said hello to each person who sang it out to you, you'd use up all your words before saying anything of significance. He carried on toward the bank of elevators, out of sight of the staff's persistent cheer. The burnished doors opened. Inside stood a tanned woman in a spaghetti-strap dress with two children and an equally leathery-looking husband. Abdulla's mother, even his aunts, would tut-tut at the expat's brazenness. They used expat women's dress as the runes by which to read the way their country was heading. The father pushed a stroller and, on his shoulders, carried a curly-headed child who reached out her chubby hands to grab Abdulla's *ghutra*. The mother clutched a shawl around her shoulders and slapped the child's hands down. Her wide eyes took in Abdulla in his traditional dress, then she glanced away. Abdulla held the elevator door open for them.

"Thank you," the father said.

"Sure," Abdulla replied. He contemplated his reflection in the closing doors. One day that might be them, him and Sangita, bringing kids to play on the beach. *Kids*. The word dredged up memories of his dead first wife and unborn baby. *Was it wanting too much, all this happiness that lay ahead?* He brushed the old fear away along with some lint on his left cufflink. Plush carpet absorbed his footsteps as he pushed open the double doors to the meeting room. A man sat at the table, drinking coffee. When he saw Abdulla, he hopped to his feet, hair flopping to one side.

"James." Abdulla grasped his university friend's offered hand, tapping him on the shoulder with the other. "Thanks for coming." Seeing him was like stepping back into the carefree years – maybe the best of his life. The two hadn't seen each other in four or five years. James had been the brightest star in their graduating class at the London School of Economics.

"Well, you know, people are always asking me to turn up to brainstorm international franchising opportunities." James's green eyes twinkled. The web of lines around the corners of his smile were new, otherwise his friend was trim, and freckled as ever, energy crackled in his grip. "Who am I to say no?"

"You were last on my list," Abdulla said, "but first to answer."

James hooted with laughter. They sat down next to each other at a table set for six with pads of paper, pencils, coasters, glasses, and bottles of water.

"Seriously," Abdulla dropped his smile, "that work you did for the pizza place is legend."

James waved off the praise. "You know the Gulf is ripe for this kind of thing. I'm glad I was on your list at all. You dropped off the face of the earth after graduation." He stretched, cracking his knuckles.

"Swallowed up by a government job and all those monotonous meetings," Abdulla muttered. "You got in fine, then. You like the hotel?"

"Stop mothering me! It's not the first time I've left home, you know." James gave him another wolfish grin. Women pretended not to notice, but that grin had likely got him upgraded without asking. "A junior suite will do—for now."

"Believe me, this is the only time you're going to get concern from me," Abdulla retorted.

"Ah, none of the famed Arab hospitality."

"When you earn it," he said with a wink. Their repartee brought back his student persona, erasing the intervening years of living the life his family had planned for him as if they hadn't happened.

"Yes, about that. This contract they sent me; it's in Arabic." James pulled out a sheaf of papers marked with Abdulla's new company logo.

"I asked my father's guy to get that translated. Sorry." Abdulla skimmed the first page. "My family thinks this business thing's a fad. That I'll change my mind," he mumbled.

It was true. His father wanted Abdulla to keep his government job even as he launched his entrepreneurial dream. "You're setting up a family, not starting out as some kid in university," Mohammed had scolded when Abdulla asked to borrow the capital to set up a business. "A restaurant is not the same thing as the neighborhood McDonald's," Abdulla had told his risk-averse father for the hundredth time, trying to explain why quitting his job might be necessary. "It's not a corner shop you open on a whim."

Mohammed's nod through the window that morning, as Abdulla reversed out of the family compound, had said that he was staying out of it. Staying out, but watching. He would incur his mother's wrath, too, if the project proved financially irresponsible at the expense of the family's reputation. First a foreign wife, and then the prospect of a failed business—lately Abdulla seemed to be upsetting everyone who mattered to him.

"The bank won't accept me as a signatory if I'm not an official employee," James said. "But there'll be major expenses coming up with outfitting. Or I can kick everything over to you, if you want."

"That'll cause all kinds of delays. And I'm going to be tied up for a few weeks."

"Tied up? While you're still working out the business plan for your new project?" James leaned an elbow on the table. "Good strategy. Play hard to get." Trust James to get to the crux of the issue, just as he did during case analysis in graduate school.

This was the real reason why Abdulla chose him as a partner. James wouldn't mince words. Abdulla flipped through the contract. "Can you just sign it, and I'll get them to do a new one? That way we can get your residence permit going."

James gave him a sideways glance.

"I know, I know, bad business practice, but I'm sure it's standard lingo."

James uncapped an ink pen and obliged with a flourish. "Whatever the sheikh says."

Abdulla grimaced. "No more of that, please."

James laughed. He passed the stack over. "Of course. The first pitching team will be here in a few hours."

"I didn't realize that was also today. I was going to show you around the city." Abdulla slid the contract into his carryall. "Still mulling over things. Not sure which tack to take." If only there was a way to be certain about the return on investment in any of their options. *There is a way,* his father would say, sitting cross-legged in the *majlis. A government pension.*

"Time for that later." James waved the offer aside. "They'll give us their ideas today, and then there are two more later this week who are leaning toward—"

"Some of the brands have restrictions on who we use. Sourcing their suppliers is going to add to the overhead." Abdulla skimmed the notes Sangita's summary notes. Her questions were insightful, analytical: what discount rules applied to multiple outlets? He scribbled his own: What were the penalties for early termination of agreements? The rules for on-selling a franchise?

"Let me show you the franchise guidelines, and then we can decide what unique overseas flourishes we want for our clientele. Everything is a negotiation," James said. They pored over the lists of available licenses for a wide variety of American eateries. "Burgers, steakhouses, pseudo-Italian chains—and there's this Korean-style chicken place. Seemingly everyone wants a crack at this market."

"Asian food is tough. People don't know what to order." Abdulla sank back in his chair, swiveling around to look at the flow chart James was drawing on an oversize legal pad.

"So who's our target audience? Because expats love Asian. *They're* not eating sushi with a knife and fork." James paused. "I saw a woman doing that on the plane. Couldn't stop staring."

Abdulla laughed at James's astuteness. He was describing exactly his mother's approach to sushi at buffets. "But locals have the disposable income."

James added a bullet to the never-ending list of things to do. *Aggregate data on spending habits.* They summarized the pros and cons of each eatery license on the list. Abdulla's eyes glazed over—the same effect his government job had often had after hours of sitting at conference tables. *Won't be like this once we open the doors,* he reminded himself. *Nothing is glamorous in the beginning.*

"Whatever we choose should be a winner, since people have disposable income and mostly eat outside their homes."

"Two years," Abdulla said, reading James's projections in the business plan. In their initial online brainstorming, twenty-four months had seemed like the blink of an eye. *Two years of the high life in fancy hotels,* he could hear his father grumble in response. *Not like you're pouring concrete,* Sangita would say. There was no one who would sympathize that a couple of years was a high price to pay. His breath came tight in his chest, pressure building in his head like descending in an airplane.

"Most restaurants close within the first five years. Two years will go by like that."

His friend's words sent a bell ringing through Abdulla's mind.

"That's half the time of any other location." The loud rumble of James's stomach interrupted them.

"You're starving," Abdulla said. A glance at his watch showed that it was past noon. The mundane details of the day brought him back to reality and away from the funnel of tornado-like worries.

"I heard about these Gulf work conditions." James checked the time on his phone. "Anyway, those design guys are late."

"All right." Abdulla mock-punched him in the shoulder. He could breathe again, one full breath and then another. His friend's irreverence was as much a part of his persona as the British accent. This was the kind of liveliness he missed at endless government meetings. "Shall we order some lunch, or do you want a break from this room?"

A knock on the door prevented James from answering. Two suited men with curly hair pushed it open. Their matching dark suits and tapered pants made them look like a pair of penguins.

"Sorry, the traffic in this area is horrendous," the taller one said.

"Yes, hello." James jumped up. "Welcome, welcome." He made the introductions while shrugging into his jacket. A uniformed hotel staffer shadowed the men in, asking the room at large what they would like to drink.

"Espresso," the new arrivals said in unison.

When she looked in his direction, Abdulla shook his head in answer to the woman's question. He sipped at the bottle of water in front of him.

The duo sat at the table, smoothing their ties. "Yes, we want to make this the destination for all the expat housewives in the country," one of the architects said. "Showcase the freshest of items. Make their mouths water."

James responded to the opening volley. The meeting kicked off with spreads in glossy magazines of sample produce bin arrangements.

For Abdulla, the word "housewife" conjured Sangita's animated features. "They should warn you that love can turn you into a glorified housewife," she'd said in one of their protracted exchanges about their new life. "You're at work, and now you're also doing deals on the side. So that leaves me where exactly? Unable to work for the news channel, because that's 'not appropriate.'" Frustration had twisted her features into a sneer at what his family thought of her preferred occupation. "Watching over my shoulder to make sure no one knows it's me putting up these 'secrets' about life in the Gulf."

"No one's keeping you tied to the house," Abdulla had said, tweaking her nose. "I sent you a few more places to apply. Research assistant or something at one of the American universities. They'd love someone like you."

She'd put her head on his shoulder.

"These projections are optimistic," James said, tapping on the dossier, attempting to bring Abdulla back to the business at hand.

He texted his teenage cousin Luluwa, the only neutral party they had to confide in. *Can you take her to Ikea?* With new furniture, Sangita would feel like the place was theirs. Women liked decorating, didn't they? His mother was always making some upgrade to a room in the family house. Getting Sangita out of the apartment and into the city should lift her spirits.

Sure, but she's not answering. Hasn't replied all day.

"Abdulla." James nudged his elbow.

"Yes?" His attention snapped into focus to find the group staring at him. "Yes."

"What do you think?"

"It sounds great," he said.

James raised an eyebrow. "Any questions?"

"I liked all the ideas." Abdulla kept his voice even so as not to reveal his frustration to the unsuspecting men at the table. "Women are a good group to target. They do spend a lot of time going out."

"Retrofitting the jewelry store won't run into permitting issues?" James tapped his pencil on the table.

"I'll look into it," Abdulla mumbled. The three of them needed each other—James with the start-up expertise; whichever design company they chose for the buildout; and Abdulla with the capital—like a three-legged stool, the whole project would topple if any one person didn't pull his weight.

The younger of the two men unfurled some sample floor plans. "All right," he said, his brow furrowing. "The proposal didn't say the size of the space."

Abdulla reached for a copy of the Request for Proposal. He'd staked everything on this idea of a franchise, going into business for himself, taking a staggering loan from the bank when his family refused to back him. "I'm starting over," he'd said, filled with the promise of a new life as an entrepreneur. *A one-of-a-kind food franchise in one of the world's highest per capita income countries—what could be easier?* He racked his brain, trying to recall what he knew from his time in the Ministry of Business and Trade. What were the rules for malls? His civil servant days were now so hazy they could have happened to another person.

"So the current store is near other jewelry stores," the architect said with the cadence of Italian-accented English. "This will not be an issue?" He echoed James's question.

"The opposite," Abdulla snapped. "People will get hungry while shopping."

The two men exchanged glances with a slight shrug, as if to say, "It's your money."

"Let's take a break," James suggested.

The architect shrugged again. His assistant, a thin, wiry young man, scurried away to check on their espressos. The older one loped out of the room to find a place to smoke.

"What are their names again?" Abdulla asked, once the room was clear.

"You okay?" James asked in a low voice.

"Sorry—you know, the wedding. Everything is on hold until then. But the bride to be ..." He rearranged the folds of his *ghutra*. Sangita would be furious if she knew he was using her as an excuse.

"Wedding." James pushed away from the table. "You didn't say. Congratulations. There are tons of changes afoot."

"Yes."

"So the family is expanding," James said. "I mean, it's none of my business ..." He put up his hands. "But when we finished the program you said you were getting married. We all thought you were crazy."

"She's not local," Abdulla said. It sounded like a confession. "My first wife, the cousin, she——"

"Right, this is the second one," James said. "We need to have a proper catch-up. Maybe with diagrams."

Abdulla hit himself in the forehead. "This is a second wife, but not like you're thinking."

His university friend put up his hands again. "Not for me to judge," he said. "Different doesn't mean wrong."

Abdulla laughed. "Ever the diplomat. You sure you don't want to go into the Foreign Office?"

James took a swig of water. "The pay is crap for an up-and-comer like me. Nothing like what you're offering!"

Abdulla shook his head, the mirth of a few moments ago dissipating. People were counting on him. James was counting on him to make them all a lot of money. "My first wife, the one I married out of uni, she died," he said.

"God, Abdulla, I'm sorry." James gave his shoulder a squeeze.

He nodded his acceptance of his friend's condolences. "Ask those guys to reschedule. I need time to think."

"To come up with more ideas like the connections between hunger and shopping?"

Abdulla laughed. "Yeah, I think we can do better than that." The photos of luxury mall interiors swam before his eyes. "I need something to get excited about. To spend two years on, night and day."

James rubbed his chin. "That's one way to go about it. If you want to create something from the ground up. Not franchise."

"Like what if we sold the raw meat and veg. What about a fancy grocery? Wasn't Whole Foods on that list?" He shuffled through the haphazard pile on the table.

"Erase our entire business plan and go in another direction?" James rubbed his hands together. "Let's get started."

"So maybe not the best idea," Abdulla said. "Let me go over the list again and think this over. Again."

"You're the boss," James said, walking him to the elevator. "I'll tell the guys lunch is on us."

Abdulla felt a pang of guilt at the sight of James standing alone in the hallway. "You could come over, but you'll have more fun here."

His partner's smile didn't quite reach his eyes, as if to say, "Invite me and let's find out."

"See you then," he said with a wave as the elevator doors closed.

James was a seasoned traveler. His previous project had had outlets that needed monitoring in cities all over the world. James could make himself at home in a new country as easily at the next expat. Abdulla made a note to take James out soon. Maybe he and Sangita could trade tips. But then again, with one at home all day and the other here to work …. He rejected that idea as quickly as it'd cropped up.

* * *

Abdulla made his way through the glittering collection of skyscrapers in West Bay. No two buildings were alike, each of them twisting to the sky like a shard of glass, the sunlight reflecting like a mirror without end. He drove through the looping set of temporary roads that doubled back on themselves into the reclaimed land of The Pearl. Apartment buildings towered above him as he sped through the underpass and into the car park. He left the bag in the car, swiping to gain access to the residents' entrance. The elevator stopped at the amenities floor. A nanny in a grey uniform was chasing dripping, dark-haired children with a towel into the elevator. The boy and girl ran from one wall to the other as the nanny admonished them.

"*Yella*," Abdulla said, in the voice he'd used when his cousins were younger.

They stilled at the sound of Arabic. The nanny draped a towel over their shoulders. The gratitude in her wide smile lingered with him after they'd exited on the floor beneath the penthouse.

Abdulla came up short at the closed door. Maybe she was sleeping. He knocked. Then took out his key to let himself in. The blues and creams of the late Fatima's sofas greeted him.

"Hello?" Abdulla called through the silent apartment. The azure blue of the Arabian Gulf shimmered beyond the balcony. *No, no one out there.* He tossed his sunglasses onto a coffee table and unbuttoned the top of his *thobe.* "Sangita?"

A muffled clang came from the hallway between the bedrooms.

"Back here," she called. "And bring a bucket."

"Huh?" He stopped short in the bedroom. Water lapped over the edges of his sandals, rising to his ankles.

Sangita stood in the corner of the room, next to the bed. Water gushed through a hole in the ceiling.

"Why didn't you call someone?"

"It's like this in every apartment on the floor," she said, flipping wet hair out of her eyes. "A pipe burst upstairs. Get a towel or something."

He went to the phone on the wall to call the front desk. "Shut off the water on this side of the building," he said in exasperation when the receptionist answered.

"Sir, yes, sir, we did, but there are many gallons."

"Get someone up here to help clean this up!" He eyed the Turkish kilim from his first honeymoon, which was sopping up water like a paper towel. Reds and blues spread into the cream in the middle of the pattern, turning it a murky brown.

"You're on the list, sir," she sing-songed into his ear. "As soon as they're done with the other apartments on your floor, they'll be along to you."

He hung up the phone in frustration. "I might as well call the maids from our house," Abdulla said, surveying the shallow lake in their bedroom.

"Don't you dare." Sangita wrung a towel out on the balcony. "We are not running to your parents for help."

He picked up a waterlogged journal from the bedside table. "Okay." The light in her eye said it was easier to give in than argue. "Let me change."

"I wouldn't go in there," Sangita called.

He snapped on the overhead light of the walk-in closet, and a shower of sparks greeted him. "What the hell?" Water cascaded from the light fixtures, across the racks of clothes, and pooled in the heels of his loafers.

"You don't think this is her ghost, getting revenge?" Sangita asked.

He leaned forward to catch the muttered words. "Not funny." The idea that they would live in the apartment he'd briefly shared with his first wife didn't sit well with Sangita—no matter how many times he told her it'd only been three months. "You could have called me." He fingered the rows of sleeved shirts and *thobes* made limp by the moisture.

"I did call you." She hung a towel on the balcony.

"When?" Abdulla pulled off his *thobe* and laid it on a dresser that was still dry, at least for now, leaving him in the white t-shirt and cotton *sirwal* pants that had kept him modest under the long translucent garment.

"Six times," Sangita said, retying her hair. Sweat beaded on her upper lip and forehead. She put her hands on her hips, waiting as he grabbed his phone from the dresser.

"Right," he said. "On silent this morning."

"Meetings," they said together.

She crossed the room, each step creating a squish. "So out of character," she said, pushing him in the middle of the chest. "Your lack of availability."

"Hey!" He stepped back in surprise, slipping in the water. He reached out to steady himself and grabbed onto her. Sangita gave a shriek as his weight threw her off balance and took them both down, water spraying around them.

"Hey, yourself." She beat her fists against him. "Sell this place. Let's at least move to one of the other towers. I feel like she's watching me."

"You don't want to play this game." He tightened his arms around her in a band of muscle. "We grew up wrestling."

"I'm dressed for it," she said. Water slid off the spandex in her yoga pants and sports bra.

He was soaked within seconds. "You've been warned," Abdulla said and rolled over, sending her into the film of water on the floor. His wet shirt stuck to his navel. "Now." He shook his head like a wet cat, sending sprays of water all over her. "You were saying?"

She shrieked and wrapped her legs around him, her ankles hooking around his. "You'll pay for that!"

"I hope I will." He glanced down at the tangle of their legs. "I like how you have me locked in here."

She tightened her grip, bringing him closer. For a fleeting second their mouths touched, and he remembered what it felt like to be alive again, the sheer, pulsing joy of feeling someone else's pulse against your thumb. He held her hands above her head and bent to kiss her.

"All the better to turn you over with," Sangita said against his lips. She brought her legs together, using surprise and momentum to roll him over until he lay beneath her. "You were saying?"

He put his hands on her hips, all playfulness gone. "I can—"

She splashed water in his face.

"What the hell?"

Sangita burst into laughter. She sprang up and ran out of the room and down the hallway.

"I don't give in that easily," Abdulla shouted after her. He pulled off his wet shirt and chased her into the living room. "You'll pay for that!" He ran straight into Sangita, who was standing in the middle of the living room. This sent them sprawling again. "Ouch," he said, staring into her heart-shaped face. Her eyes focused beyond his shoulder.

"*Salaam.* Oh, sorry. Sorry," his mother said.

They snapped apart.

"*Yema,*" Abdulla stammered at the sight of his mother in their living room.

"I was here having a coffee, so thought I would say hello." Maryam kept her gaze above them, staring out of the sliding glass door. "You didn't answer your phones. The door was unlocked."

Sangita disappeared into the bedroom. She re-emerged with towels, handing two to Abdulla. He wrapped one around his waist and over his soaked pants. She folded herself in a bathrobe.

"We're, ah, having an emergency," he said. "Pipe burst upstairs, and these two floors are flooded." Water dripped into his eyes.

Maryam looked from one to the other. "You'll come home. Until they get this sorted out."

"I'll go to a hotel for a few nights," Sangita said. "The Hyatt is close."

Maryam snorted. "Nonsense. This is going to take months. The mold in here." She sniffed. "You'll come home. Use Ahmed's house. I'll send Anita. See you at home." She gave them both the look she normally reserved for errant children, then swept out of the room.

Abdulla followed his mother to the hall, making sure the front door had clicked into place and locked before he returned and collapsed onto the sofa.

"No," Sangita said, her voice half moan, half whisper. "Not in with your family. They hate me!"

"You said it yourself; you don't like living here." He tugged at her arm, pulling her down onto the sofa next to him. "Besides, not true about the family." He kissed her cheek and used the collar of the bathrobe to wipe away a few drops of water. She leaned toward him, turning so their noses were inches from each other. "They need a little time," he went on. "How it happened—even yours aren't thrilled at the idea of a Muslim in the family."

"Let's not do this again." She pressed her forehead into his. Droplets shone on the tips of her eyelashes, but whether from the floor or tears he couldn't be certain.

"We need to make this place over," Abdulla said. "Now you can decide how you want everything."

"Argh." She slid down his chest and rested her chin on his breastbone. "It's the master bedroom," she said. "I can use the spare."

"Ouch," he said. "Who has such a pointy chin?"

She dug it in deeper. "Will they even let us stay together? The wedding is still a month away. I won't be in Ahmed's house alone," she warned. "I'll stay here. Everything's fine."

"My father's house is right next door. I'll go back and forth to sleep.

Otherwise I'll be there with you at Ahmed's." Abdulla slid his hands up her arms inside the robe.

"I still can't explain to my friends the difference between being legally married and waiting for this reception to be official. Am I your wife or not?"

He laid his head on the back of the sofa, staring at the ceiling. "I know this hasn't been ideal. And yes, once we signed the marriage contract you became my wife. But people's obsession with these massive weddings means we'll only be properly sealed and delivered after the reception. Four weeks," he said, holding up four fingers. "That's nothing."

"Don't use that tone with me," she said. "We are not negotiating. You'll be at work all day, and next door most of the night, and I'll do what, exactly, in the bosom of your family?" She tugged her arms away.

"Whatever you do here during the day. Everything is a negotiation." He held onto her elbows, not allowing her to slide away. "Besides, you might start working soon." The business axiom had sent his thoughts racing. "And I owe you a honeymoon. We'll go as soon as the wedding is over."

"A month?" She said. "A month away? London?"

He scrunched up his nose. "Something more original, surely?"

"Where we met." Sangita played with his earlobe. "Memory Lane. Where the Arab cast his spell on me."

"Getting nostalgic." He caught her fingers. "Not exactly how I remember it. That tickles."

A crash in the kitchen saved him from having to confess the truth. There was no way he could take a month off work then, not even a few weeks.

"Holy hell." Sangita stared at the gaping hole in the ceiling. Exposed wires and tiles tangled through the opening, along with a trickle of water.

"Don't touch anything," he said. *So much for a relaxing night at home.* Another thud. A cabinet came loose from the wall. *At this rate, we won't have a home at all.*

Chapter Two

The cacophony of honking from downstairs persisted through Hind's apartment door. She unwound her *shayla,* pressing a handkerchief to her neck to mop the sweat. Life in a headscarf was not ideal in India, even in the western city of Mumbai, but she couldn't go to work at the consulate any other way, not with all the other Qatari staff there.

Home. Well, after a fashion. The three-bedroom apartment was more like a rattling cage than a house filled with the smells and sounds of family. A cage full of sandalwood furniture and silk carpets, decorated by the previous staffer's wife, whose tastes tended toward the curatorial rather than the modern. Hind half expected someone to come through the embroidered drapes and burst into an old Bollywood film song. But there was no Romeo. On weekends she could go an entire two days without speaking to another human being.

No one expected her for dinner; no one begged her to go to the mall; no one demanded explanations of where she was going and when she'd be back. Hind slipped on a loose cotton dress, the kind she might've worn in graduate school in the sweltering heat of London then had pushed away in her closet at her father's house when she'd thought she was returning home for good. She turned the television on to the Food Network and set about shedding the grime of the city, transitioning to her evening alone.

She poured herself a glass of water and contemplated the view of the street from her high-rise apartment. All around her glass-fronted buildings rose from the concrete, their scaffolds like fingers reaching upwards in a way that reminded her of the skyline at home. She could see the snake of the road winding back on itself, the cars bumper to bumper. Two boys sat on an unfinished rooftop a few buildings over. Their bony shoulders and scruffy pants spoke volumes about the legitimacy of their presence there.

With construction halted for the day, the boys were alone on the terrace with construction tools strewn around them in haphazard piles.

They should be in school. She'd traveled once to India before moving here for work. To the south, on a lark, with Sangita's brother to visit his family's charity project. One last breath of freedom before her life was forever linked to a husband, Abdulla. She sipped her water, swallowing hard as she recalled her indignation on that first trip to India, a year ago, when street children knocked on the windows of their car during stops at traffic signals. Their eyes pleaded with her from emaciated faces while they hawked candy and plastic toys. "They should be in school," she'd said one hot summer afternoon, surprised by the persistence of the children racing from car to car, rapping on passenger side windows.

Sangita's brother had rolled his eyes at her. "Of course they should be in school," Ravi had said with the same tacit honesty she knew from his sister, her friend. "And those with parents and money are." When the cars began moving again, he'd waved across the street toward groups of girls in pink-striped uniforms walking home, their braids bouncing with each step. He tolerated so much of her confused judgement, her constant wondering why kids weren't in school, how old they were, why couldn't the government intervene?

Now, she wanted to fling open the window and ask the boys on the street below similar questions. Would they understand English? One boy said something to the other. His friend's face clouded over, eyebrows knitting together. He jumped up and pushed the first boy on the shoulder. Hind gasped, as her mother would've done, and put her hand on the window. The other boy ducked beneath his friend's outstretched arm and swiped his legs out from under him. *It's a game.* She relaxed.

Months here, and you're still living with assumptions. Ravi's voice rang in her ears as if he were standing in the apartment. That trip was the most rebellious thing she'd ever done—other than setting conditions to her engagement that her parents hadn't necessarily approved of, and almost falling in love with a stranger. *Almost.*

The clock in the hallway struck six, shaking her out of the downward turn of her thoughts. The boys below had also moved on. Hopefully to a family waiting for them with dinner. Six o'clock. Which meant it was three in the afternoon back home in the Gulf. Khalid and Saad would be home from school, trying to find mischief. Knowing them, they would succeed. The amazing thing was that most of the adults in the family didn't seem to notice. She turned from the window and wandered across to an overstuffed sofa, her one introduction to the room in the months since she'd moved in. Any further upgrading would require a total overhaul, and she had neither the energy nor the vision to completely redo the flat.

She swallowed past a constriction in her throat at the thought of home, the family compound, her best friend living in her home country with her former fiancé. *As Abdulla's wife.* She prodded at the thought, turning it over, to see if she found any regret, glee, anger. She felt nothing more than a prick of sadness. From her sister Noor's daily updates via Messenger she knew that Sangita had moved into the apartment on The Pearl. Hind knew what that life was like. Though, in the silence, she couldn't say that this was much better. *Of course it is. You can do as you please. Stop being melodramatic.*

Hind flipped through the TV channels. *So much food and no one to eat it with.* A video sequence in which a thin, long-haired heroine gyrated next to the muscular hero. She watched them for a moment to see if she could detect what it was her mother loved about the endless Bollywood films shown at home, dubbed with Arabic subtitles. Two minutes in, and she couldn't trace the appeal. Who would have thought she would find herself hankering for human contact in preference to solitude?

She could go to the *khaleeji* ladies' dinner tonight. The invitation winked at her from the carved wooden coffee table. A dinner for all the wives of the Gulf diplomatic community. The idea pressed her further back into the cushions. All those Gulf Arab women, wearing as much gold as they could fit onto their fingers, wrists and ears, choking their necks like leashes. *Yes, we are going to Kerala for Eid. So nice. On the boat we had a cook and a maid!* She could hear versions of the same conversations women had in the *majlis* at home. Leaving home to be surrounded by people from home—it was more than she could face. Her phone buzzed with the sound of a Skype call.

"What are you doing?" Noor's worried face peered at her sister from the small screen.

"Relaxing," Hind said. "Stop frowning so much, you'll get wrinkles."

Although there had not always been these hundreds of miles between them, the impulse to needle each other was nothing new. Instantly Noor's face relaxed. Hind laughed, her voice echoing through the apartment.

"Are you coming home for Eid?"

Hind rearranged her limbs, delaying answering. She didn't like the hint of a double chin she noticed in the smaller box to the right. In London she'd walked nearly everywhere, whereas now, her official driver escorted her constantly. She'd have to look into the hotel gym she'd heard someone talking about in the office. Finally she replied to her sister's question. "To go around on visits and have everyone ask if I really know what I'm doing?"

Noor pouted. "Well, I miss you."

Hind felt a rush of pleasure at the thought of being missed. Even if it was only by her sister. "What's new there?" she asked, in as neutral a voice as possible.

"Same," Noor said. "Though they're having a sale at Blue Salon."

"Right."

"Oh, and the foreigner is trying to get pregnant."

So. A baby would really make things final. Hind fiddled with the remote control. *Divorce would be a much messier process with a child.* "How do you know? Luluwa told you?"

"No way." Noor's face came closer to the screen. "*Yema.* Auntie told her."

"You're still not talking to Luluwa?" Hind was glad to switch the subject away from news of Sangita. She frowned. "That's your best friend."

"Now and then. Family lunch." Noor shrugged.

"Don't punish her on my account," Hind warned. "She had no part in what happened."

"Come on," Noor protested. "Nothing will ever be the same. That woman took Abdulla. How are you ever going to get married now?"

The end of the known world! "I'm losing the connection," Hind said. "Talk to you later." She signed out of Skype before her sister could say another word. Hind lay back on the sofa cushions, Noor's words ringing in her ears. An ocean away, and still nothing had changed. They were still asking the same questions. *When would she marry? Who would she marry?*

She turned up the volume on the television in an effort to drown out the pressure from her family, their fingers reaching out across the Arabian Sea. Her phone buzzed again. She eyed it. How many times could she tell Noor to back off without hurting her sister's feelings?

Come laugh with the ladies! The Aditya Mittal Show.
Tonight! The Canvas Comedy Club.
Ladies enter free! First drink is on us.

She laughed at the exuberant punctuation in the text. All it was missing was a few emojis, and it could have been something from one of her male cousins. Well, that and the mention of alcohol. This was exactly the kind of thing families back home had in mind when they tried to stop their daughters traveling abroad.

Come laugh.

She turned off the TV, pointing the remote as if it were a magic wand. A measured rebellion never hurt anyone.

Chapter Three

After several hours of sopping up water or sloshing it toward the nearest drain, at Abdulla's urging Sangita put a few days of clothes and toiletries into a suitcase. "They're giving people temporary shelter in other units," she said.

"In other towers. If you're going to move to one of those, might as well come home," Abdulla said as they got into the car. This was the answer his mother would give if he tried the argument with her. "Besides, this will be good. Make it easier to plan the reception."

Sangita snorted. "Like they care what I think."

"They're not showing you the samples of stuff?"

"Because they care so much what I think." She folded her arms and fixed him with a level stare. "They were nicer to Fatima, I guess. Since she was family."

He pretended to watch the road. His dead first wife's name fell so casually from her lips. Falling in love again dislodged the splintering loss of Fatima and their unborn baby. "I mean the favors, the table settings, the napkins." He improvised the list from his memory of the night he went to claim Fatima from among all their female family members and friends. Remembering his first wedding reception was like itching a scar.

"You prefer pink over eggshell?"

Arriving in the neighborhood at dead of night made it feel like they were thieves returning to their lair. Abdullah braked hard to avoid two teenagers barreling around the corner on a four-wheel ATV.

"Slow down!" he shouted. He lowered the window and said it again. "Oh my God, that's Saad!"

The boys gave him a wave. Abdulla's brother bounced in his seat behind Khalid, Abdulla's nephew.

"What are you doing out so late?" Abdulla called across to them.

"Somebody gave *Ubooy* this, and they said we could use it." Khalid revved the engine.

"At midnight? I think not," Abdulla said.

Sangita, her eyes wide on his face, pressed against the car seat so they could continue their heated exchange. "This is teenage angst?" she whispered.

He squeezed her fingers to say this was not the time for one of her anthropological enquiries.

"We were going in," Saad said. The cadence of his words gave them the whiny quality of a much younger child.

"Who's she?" Khalid asked in Arabic.

"Get in the house now," Abdulla said in an even tone.

"That's my sister-in-law, remember," Saad muttered in dialect to his cousin. "Be nice. They're happy."

Abdulla flushed. His brother was sticking up for him, something he hadn't realized he needed. Gauging the mood of an adolescent was like trying to read your future in the grains of Turkish coffee—murky, haphazard.

"*Salaam alaikum*," Saad said. He flashed a grin at Sangita, who gave him one back.

"He looks like you," she said, pointing at Abdulla.

"I'm better-looking," Saad said, his chest puffed with pride.

They laughed at Abdulla's expense. Khalid continued staring until an elbow in the rib prompted him to echo his cousin's greeting.

Abdulla cleared his throat. The boys guided the ATV back inside the gate, parking it next to the row of family SUVs before they slunk toward the house. Saad gave a departing smile full of teeth.

"Nice to know someone's out having fun," Sangita said, her gaze on the retreating boys.

Abdulla said a silent thank you that she hadn't yet learned enough Gulf dialect to make out the boys' exchange. "Anyway." He brushed the side of her cheek. "This is only temporary. They'll fix up the place, and we'll be married, out of here in no time."

"In no time," she repeated, squeezing his fingers so hard he did a double take.

The darkened windows of the other three houses in the family compound surrounded them like unseeing eyes as they approached the one that had been Uncle Ahmed's. Set back from the circular driveway, the two-story concrete structure was nestled between his father's house on the left and his grandfather's on the right. They crossed over the patch of grass where his brother and cousin played football. Abdulla opened the front door.

The smell of Dettol disinfectant emanated from the floors. His footsteps rang through the marble entryway. Yellow light from the courtyard spilled across the cream walls of the empty room to his right. The last time he'd been in this house was when he'd learned of his wife's death in a car accident. Uncle Ahmed had left the family shortly thereafter, marrying a new wife and abandoning his surviving daughter, Fatima's sister Luluwa. Even Ahmed's brothers—Abdulla's father Mohammed and Uncle Saoud—couldn't talk Ahmed out of the guilt of walking away from an accident that killed his daughter and unborn grandchild.

"Has anyone been here in years?" Sangita shivered and rubbed her arms.

He pushed the dark memories away. "All to ourselves," he said with a false note of cheer. When he snapped on the central chandelier, a light bulb popped.

"Aaah!" Anita, the family's long-time housemaid, bobbed up from a sofa in the sitting room.

Sangita gave a yelp and clutched Abdulla round the waist.

"Oh, sir, it is you." Anita dropped the folds of her floor-length printed housedress.

"Sorry, Anita." Abdulla squeezed Sangita's arms, willing away the gooseflesh on his own.

Anita sniffed. "I waiting. Your mom say you coming." She gave them both the once-over.

He was thankful for the dim light. Anita would report back every small detail, as his mother and aunts had trained her: "Jeans and t-shirts, both of them," she would whisper. "Standing very close."

"I'm exhausted." Sangita didn't bother with any other lights. She marched upstairs, hanging on to the railing, and trailed into the first bedroom on the corner of the landing.

Anita scurried after her. "No, no, you go in the big bed, ma'am. This way. I change all the sheets today."

Sangita shook her head. "It's only me for now. I'll stay in here."

Abdulla lugged the suitcase after them. He leaned it against the wall next to the doorway. They contemplated the mauve walls and matching lace-edged bedspread. Fringes hung from the pillowcases like hair. "Her mom did this room for her after the accident. Lulu rarely spent time in here."

"I didn't take her for the girly type." Sangita sat on the edge of the bed and fell backward onto the duvet. "Still, no posters of Justin Bieber."

"You need anything else, sir?" Anita's head bobbed in the doorway.

Abdulla shook his head, thankful when the maid left without any follow-up questions. In the semi-dark, a sliver of light falling through the window caught Sangita's high forehead and full lips.

"Lulu's changed a lot from the girl who grew up in this room." Abdulla sat next to Sangita. As always when they were close, electricity hummed between them. Was it the late hour or were those shadows under her eyes? He brushed strands of hair off her neck. "We all have."

"Could be worse." She turned her face toward him. "I could be in Hind's room, in your Uncle Saoud's house. That would be weird." She pressed a kiss against his palm. "Though if she were here, I'd be having a lot more fun."

Abdulla snatched his hand back as if she'd bitten him.

"I mean, if we were speaking, and she were here ..."

One thing that could kill his desire was the mention of his other cousin, the person who'd inadvertently introduced them. Hind, with whom Sangita had shared that apartment in London.

"And if she hadn't been the whole reason we met." Sangita gave a small smile at the irony.

Hind had been the family's choice as a second wife for him after Fatima's death. Neither Hind nor Abdulla had had their hearts in it. And their broken engagement had led to Sangita's presence in his life—a fact that everyone in the family overlooked, but no one wanted to forgive. "I'll see you tomorrow."

"We can't pretend she doesn't exist," Sangita murmured.

"I know." He rested his forehead against hers. Their breath mingled for a few moments. "It's a lot to take in. I didn't ..." There was no fair way to end the sentence. He tugged at the ends of her hair to distract them both.

"Didn't realize you were moving me from the apartment where you lived with your dead wife into your dead wife's childhood home. Yards away from where my best friend Hind, your now ex-fiancée, grew up." Sangita laughed, though it sounded like a cough. She ran her fingers up and down his arm.

Abdulla closed his eyes. "This is all going to be fine," he said. "Wedding, launch of business, multimillion-dollar tell-all ..."

"Then we go and live in Fiji!" She bounced onto her knees on the bed.

"Fiji …" His smile faded at the impossibility of the idea. Even if they managed to accomplish the rest of their wish list, living so far away from his ailing grandfather was inconceivable. Beating the odds, Jassim hung on, though his quality of life shrank by the year. Again, the torrent of negativity swirling up threatened to engulf him.

Sangita grabbed his hand. "You're shaking."

Abdulla squeezed her palm. He didn't have words to put the storm of emotions in order. "Why don't you shower? Who would have thought a flood of water could make things so dirty."

She crawled to the top of the bed fully clothed and slipped under the duvet. Her face left a smudge on the cream pillow. "Time for that tomorrow." She waved him away with a big yawn. "Go to your room." She rolled onto her side, knees together, with hands tucked under her cheek. In repose, all her defenses down, she looked like a child.

"Soon my room will be here with you." His phone buzzed with a text from his mother asking if everything was to their liking. A thinly veiled admonishment that it was time for him to leave Sangita and come home. "Good night," he said to his bride, who was already asleep.

* * *

For Abdulla, the rhythm of family life—with every moment on the premises under surveillance—was as familiar as slipping into his favorite pair of sandals. But now every day was different, because everyone else was pretending there wasn't anything unusual about a woman living in his uncle's house on her own. The collective silence became a pebble he couldn't shake from his shoe. Instead of welcoming Sangita into the family, they embraced him alone, as if he'd returned from a war. His mother acted as if he'd just popped back home from his university days in the UK, not as if he was marking a stage on the journey to setting up his own household.

There she was, setting out his breakfast in the morning instead of letting the maid do it, asking him when he might be around for dinner. He stayed up every night, poring over pages of data, pushing away the whispers that he was making the biggest mistake of his life. *No risk, no gain,* he reminded himself over and over again, trying to override the accelerated heartbeat thudding in his ears. He lost track of the number of times the fajr dawn call to prayer had jolted him out of his drooling over folders filled with business plans for yogurt-smoothie-juice shop hybrids and the like.

Between his mother's renewed attentions and James's endless texted requests for information, he hardly had time to talk to anyone else before heading out the door—especially not Sangita, who was waiting for her morning "hello" next door in his uncle's house.

"So you like these invitations?" Maryam passed the cards over to him as he adjusted his *ghutra* and *agal* in the hallway mirror.

"Sangita says they're too plain."

Maryam made a tsking sound. "We are not a flashy family. She wants red. Maybe a flourish here or there, but red? Imagine."

"It's her wedding," Abdulla said. "Give her what she wants."

"You can't be serious." Maryam pressed the card to her chest. "This is our wedding. The union of two families."

The bleat of his phone interrupted Abdulla before he could reassure his mother that in fact he was very serious. He pressed *Decline* to the unknown number. "When you put it like that—" The line lit up again.

"You've got to get your head on straight," James said, the second Abdulla answered. "They'll go with someone else. And no one in food will want to work with us if we pull out now."

"James, hang on, I'm coming in," Abdulla said. He slipped the phone into his pocket and turned to his mother. "*Yema*, be nice. This is the only wedding she's going to have. And if you had a girl, you could have chosen. But you have sons." He pressed a kiss to her forehead to lessen the severity of his words. His phone vibrated against his leg. *Same unknown number.*

"Hello?" Abdulla said sharply.

"Is this Mr. Mohammed, guardian of Saad?" A woman's equally clipped tone rang in his ear.

"That's my father," Abdulla said. "He's traveling." He climbed into the car. James was sending him a stream of sketches of dollar bills catching fire.

"You are?"

"Abdulla," he said. "I'm the guardian when my father is traveling. Is it a fever?" The international schools never called unless a kid was sick. "I can send the driver."

"No, Mr. Abdulla, I'm afraid Saad has come to school without his lunch," the woman said. "He's got nothing to eat."

"Well, he must have money on that band thing," Abdulla said in disbelief. The boys' school issued each student a wristband to swipe in and out of the building. Keeping track of it was a full-time job for Anita.

"Apparently he's spent it all, buying pizza for his friends last week."

Abdulla pinched the bridge of his nose in frustration.

"If you're near a computer, you can add money online right away with your family login details."

Abdulla stared at the minute hand of his watch. Was this what parenthood was all about? He had no idea what their login might be or where to start guessing.

"Perhaps we can call the boy's mother?"

"No, no, I'm coming," Abdulla said. His father would be furious if he thought Abdulla was shirking his responsibilities to the family, especially for his non-existent business. "I'll be there in twenty minutes."

"We'll see you when you get here," the woman said. The line disconnected before he could say another word.

"I'm going to be late," Abdulla said to James through the car's Bluetooth.

"Picking out drapes with the missus?" James said and texted a sketch of a store with empty aisles.

"Something with the family," Abdulla mumbled. "I'll call you later." He pulled out into the traffic, wondering where he could stop along to the way to pick up some snacks for his brother.

* * *

When he got to the school, the African guards smiled in greeting. Abdulla handed over his ID. He went through the metal detector, remembering his own grade-school days, when drivers would lounge around the waiting area until they could pick up their charges. The guards buzzed him through the heavy security door—reinforced to minimize a bomb blast.

Abdulla stood on the threshold, staring at the brick courtyard. The friendliest of the four men in the guard station jumped up, asking where he needed to go. He then led Abdulla toward middle school with a long-legged stride, past the outdoor swimming pool and along the side of one of the two libraries—as announced by the books painted on the exterior walls. Saad should be turning into a Da Vinci, Abdulla thought as they strode through a hallway littered with student creations inspired by Salvador Dali. Not some kind of absent-minded loafer. The grocery bag swung against his knee.

"Cafeteria," the guard said with a blinding grin, his white teeth sharply contrasting with his black skin. They stopped outside a glass-enclosed atrium.

"Thank you," Abdulla murmured. He entered the rectangular room, which had an oval space at the end where kids sat at long tables chattering like a group of trapped chickens. He spotted his brother hanging off a bench that ran along the side of a table. "Lunch." Abdulla slung the deli sandwich and bottled water onto the table.

"Uff; I wanted McDonald's." Saad covered his face with his hands. Red paint dotted the cuffs of his *thobe*.

"You're filthy," Abdulla said in a low voice. "Roll those up."

"Hello, are you Saad's father?" The teacher's gaze raked over his traditional dress, her eyes as blue as the waters of the Arabian Gulf.

"No, I'm his brother," Abdulla said. "Sorry about this. Won't happen again."

"Yes, of course." She nodded in the direction of the table. "You can reload the bands online."

"Hm." Abdulla's brother made no movement toward the sandwich.

"Could I talk to you for a few seconds—if you are one of Saad's guardians?"

"Yes, sure." Abdulla followed her a few steps away from the table of kids, who carried on boasting about who was fastest in P.E. He leaned forward to catch the teacher's words.

Apparently, she recounted in low tones, Saad had been baiting one of his classmates for over a week. "One of our core values is respect," she said.

"Right," Abdulla said. "I mean, kids joke around a lot. Maybe the boys are a little rougher than they should be." Visions of his school days flashed back to him. There was always a group prowling around looking for the weaker ones. Back then, in the government schools, there was a hierarchy of who preyed on who. Local kids harassed other, non-Gulf, Arab boys, who in turn would tease the odd Indian or Asian kid who was getting a free public education by studying in Arabic, unlike all the other expats who went to private international schools.

"His classmate's family is from Germany. Your brother has been calling him a Nazi."

Abdulla glanced over his shoulder at the table. Which of the kids was it? The skinny blonde one? He murmured his apologies. "You know we don't cover World War II history in the local primary schools. The novelty will wear off."

"The novelty"—the teacher pronounced it as if it were a dirty word—"should not be used to categorize students. Everyone is free to learn here."

"Yes, of course," Abdulla mumbled. "I ... you know, I studied in the UK for university, and I hope my brother gets to see the world too."

"You did? Where?"

"Did you tell the other boy's parents?" Abdulla searched the room for another set of adults.

"They're also traveling," she said. "We'll send them a note after the boys meet with the counselor."

"I'll be sure to talk to him. So that Saad realizes his error." Abdulla cleared his throat.

"Yes, and we'll be talking about respect in class as well. I wanted to bring it to your attention, since his parents don't respond to email."

"Sure." Abdulla wasn't going to waste his time explaining that his parents' generation saw the school as an island. Children were sent there to be educated, at the discretion of the teachers.

"May I have a moment with my brother, please?"

"Ah, yes, but we're finishing up now."

"Okay." Abdulla waited as she motioned Saad over. The rest of the class threw away the remains of their lunch and packed up their bags.

"What a weird thing to fixate on," Abdulla hissed when Saad was in earshot. "Why would you call that kid a Nazi?"

Saad gulped. "Do you know what the Nazis did? They killed millions of people. Women and children and J—"

Abdulla put up a hand. "Listen, you can't go around talking about Jews. You're an Arab. You live in an Arab country." He was turning into his father already. "Don't forget who you are." And he didn't even have any children of his own.

"So killing people is okay? Because they're the enemy?" Saad's voice rose. The teacher gathered everyone in the hallway, redirecting their attention to herself.

Abdulla grabbed Saad by the shoulder. "I can't deal with this now. I have to get back to work. Never speak of this to anyone again. Ever. Do you understand?" He gave his brother a shake. "You're not a kid anymore. You've got to take things seriously. Next time you forget it you can go without lunch."

Saad nodded, his chin wobbling.

Abdulla raced past security as fast as he could. His face flushed, even though the guards couldn't possibly suspect what had brought him onto the campus. His tires kicked up a stream of dust across the dirt parking lot. *Firefighting, from one crisis to the next—that's what my life is turning into.*

Chapter Four

The press of bodies made Hind blush. She turned toward the window, grateful for the rush of air that stirred a few of the older women's shawls. At home, no local woman would step aboard anything so crowded. Even the metro in Dubai ran empty, or full of expats, despite the pink cars designated for ladies. Taking the train to the south side of town this evening had been a lark. Another foray in her program of micro-changes. A dozing child rolled on his mother's shoulder, and his shoe dropped onto Hind's lap. The mother stood staring out the window at the city speeding by, not responding.

"Um …" Hind fumbled with the shoe; a set of Velcro straps were presumably meant to fasten across the foot. The sleeping child was no help, and if the shoe somehow fitted, Hind would have loved to see a demonstration of someone putting it on. "Do you want to sit?" she asked the mother as the train skidded to a stop.

The woman slid onto the bench, taking the shoe from Hind with one hand and deftly slipping it back on the infant's foot without missing a beat.

Now that she was standing, Hind reconsidered her evening out. Women stood in groups chatting to each other or with young guys, showing each other videos on their phones. The constant rumble of voices was quite unlike the ever-present blanket of silence on the Tube that Hind remembered from years visiting and studying in London. *Life.* The riot of colors in the women's clothing—even the men's—striped bright yellows and neon greens that hurt your eyes. She tugged at her pink kurta and black jeans that would've been the envy of any ladies' gathering at home. Here she felt dowdy with her full sleeves, standing next to the women in their sleeveless blouses. Pressed every which way by people of all sizes, she felt relief rather than disgust. The perfumes and deodorants, mixing with sweat, woke up her senses as if from a long slumber. She exhaled, holding her wrist up to her nose. How many weeks since she'd been around this many people? Back home, there were only a few ways you would describe someone: light, dark, black. A palette of skin tones that went way beyond such limited vocabulary crushed into the carriage with her.

The app on her phone buzzed. This was her stop. She joined the crush of bodies exiting, leaving the mother and son both lost in slumber. The crowd emptied out onto the platform, pushing against the people trying to get in, like a surge of fish going upstream. She walked behind two girls linking arms and chatting to each other in Hindi. *Language.* Another thing on her checklist for a successful life away from home. Hind climbed the steps with them. The same impetus that had once driven her to invite a near-stranger to share her apartment in London now flooded her with gratitude for strangers once again.

She picked up her pace with an energy she hadn't felt in weeks. Out on the street traffic crawled by, horns blared, and moped riders held on tight to their helmeted drivers. She smiled as a small girl with swaying ponytails waved, sandwiched between her mother's belly and her father's back. The app led her to the comedy club's entrance. She took a deep breath before pushing past the swinging door.

A man in a tight black t-shirt stamped her hand. Hind paused for a minute, coughing at the cigarette smoke that singed her lungs. *This was a mistake,* she thought with a sinking feeling as her eyes adjusted to the semi-dark interior of the bar. A single microphone stood at the center of a stage at the front. Cocktail tables scattered throughout the club, and people in pairs, trios or larger groups chatted and held bottles of Kingfisher beer.

At the sight of the alcohol, Hind heard her mother's voice echoing in her ears—*Astaghfirullah!*—asking forgiveness for having raised such a daughter. For most of her life so many choices had been made easy for her. No dating. No pork. No alcohol. She broke into a sweat. Those things were each there for the taking now—if she so chose. Did she want any of them? Or none? As on that fateful trip with Ravi, she shied away from making any decision that would go against her upbringing. *Better to flee and remain the person everyone assumed you were.*

"Going so soon?" The guy at the door looked up from his perch on the stool.

"Oh, I was meeting friends. They're not coming." His blank stare egged her on to say more. "Birthday plans. You know, she changed her mind." She forced a laugh.

"The birthday's over there." He pointed a pencil toward a knot of young women standing by the front of the stage.

"No, I don't think …"

"First act will be on in five minutes," he said. "She's good."

"Ah …" Hind fell back a step as another group swept into the club. She allowed them to pull her along in their wake, thinking she'd make another attempt to leave when the bouncer was not so interested in her entertainment. The girls were speaking English. And in the glare of the swiveling stage lights, Hind saw that they were closer to her age than the barely-out-of-high-school girls at other tables. Instead of squealing and reaching for each other like teenagers, these women stood around ordering sodas and eyeing the food menu.

"What bank are you with?" a chubby woman in leggings and a t-shirt asked.

"Oh, I'm a diplomat," Hind said.

"Ah, traditional wear all day." She gave Hind a once-over. "Saris?"

"Uh, no." Hind realized with a start that the woman thought she was Indian. For some reason, this helped her relax. What if she were just one of the dozens of women here to grab a drink and blow off steam heading into the weekend?

"You definitely could pass," Ravi used to say to her each day when they visited the children in the village, installing computers for the first-ever lab in the school run by the orphanage.

And so I shall, she thought, grabbing a handful of peanuts out of the bowl in the middle of the nearest table. "Coke," she said hastily when the waiter came to take her order.

"Rum and coke?" He peered at her while tapping her order into a hand-held device.

"Soda only," Hind said.

He gave a shrug and turned to the group one table over.

She scrolled through the Instagram feed on her phone to avoid looking as forlorn as she felt. The low rumble of dozens of conversations and instrumental background music was better than the news anchors keeping her company in her apartment. But this prickly feeling of being around people yet utterly alone might possibly be worse.

"Haven't seen you here before." A guy in a shirt that stretched open over his broad chest stood next to her at the table.

"First time," Hind mumbled. Her first time in a bar. Only to discover it was kind of like what they warned you about in grade school. Men came up to you without a thought. What would she do if he threw his phone number at her on a piece of paper, like the boys did in the malls at home? Would she tear it up in his face and storm out?

"Yeah, me too. Not my scene. Waiting for my girlfriend." He reached for the pile of nuts in the glass bowl on the table.

She relaxed a little, sipping cautiously at the soda the waiter brought over.

"Whiskey, neat," the boyfriend said without preamble.

The waiter nodded as if this were a decent order.

Hind turned around, giving her back to the man, and the table, a faux pas her mother would have castigated her for—in the *majlis* or at a party. *If only she knew her daughter was in a bar …* Hind chuckled to herself. She had to find another table before the whiskey arrived, that much she knew for sure. Going out to a bar, a guy coming up to you, and alcohol—she didn't want to overdo it on her first night out. The group of women who came in shortly after her had taken up a row of seats in front of the stage. One aisle seat was empty. Hind slipped in among them, her dark hair blending inconspicuously among a sea of similar shades. Was this the kind of thing Ravi did on a Friday night? She didn't have much time for any further wistful thinking. A short man in snug jeans and a black button-down shirt took to the stage amid a chorus of whistles.

"You should cheer," he shouted into the microphone. "Wait until you hear what we have in store for you!"

Chapter Five

Luluwa smirked at the blonde woman across from her. The young American's neck couldn't swivel fast enough to keep up with the parade of glamorous dresses as their owners marched to their seats. She gaped at the plunging neckline of a woman in five-inch Louboutins—a cousin by marriage through one of Luluwa's aunts—who flicked her eyes in greeting as she minced past their table, breasts and hips swaying. Green satin clung to her ample figure and stretched across ponderous arms. Her chin jiggled as she moved beyond them to a table more worthy of her attention.

Sort of like watching a tennis match, only boobs instead of a ball.

"Is this what everyone wears under their *abayas*?" the American asked, her blue eyes pools of wonder.

"No," Luluwa laughed. "On a normal day we wear pajamas."

Trays of welcome sweets, little nibbles of *fatayer* and other appetizers, marked the second hour of waiting for the bride to make her appearance. When she did come, would her soon-to-be cousin-in-law Sangita manage not to smile, since people would think it was bad luck?

A server of indeterminate Asian features—Indonesian if Luluwa had to guess—arrived at their table and extended her right hand with a gold-rimmed *finjal,* the tiny cup for Arabic coffee. "*Gahwa, ma'am.*"

"This is the size of a shot glass," the American woman said, accepting a steaming cup. At Luluwa's blank look, she sipped the liquid. "Ouch, that's hot."

Another head-scarved Asian woman followed close behind, toting a basket of chocolates wider than she was.

"*La, shukran,*" Luluwa's table companion said with a smile and shoved the bulging wicker tray in Luluwa's direction.

The rituals of coffee and sweets repeated at the thirty or so tables scattered throughout the room. This first wave of hospitality was like an army, an army hired by the aunts.

"Oh, Godiva!" A woman with pudgy fingers one table over recognized the Belgian brand and reached for a wrapped square from the welcome sweets.

They could have at least got treats from Patchi, the Lebanese chocolatier. Luluwa itched to text this to someone, anyone. Noor would be all too happy that her sister's ex-fiancé was being slighted at his own wedding by his own family.

"I should be taking notes for my wedding," giggled Mary, an exchange student from the university's main campus in Texas. Her accent was like cotton candy, sweet and easy on the ear. Her brown hair and eyes gave her a mousy look, friendly, yet easily passed over.

"Not like an American at all," her cousin Noor had said in bemusement about Mary the first time they'd bumped into each other at the café in Luluwa's university building.

"Well, I'm not your fashion plate either," the coltish Luluwa had replied, not sure who she was defending, herself or Mary, or both.

"You; you have potential you squander," Noor had retorted, flicking a hand at Luluwa's high cheekbones and shoulder-length hair that tumbled from beneath her scarf. "Don't use youth as your excuse."

The fact that sixteen-year-old Luluwa was in university at the same time as her slightly older cousin rankled. Skipping a year in elementary and a year in high school had seen Luluwa tutoring Noor through their finals together.

"How memorable!" Mary sighed heavily, the gust of air ruffling her low-hanging bangs. She wore black pants and a hot-pink silk shirt. If she'd been local, people would've thought she was a *boya*, a girl pretending to be a man, and Luluwa her girlfriend. But Mary's milky skin announced her foreignness and, with it, an excuse for her style of clothing.

"They're all the same," Luluwa murmured. Mary had no way of knowing that this wedding was not like the dozens of others that would take place this month, many this week, even. In most of the others, cousins were marrying within the family to the delight of their parents and the tribe. She could see why Mary would be fooled, and hoped the others in attendance would be as easily convinced.

Azure blue curtains draped the walls. No fault there; they'd spent the extra money to decorate the hall. A fifty-meter catwalk ran all the way down the middle of the room, an exposed tongue on which the bride would tread her journey to the mouth. The bride and her family and friends had ample room to display their happiness. The imposing sofa at the top of the platform, where the bride would greet her guests and could sit with at least fifty people, was a yawning expanse of white leather.

The main problem was that there weren't fifty people who would sit there.

"Most people are in their pajamas," Luluwa said, "when not at parties. Under their *abayas.*"

Her companion's blue eyes squinted doubtfully as a red-chiffon train with a rear view Kim Kardashian would have envied sashayed past. "Pajamas?"

"At least, I know I am," Luluwa replied. She scanned the room for signs that the family were taking this marriage seriously. There weren't many. At least someone, probably Aunt Maryam, had seen to it that the initials S and A, entwined together in a cream seal, were plastered on the back of each chair.

The persistent blue-eyed woman—*what was her name? Susan? Alice?*—scooted closer to the other university professors, who were huddled together at the south end of the table. They whispered together like teenage girls, taking sidewise glances at the lacquered hairdos at the tables that surrounded them.

Overt ogling by the three hundred local women in attendance rewarded their discretion. As animals would in a savannah, the locals stared back from their tables without any attempt to hide their gaze.

Luluwa sat with the Americans Noor had invited from her university, but her cousin was nowhere in sight.

Angela, a waifish blonde, kept tugging at her hemline. "If I'd known, I would've had a longer one made," she muttered. Her specialty was dressmaking, or some such, in the fashion department at Noor's university.

All the Westerners had worn short dresses, and their legs stuck out like cream twigs in the forest of satin and chiffon filling the ballroom—far more conspicuous than the other *ajnabiya* at Luluwa's table: the darkest woman in the room, her petite Indian frame nestled in the curve of the ballroom chair.

Abdulla's new mother-in-law was the recipient of disapproving glares directed at the back of that chair in particular.

How different this wedding was from the henna-laden, dance-filled affair her sister Fatima had had. Tears stung Luluwa's eyes at the memory of Fatima on her way to the bride's seat at the *kosha*, the bodice of her dress heaving with nervousness. Little more than a girl, Luluwa had held her breath, restrained by their mother's firm hand from darting forward when her older, and only, sister swayed as she stepped onto the front of the long catwalk. Twelve-year-old Luluwa had gasped, her worry mingling with the band's cry, like a call to arms, "*Aeeeeiii Mohammed!*" The prayer to ward off the evil eye thundered through the room. The prayer evidently hadn't worked, since at the height of her sister's happiness, three months into married life, a baby on the way, she and her unborn child had died in a car accident.

Luluwa bit her lip to halt the familiar train of thoughts. "Focus on the present," the counselor at her American-curriculum high school had said. It wasn't all that different from the Muslim idea that life was best left to the living, which was the rest of the family's advice in the months and years since her sister's passing.

In the present moment, Sangita's mother pushed up from the table and went to the closed double doors of the ballroom. No, this wasn't four years ago. This wasn't Fatima's wedding with her Aunt Maryam throwing one-riyal bills on their friends and family, dancing with joy that the first cousins of their family were getting married. Hessa, Luluwa's mother, wasn't here this time. Wasn't here yet, she corrected herself, texting her mother for the fifth time since the receiving line had opened two hours ago.

The phone buzzed with her reply. *They messed up my hair. I'll be there soon.*

A lie. An evasion. Luluwa tapped the edge of the phone's corner on the table. She couldn't blame her mother. How could Hessa celebrate her nephew's new wife when her daughter lay beneath the ground? Would she stand by and greet him with a smile as she'd done when he came to claim her daughter as his bride?

The double doors at the back remained closed.

There was still no sign of the bride.

Aunt Maryam led the other woman by the arm in what should have been a moment of great joy for the two mothers. Their children were getting settled. They were now relatives by marriage. But this was not the in-law of her aunt's choice. Luluwa leaned closer, mimicking her aunt, who was bending to hear what the much smaller woman had to say.

The Americans' attention had turned to sizing up the other parts of the reception, moving from the human bouquet to the towering floral decorations spurting out of two-foot tall, narrow-necked gold vases—the only detail Sangita had been allowed to choose. The rest—the low-slung white sofa at the top of the dais, the Sudanese wedding singers, the favors, boxes of dates with intertwined initials—was all arranged by the aunts. Taste on a budget, Luluwa knew. She hoped it wasn't obvious to the other attendees that instead of spoiling the bride in welcome to their family, the in-laws were doing what was required, but no more, going through the motions, hoping the groom would get over his romantic notions.

"You're so busy, dear, fixing up your house. Let us worry about this," Aunt Wadha had said to Sangita in a soothing voice.

Sangita had acquiesced, while murmuring about receptions in India and the United States. Luluwa had stood tongue-tied. The funny, charming and, it must be said, loud personality her sister's husband had fallen for had transformed into a demure maiden faster than a Disney princess. Luluwa couldn't intervene. For one thing, she didn't have the knowledge. Her own mother was hoping to move on to a new family, as a second wife for an older man with no children. In the Gulf women had children into their early forties, so her mother still had a chance to start over.

Meanwhile Luluwa's uncles were content for her to remain under their father's roof, toiling away in high school and then university. Luluwa's life would remain on the back burner so long as everyone avoided discussing what to do about Hind, her errant cousin, determined to live her dream of working for the Foreign Service in India.

"More food?" Angela gasped, pulling at her waistband. "Why start with an hour of chocolates if there's real food?"

The hotel's waitresses brought out the dinner plates, swarming each section like ants in their black pants and shirts, their Filipino nationality a uniform of its own. Luluwa had long stopped noticing details like this, that the band were Sudanese and the sweets servers Indonesian, but Sangita had called it to her attention in one of her lengthy analyses of Gulf wedding planning practices. The women at the next table sliced into their steaks as soon as the plates arrived. They chewed like cows masticating the same piece of meat over and over, their lips flapping open like barn doors.

"I'll go check on the bride," Luluwa said to the professors, and she strode away before anyone could ask her any more questions about whether all the hair they saw was real, or if Luluwa's blue sequined Saks Fifth Avenue sheath came in their size.

She pushed at the padded door and past the gauzy blue fabric that someone, probably the hotel wedding planner, had found romantic, evocative of a French boudoir.

"Where are you going?" Aunt Wadha's hand came around her waist and cinched her to the older woman's ample form like a vise.

"I was going to check on the bride," Luluwa stammered. "Isn't it—?"

"She's fine," Wadha said, turning Luluwa around.

"Should we tell her to—"

"You and all your friends should be dancing," Wadha said, shooing Luluwa toward the two steps leading up to the catwalk.

"I—"

"Aren't you happy for your cousin?"

"Yes, *Aamti,* of course."

"Then go, go. Dance."

Luluwa faltered, her foot on the first step. She and her friends were supposed to be crowding the dance floor, showing off their best angles, marketing themselves to all the mothers, aunts and sisters sitting on either side of the catwalk as suitable brides for their young men—showing that marriage was on their minds.

The drum started again, the all-female band buoyed by the sight of a dancer. A dancer meant money: money raining down on the dancer while the band members and hospitality crew scurried hither and thither to gather up as much as they could. Luluwa made her way up the steps, cursing the lonely years since Fatima's death, the years she'd spent in the office of the guidance counselor or hanging around Abdulla like—his father had warned, when he thought she was out of earshot—a baby camel. She had no real friends among her classmates, not at university.

No cousins, Hind or Noor, to hide behind.

She'd made herself a pariah amongst the local girls she'd gone to high school with by declaring mechanical engineering as her major. Most of them were studying something more sensible, like international relations, that didn't require working with men but led to jobs in government ministries that were gender-segregated. So much for international universities right in your backyard to broaden your horizons. Ostensibly she and every other local girl could choose their own path from the comfort of home, without having to go abroad unchaperoned.

"Yes, yes, yes, yes," the singer crooned, encouraging the guests to crowd the dance floor.

Luluwa proceeded down the catwalk, moving her shoulders, legs, and waist as she'd seen hundreds of other women do at countless family weddings. The beat was slow, her steps stilted, the dance designed to show her off to maximum advantage. No Hollywood gyrations here. If only she could close her eyes, be twelve years old again, trailing in the perfume of their mothers and sisters, chasing Noor from this basket to that, looking for the tastiest sweets, this whole spectacle a game, a reason to get dressed up, nothing more. If she could close her eyes and execute moves like Beyoncé or J-Lo, anything to make these moments speed up, pass in a blur of shaking hips and swinging hair. She turned to look at the top of the room and the sofa Sangita would occupy; its white leather spread like wings behind her. A few others joined her at the foot of the catwalk: high school girls, giggling; there for a good night out, a female wedding party being the one place their conservative parents would let them go. Certainly not the malls, where all the casual flirting took place and assignations were made.

Two dyed blondes, their angular faces beaming, brushed shoulders, shimmying nascent breasts. Buoyed by the small crowd, Mary popped up next to them, shaking her hips with a wide grin. Aunt Maryam came to shower them with one *riyal* bills and a tight smile. For her son's wedding, she had to pretend happiness and keep the tongues from further wagging.

"Slowly, slowly," Luluwa said, taking Mary by the hand. She swayed, hoping to slow her friend's shimmy, honed in a nightclub by the looks of things, into a rhythm more suitable for *khaleeji* audiences.

"Oh, sorry." Mary reached down to pick up a bill that had floated under her foot. She gave it to the woman with henna-stained finger tips crouching to sweep up all the bills. The woman took it without raising her head and moved away to collect more bills. She waited for a few others to move their feet before snatching them up.

"No, let her get it on her own," Luluwa whispered, grateful when the song ended. She speeded up her exit down the catwalk, pulling a confused Mary in her wake, back to their table.

"Seems so weird. Why do they have those vests on?"

"They work for a charity," Luluwa mumbled, keeping her eyes straight ahead as the guests stared unabashedly at her and the American in her knee-length dress. "They get to keep everything they collect."

Aunt Wadha was crossing the room to intercept them. Luluwa cut a diagonal line through the tables to avoid her.

"Why not donate it?" Mary stumbled as she tried to squeeze herself between a set of chairs, their occupants immobile. "I mean, plastic bags in a room full of this—" Mary gestured at the billowing tulle draped around the room and the towering floral centerpieces.

Her question went unanswered. Arriving at the table, Luluwa grabbed a glass of fresh juice from the Filipina waitress.

"You're brave," Angela said to Mary. "That was like the Virginia reel."

"So fun," Mary giggled.

Luluwa gulped down a river of liquid strawberries.

Angela craned her neck towards Luluwa. "You know, line dancing, practiced steps, deliberate movements."

"Not really," Luluwa mumbled. Her science classes did not cover the minutiae of American society. Nor, for that matter, did her history or English electives.

The music stopped. A flurry of hotel staff gathered at the back of the room.

"She's coming!" Luluwa said so loudly that women at the next table turned around.

"Oh, the bride?"

A fog machine started as the lights dimmed. The fog built up, clouding the doorway.

"So dramatic!"

Or they're hoping to hide the fact she isn't local. But they'd need a lot more than smoke and strobe lights. There had been no bridal slideshow of the henna or engagement nights. Sangita had preferred—or been coerced?—to keep those pictures private.

The door swung open; two women in black hotel uniforms pressed it back against the wall.

One second, two, and then she emerged—the prow of a ship breasting a storm. Her face was composed, her hair in a coiled braid around the crown of her head. She wore a blood-red sari, heavy with gold embroidery. Luluwa felt the collective gasp. She clutched Angela's bony wrist, dropping it when the woman turned to her questioningly. Sangita hadn't used the fabric to make a wedding dress, as she'd said she would. Nor had she chosen any of the dozens of dresses they'd considered as alternates in the pages and pages of magazines they'd pored over.

Sangita's procession walked swiftly from the entrance up the catwalk. She didn't pause for the videographer; she didn't have to tug at a train. The camera on the boom arm oscillated ten feet above everyone, catching the shocked expressions. *This was one video they'd have to destroy.*

Sangita, oblivious to them all, held her head high and marched toward her seat at the *kosha*. The sari shimmered in the light, the fabric riding on her undulating hips, exposing perfect abs at every other step.

"How could this have happened?" Luluwa muttered, as the Americans ooh-ed and ah-ed at how well-chosen red was for the bride's skin tone.

"At least she's fair and not dark like some of them." Noor slid onto Luluwa's seat, nudging her to move over. "I told her it wasn't the best choice," she added, in Arabic, reaching for the basket of bread rolls.

"What? Where have you been?" Luluwa hissed. "I could have used your help."

"I did my best," Noor said, chewing a mouthful of brown bread. "She needed me more, but as you can see," she tore off another chunk, "she didn't take my advice."

"Well, probably because of the source."

They exchanged glances.

"Messenger, not the message." Noor motioned to a waiter for a dinner plate, even as dessert, an assortment of cakes, was being placed on each table.

"She wasn't having it."

A heavy gold choker encircled Sangita's delicate throat, radiating spikes across her sternum.

"We have to go to her," Luluwa gasped, coming to herself as the bride reached the end of her walk. "She doesn't know what to do. Come on!" She jerked Noor up and away from the empty plate. Luluwa linked arms with her cousin and pulled her along with a peal of fake laughter, weaving the most direct path to the steps at the front of the stage.

Aunt Maryam was already there—Allah be praised—with Sangita's mother, who dabbed at tears with a tissue spotted with her brown foundation.

Tears of happiness, or ... Luluwa swept into the photo, taking the chance to squeeze Sangita's arm. The bride's uncomprehending glance said she hadn't recognized the nerdish Luluwa without her glasses or ripped t-shirts.

"It's me," she said with a wink.

"Wow," Sangita replied shakily. "Lulu. Hi."

"This way, this way," insisted the Lebanese photographer, her arched eyebrows raised in a permanent state of surprise. "Closer. Closer, please."

No one moved an inch. All the aunts were present now, hands at their sides. Luluwa's mother, Hessa, stared at the camera without even the wan smile Aunt Maryam had managed.

Luluwa stretched her lips as wide as they would go, emotions swirling in her chest, making it hard to breathe. Noor leaned into her when she started to sway.

The guests crowded the platform now, paying their respects to Aunt Maryam while flicking a glance at the red sari-clad bride. No dress to gossip about here—the bodice too low, the waist impossibly slim. No, the bride herself would be the central subject of the wedding's deconstruction in the days to come.

You better get here as soon as you can, Luluwa messaged Abdulla. *This cannot drag on.*

Sangita continued to sit on the sofa, where she would wait for Abdulla in front of a sea of women's faces, hundreds of them, their eyes taking in her hair, her makeup, the pattern work on her gold necklace, dangling earrings, the tiered stacks of bangles.

Tongues were already wagging: the lipstick was too red, the gold sandals too simple, the hair couldn't possibly all be hers.

Aunt Maryam's brave front continued. She sailed from table to table, greeting their family friends.

Her phone buzzed as if surprised at the irregularity of the evening. *I've been upstairs the whole time. Should I come now?*

Yes, she replied, without asking the dozens of questions she would soon have the answers to. *Did you see the sari? Is our family with you? Which of the boys is coming?*

Luluwa passed a glass of water to Sangita. Her mother had joined her on the sofa. Sangita sat still, so still that she could've been a local bride, worried about attracting the evil eye. Her eyebrows were plucked into symmetrical arches; her face remained impassive as she surveyed the audience who'd come to see Abdulla's strange choice of bride.

The black-haired hotel staff bobbed through the guests like corks. Women reached for the *abayas* on the backs of their chairs. Younger ones went to the collection area in the lobby to cover up. The sea of multicolored finery vanished, to be replaced by a single hue: black. From head to toe, the women were covered from the prying eyes of the male party about to enter.

The Americans clustered together at their table, no doubt mourning this change that hid the ostentation they'd found so fascinating.

And then the doors swung open again, this time with no fog, no strobe lighting. On the groom's arrival the female singer's voice rose in volume to fill the room with a piercing blessing. Abdulla, Uncle Mohammed, Uncle Saoud and Luluwa's prepubescent cousins Khalid and Saad strode into the ballroom. Khalid and Saad smiled as their heads swung from side to side, trying to pick out women they knew in the crowd. Kids loved weddings more than the adults did—like the younger girls running around the room.

Luluwa's father, Ahmed, hadn't come. Luluwa noticed a deflation in her mother's posture. Her uncles, Mohammed and Saoud, flanked the groom, their eyes trained on their wives. Her cousin Abdulla, more like a sibling to her, stepped up eagerly onto the platform, ready to march his way forward to claim his bride. Uncle Mohammed put a restraining hand on Abdulla's sleeve, pinching the five fingers of his other hand together, gesturing for a more measured pace. His son only had eyes for the woman in red at the end of their walk.

Sangita rose as Abdulla approached across the distance, his legs making strides as long as the hem of his *thobe* would allow. Her uncle put his arm in the crook of Abdulla's elbow to slow him down once again. *Wouldn't do to look too eager.*

Had his eyes shone for her sister the way they were trained on Sangita? He reached her and stood next to her without touching, despite the intensity of their eye contact, as the photographer's camera flashed. The camera on the swinging boom closed in on them, the arm bent at an awkward angle.

Luluwa went to have her photo taken with the bridal couple. Khalid and Saad jostled each other, their elbows jutting out at her. "Stop squirming," she hissed.

The boys were not at all intimidated by the hundreds of women and the loud music; if anything, they seemed to be encouraged by the razzmatazz. Preening in the presence of so many adults, they flipped their *ghutras* this way and that, as if they were not pieces of cloth but extensions of their hair.

Abdulla finally sat down, Sangita next to him as if she were a doll.

"Water," Luluwa said, passing them a tray with two bottles.

Abdulla twisted the cap off one of them and gulped down half of it. Aunt Maryam shooed Luluwa away from hovering. Her uncle gave her a brief smile, said something in his wife's direction, and made his way back down toward the door.

"Boys," he called sharply, when Khalid and Saad showed no signs of ceasing their endless posing for the photographer. They left without further ceremony, the boys too young and her uncles too scrupulous to search the crowd for any negligently veiled women or uncovered foreigners.

Luluwa sat next to Sangita's mother, whose bangles tinkled as she toyed with the silverware.

"It's so hot up there," she said.

"The lights," Luluwa said sympathetically. She waved away the uniformed Indonesian waitress who offered yet another tray of sweets, this time cake pops with a blue dusting. She had gone with Sangita and Aunt Maryam to pick out all the sweets; the cake pops had been her idea, a personal touch in the impersonal bridal machinery.

Sangita's mother fretted. "She seems tired."

"We were up early," Luluwa said. The two women watched the bridal couple as everyone else in the room watched them, their glances alternating between the bride and her mother, everyone eyeing the dark skin that bespoke their Indian ethnicity. "At least he loves her," Luluwa said.

Abdulla's hand lay on the couch between their legs, his pinky finger touching the back of Sangita's palm.

"They'll need more than love," Sangita's mother muttered. She pressed a napkin to her mouth as if to keep herself from saying more.

Luluwa's mother, Hessa, would say the same thing. The ravages of her sister's death and father's divorce had shattered the illusion of their comfortable family life. "Get your education," her mother repeated at their monthly dinners in her brother's house, prepared by her one remaining housemaid. "Then you won't have to depend on anyone."

Luluwa had taken her words to heart, all too conscious of their searing relevance to her life. Her mother depended on her father's monthly payments, which would cease in the next year or two after Luluwa married. Hessa had only a high school diploma. A primary teacher's salary was not enough to support the lavish lifestyle she needed to keep up with her friends who had jobs in telecoms or oil companies.

"Back in my day," Sangita's mother said, "marrying a Gujarati when you were from the south was the most rebellious thing someone could do."

"It's in her blood then," Luluwa said. "Going to new places for love."

"That's what her father said." Her mother managed a laugh. "Abdulla told them not to bother with the men's wedding. 'Standing around drinking tea,' he said. 'We'll get together another time.' I hope it's not a delaying tactic."

Luluwa saw the passion in Abdulla's eyes and no sign of the disappointment or anger another groom might have felt at what Sangita wore. The couple were chatting now, phrases out of the corners of their mouths while continuing to face forward.

Love or a career.

She ate a forkful of rice.

Sangita and Abdulla stared ahead, submitting to their status as the focus of all the curiosity in the room. Luluwa wondered if women really had any more choices today than in previous generations.

* * *

The jinni pounced on the rat; its neck snapped in his jaws like a twig. Blood filled his mouth and coursed down his throat. He clutched the body in his paws, holding on tightly as the muscles twitched in death. His first kill in many months. Rats down on the docks were large, their tails as long as the body of his feline host.

"Nothing," the diver said. She tore off her mask and swim cap, black hair disappearing against the black wetsuit.

"Every day, the same. For months. Like we're caught in a net." The man in the dark suit paced back and forth. "I don't see how that's possible. The records say the ship sank just before docking. It must be here."

The jinni rolled his eyes at the human. If this man could find a few months of sitting dockside so trying, he would surely never have endured for forty years as he, the jinni-cat, had done. Yet as long as Benita lurked in the depths, trying her hardest to surface, he would stay to protect the ship and pay his debt.

"During a storm," the diver said. "I keep telling you, that was the biggest storm of the decade. That boat could be anywhere between here and the Arabian Gulf." She took the towel someone offered her and wrapped it around herself. "More likely nowhere. Wooden boats don't survive forty years in salt water." She bent her head to the left, shaking out excess water. "I'm off this project," she said. "They've got work for me on the Great Barrier Reef, measuring the bleaching."

"I'll double the money," the man wheedled. "Just a little more time."

"Three months of searching and still nothing." She shook her right ear over her shoulder. "I'm not going to waste my life chasing some legend of a pearl when there's real work to be done." She walked away, leaving the man in the suit sputtering.

The jinni gave a satisfied meow and licked his paws. Humans were such an interesting species. Amazing that things with such short attention spans survived this long.

"Aw, kitty." The diver bent down, crouching onto her knees. Her green eyes shone incandescent in the dock floodlights. "That can't taste good. You're well-groomed for a street cat." She reached out to stroke him between the ears, but the jinni forced himself to back away. That which he longed for had trapped him in the first place—his fascination with this parallel world, the world of humans.

"Come home with me," she crooned. "You shouldn't be out here. Milk and tuna and not so many smelly men."

He stiffened. As much as he wanted it, wanted her, wanted to transform out of this body and follow her home, he had to stay. She came near enough to pick him up. He arched his back, hissing.

"There, there, I won't hurt you," she whispered.

His hind paws paddled against her forearms; the rubber of her wetsuit fortunately prevented them from touching him directly. The carcass of the rat dropped to the cement floor.

"We'll be home and warm in thirty minutes."

The jinni closed his eyes in frustration, trying to erase the words from his memory. He gave her arm a nip. Not enough to break the skin, but so she felt the points of his incisors through the wetsuit.

"Ouch!" She dropped him and stepped back. "Have it your own way, then." She spun around, leaving both the man in the suit and the jinni to stare after her.

Khaldoon sighed, returning to his unfinished rodent meal. He had to stay. No choice until his debt was paid and the man who saved him had the chance to live out his natural life, dying only when it was his time, not a second before. Benita lurked in the waters below, desperate to be found, but if found and released, she would wreak havoc on everyone associated with her capture in the pearl, human and jinn alike. He was the only thing stopping them from discovering the ship. And in order for his power to work, he had to stay right where he was on the dock.

Chapter Six

The week after the wedding wore on with more deliberations, James continuing as devil's advocate and Abdulla avoiding the Italian architects in the hotel lobby.

"So, boss, we're going to need a few people," James said. "You know, to start processing orders, tracking shipments etcetera when we sign with someone."

Abdulla sighed and pressed his fingers to his eyes. "Have someone in mind? We can't get another expat. Overhead is too high."

"There are a few temp options." James slid some resumes over to him. "And I think I should move out." He produced a sheet with projections for the hotel suite across the next three months.

"Rent in this area is going to cost you at least twelve thousand," Abdulla said. He flicked through the resumes of several women. Their faces peered up at him from the photos included in their applications, the practice not yet politically incorrect in this part of the world. Most of them were Filipinas. A few Indians. All of them posed unsmiling against plain blue or white backgrounds.

"Nineteen," James said. "If I want a spare room."

Abdulla gave a low whistle.

"I've found a place for half that."

"No way," Abdulla said. "Does it have a bathroom?"

"I'm getting roommates!" James grinned at him, his head propped between his hands.

"Huh," Abdulla said. "Women?"

"Nothing like that." James straightened his collar. "I mean, for now anyway. No, these guys got here a few months ago. They're working on the turf for the stadiums. And it'll bring our costs down."

"You met them where?" Abdulla regarded his friend across the table.

"Well, Dad, I met these fine young Americans downstairs in the Library Bar. We did drink a little."

"Go ahead and drink. You're not Muslim," Abdulla shrugged. He gave his friend another look. To move in with strangers, willingly, as an adult—well, they were on opposite trajectories. "James, I didn't realize you were bored."

His partner's shoulders sagged. "It's hard going, this place, Abdulla. Everyone is always 'Yes, sir; can I help you, sir?' I can't cook anything. Laundry takes at least a day. Don't ask how much it costs. I have to call for help anytime I want to go anywhere."

"Not like central London."

The two of them stared out the window morosely.

"Sorry, I don't mean to sound like a whinger," James said. "Can I get deported for being unhappy in the land of luxury?"

Abdulla laughed. "Go, enjoy your Americans." His thoughts, as ever, skipped to Sangita. If a seasoned professional like James was finding it hard being cooped up in this luxurious accommodation, no wonder she railed against her secluded life. *Roommates and drinking—well, those are out,* he thought. If those were the best ways to make new friends, he would need to come up with some alternative strategies. "You know what, let's get out of this place altogether. A real office, like a real start-up."

We need an admin—the words were on the tip of his tongue. He could pick up the phone and tell Sangita about the vacancy. But then then there would go his private space. His space away from her and the family, and the newness, and all of it. "Pick whoever you want." He slid the resumes back at James. "I'm going to find us an office."

James nodded. "That's the spirit! Who needs all the glamour and none of the ease of starting out? Didn't your dad help build the oil wells with his bare hands in the hot sun working for the British?"

Abdulla gave him a blank stare. "No, my grandfather was really into pearling, so he wouldn't let my father go into oil until it was almost too late. His brothers stayed on the ocean as long as they could. Finally Grandad gave his blessing because his boat sank off the coast of India."

"Oh, you guys, always rebelling." James gave him a salute. "Seriously, thanks. I'm off to pack my bags. Unwashed dishes and dirty bathrooms, here I come!"

Abdulla spent the rest of day looking at offices in the West Bay district for rents double what they were paying for James's suite at the hotel. "We are a start-up," he repeated for the umpteenth time to yet another Lebanese sales agent in tight black jeans and button-down white shirt. "We can't take on high overhead costs right now."

The guy ran a hand over slicked-back hair. He eyed Abdulla's cufflinks and *thobe*.

This isn't a negotiating strategy, Abdulla wanted to shout. He gave up after the third building. He'd have to find a place the way most people did anything—everything—here. He called his Uncle Saoud. The two had made an uneasy peace since Hind's move to India to work for the Foreign Service in the consulate. After the pleasantries, Abdulla came down to the favor. Did Saoud know of any reasonably-priced office spaces? He would get back to him, his uncle said.

In the pause that followed, neither of them said a word about the woman living in the family compound while Saoud still had two unmarried daughters—Hind and Noor. Many considered Hind a divorced woman, and therefore to be shunned, though she and Abdulla had never lived together during their engagement. And neither man acknowledged that, in the face of Abdulla's own father's blatant disapproval of his actions, this call was a cry for a father's help.

"Thank you," Abdulla said.

* * *

Hemmed in on both sides by parked cars, Abdulla drove through the neighborhood, yawning, then braked to make the turn into the family compound. Parking in front of Uncle Ahmed's house grew easier by the week. He brushed aside the memories. *A new wife, a new life,* he thought to himself, playing with the adage "happy wife, happy life".

And a longer game of hide and seek. Finding her in this much bigger place proved harder than in the two-bedroom penthouse apartment. He marched into the living room. Maybe today she'd be watching television and doing her nails, like his cousins did when they were teenagers. *What do women do at home all day?* He stopped short at the sight of a petite Ethiopian woman in matching pink shirt and pants, a white frilled apron tied around her waist, sitting on the floor of the kitchen.

She scrambled to her feet. "Sir, yes, sir: you want tea?"

"No, no," Abdulla said, backing away up the stairs.

She folded back into a seated position on the tiled floor, eyes downcast, like a toy that had run out of battery.

"Here you are!" He burst into Luluwa's old bedroom and found Sangita on her laptop. He blinked for a second at the all-white bedding. "You changed the sheets. And did you know there's someone sitting in the kitchen?"

"Lulu took me to Ikea." Sangita lifted her eyes from the computer. Pop music blared from the computer's speakers. "That's the maid your mother hired for us."

"That?" He sat on the footstool in front of the dresser and removed his cufflinks.

"Sally."

"Sally can help you with cooking and keeping the house clean."

Sangita slapped her hand on the other end of the dresser. "I don't need help cooking and cleaning! You said we weren't going to stay here that long."

"Maybe she can keep you company."

"Girls! Who run this mother? Girls!" blasted from the computer

"Turn that down."

She regarded him balefully over the edge of the computer screen.

"Please." The bassline of the song throbbed in time to his headache.

Beyoncé's lyrics faded. "I outweigh her by at least thirty pounds and can speak English in full sentences. What do we have in common?"

He rolled up his sleeves. "That's not very liberal of you." He waited, expecting a tirade, even as he wondered what argument would convince his mother to send the maid back to the agency. "You won't believe what Saad did."

"Egged the house next door because he has a crush on the neighbor?"

"I don't think he's noticed girls yet," Abdulla said. "Besides you." He perched precariously on a beanbag chair in the corner. "This is new. How does it work?"

"Lean the top part up against the wall."

He maneuvered it into place and leaned his head back. "Not bad. Could I get ten minutes please, Madam Writer?"

"Anyway, about Saad." She turned away from the machine, giving him her full attention.

"He's obsessed with the Nazis."

"You don't have to make stuff up so I'll talk to you."

He arched an eyebrow.

Sangita covered her mouth. "Okay, you're not making that up. He what? Wants a swastika on the ATV? Palestine to return to the people? He's got a point."

He folded his hands behind his head, pretending to contemplate a spot on the ceiling.

"Tell me!" She crawled over to his spot on the floor and pulled on his foot.

"No, no. Nothing political. He's calling out some German kid in his class." Abdulla swung his foot away from her as Sangita raked her fingernails across the arch. "I blame you Americans. Putting these ideas in his head at school."

"The British are who you should blame—for the mandate." She shrieked as he pulled her into his lap and tickled her under the arms. "So—" She fought back by digging her elbows into his side. "He went to history class, and now thinks—"

Abdulla flipped out of the beanbag, taking her with him. They lay panting on the floor. He pulled her hair out of his mouth. She stilled. They lay nose to nose. "Never mind all that. Which do you think we should do, a restaurant or a grocery store?"

"Um, both." The levity disappeared from her tone. "This town needs more of almost everything. People are pouring in here at a rate of thousands per month."

He rolled over onto his back, staring at the ceiling, hands folded on his chest. The weight of the question pressed him into the carpet. This was why he valued her; she brought an unexpected perspective on everything. "Okay, so I asked that the wrong way. Which one do you want to hear about every day for the next two years?"

"Neither."

He laughed. "Maybe I can get my old job back at the ministry."

"You could try," she said, chin quivering. "At least you have that option."

"I won't say Indian restaurant. I know you're a terrible cook."

Sangita burst into tears. She pushed away from him to make her way back to the dresser.

"Wait, wait." Abdulla rolled up from the floor and over to the footstool. "It's true—I mean, it's a joke, anyway."

"No, you're right. That's the point. I'm here all day alone, and I'm not very good at much."

"You were alone back in the apartment," he said. "And you have Lulu. How was the Ikea run, fun?" He struggled to find a way to restore the humor of a few minutes ago.

"She's a kid." Sangita hiccupped. "Plus she has homework, and friends and stuff. Even she can't babysit me all the time. You don't understand anything." Tears splashed on her t-shirt.

Truer words were never spoken, he thought, his heart clenching at the sight of her tearstained face. "Explain it to me." He drew her into his arms and rested his cheek against her hair. "Use words I can understand."

"At The Pearl, I could go down and walk around. I sat in cafés. Sure, alone, but there were people around. Here, it's like I'm trapped. I don't drive; I can't leave this place, and if I walk outside, it's like … like everyone is watching me." Her voice rose. "Now your mother sends me a minder. The maid is a spy. You know they report everything." She ended in a wail.

He pulled a wad of tissues from the box on the dresser and pressed it under her eyes. "You can choose your own maid," he said. "I'll ask her to return this one, and then you'll interview a few, find one you like—"

"Then this woman will be out of a job!" She banged her head against the dresser.

"Wait." Abdulla took her by the shoulders, pulling Sangita up so they sat looking at their reflections in the mirror. "What is really going on?"

Her chin trembled. More tears dropped into the hollow of her clavicle. He brushed them away, his hands remaining on either side of her shoulders.

She nibbled at his fingers. "Your aunt told me Maha is pregnant."

"Maha? Maha … I don't know this person." He flicked her in the cheek. "Which means neither do you."

"She's a neighbor or a cousin or someone."

"And she's pregnant."

"Ding, ding, ding." She went limp in his arms, all the mirth drained out of her. "This is what I'll be now. A baby machine."

Better than a whining machine—don't say that! "You're writing; you're busy."

"I need people," she said, hands clasped together.

"Why don't you look for a job, then?"

"I found one." She turned the screen to him. It showed the country's international news channel, an English-language offshoot of the long-existing Arabic one.

Was this a setup? He eyed her as she knuckled away tears that were as wet as rain. "Fine, go ahead." Abdulla stood and came around to face her, kneeling to tip up her chin. "Is that what you want?"

"But your family, your mom, they think those women wear too much makeup, and the hours are too long." She blinked at him, dabbing at her nose with the tissue.

He shrugged. "We'll deal with that as it comes."

Sangita grabbed her computer. "You can't take this back, you know. If I hit

Send, that's it. If they make me an offer——"

"Where did the raging feminist go? Can we get her to come back? Because this damsel in distress sucks," he said.

She laughed, as he hoped she would.

He let out a pent-up breath. "Get an interview first." *Wouldn't it take a while? Did they even reply to those online applications?* "Come on, I want to show you new plans, for a grocery."

"Wasn't it going to be a restaurant?" She gave each of her eyes one more dab.

"That was doomed from the start. This is different." He tugged on her hands, pulling her up.

"You're as bad as a teenage girl," she said. "Changing your mind every six months."

"I thought we didn't insult women."

"Uff; whatever you do, it had better make money. We can't stay at your uncle's forever."

Later that night her words kept him tossing and turning. The promise of a new life with a bride of his own choosing seemed to be slipping through his fingers.

Chapter Seven

An array of women in colorful saris greeted Hind in the main entrance of the consulate—none of the Western brands that had shimmered in the lights of the comedy club. The local staff, middle-aged Indian clerical workers, their hair neatly oiled and parted straight down the middle, wore traditional dress at work, while young people streamed past the windows in jeans and suits. Hind walked through the open space behind the welcome area and up the stairs, heading straight for her office in the corner. She murmured hellos in reply to the women's tentative greetings. *And expats say getting to know locals is hard.* Without shopping or studies to distract her like during her London years, she was at sea for social connections in her life as a diplomat.

In public, with unbound hair and bright patterned blouses, she blended in. In the office she pulled a pink scarf over her hair. As the only Gulf Arab woman in the office, she covered up around her colleagues lest someone set tongues wagging among relatives back home.

Hanosh, his skin looking extra pulpy that morning, came in to see if she wanted coffee.

"Where is everyone?"

Hanosh ducked his head. He never looked her directly in the eye, even when answering a question, a habit Hind found amusing and infuriating at the same time. "They said they'll be out."

"Out?" She stopped logging into her computer. "Out as in where? To the market?"

"Out as in to Goa, madam," Hanosh mumbled. He shut the door before she could ask another question.

Hind swiveled in her chair to stop herself screaming. The otherwise all-male consulate staff had done it again. They had left, without notice, for a holiday, leaving her alone with all the work. She could see, through the blinds of the internal office window, the line already forming to apply for visas. Well, what would've been a line in England, anyway. About a dozen men stood in the waiting area, much too close together, taking only the space five people would've filled in London. They peeked at each other's documents, unabashedly eyeing the reasons for their visa applications, trying to catch details of each other's contracts.

Hanosh made his way back in. The coffee sloshed in the cup as he set it on Hind's desk. He stood in front of her, hands clasped behind his back, legs slightly apart. She wasn't sure who had taught him this particular pose, but she tried not to grimace as she forced a sip of the sludge he'd prepared for her.

"Excellent." She smiled.

He relaxed, but only in the shoulders. "Who do you want to start with?"

"Right." She sighed with such feeling that his eyebrows shot up in sudden concern. Hanosh clearly felt responsible for Hind's happiness. "Whoever you think," she said.

He brightened and, from his shirt pocket, produced a folded list bearing the names of twelve companies and their representatives written in pains-takingly neat block letters.

"Srikumar," she said. "Tata Industries. Send him in."

Hind braced herself for the daily deluge of visa applications for hundreds of laborers requesting authorization to work in Qatar.

Srikumar, a tiny mouse of a man who made Hanosh appear the picture of robust health, slunk in, bowing to Hind several times. His eyes bulged at the sight of her scarf before taking in her watch; she endured his gaze in a way she never would've tolerated in any of the malls in Doha. Instead of sitting in the chair facing the desk, he stood. The papers rustled in his hand.

"Tata Industries wishes an audience with the consul-general," Srikumar declared in a tremulous voice; his mustache quivered with the effort.

Hind fidgeted with the pen on her desk and gave the standard reply, the one that had become rote in the months she'd lived here. "His Excellency asked me to take this meeting on his behalf." No one wanted to meet with a mere first secretary.

"We are being of a sufficient size to be commendable for such a meeting." Srikumar puffed up several inches.

"Well," Hind said, "if you have urgent visa applications, you can let me have a look."

He glanced between her and Hanosh, who gave him the side-to-side tilting head bob that puzzled Hind no end.

"It means yes, no, maybe, I heard you, mostly," Sangita had explained. At the thought of her friend, Hind flinched.

"Okay, okay." Srikumar sat down; a cloud of talcum powder floated up around him. "Thank you, thank you." He passed her the file, careful to make sure their hands didn't touch.

Hind tuned out the obsequiousness as part of this dance that was meant to result in as many people being sent to her country as possible. She thumbed through the pile of applications as thick as her master's thesis. Men with full heads of hair, their youth etched in the fine bones of their jawlines, stared out at her from their photographs. None of them smiled, but all of them gazed directly at the camera, unblinking. She knew what greeted them at the other end of their journey: blue work overalls, buses without air-conditioning, shared rooms, shared toilets, in some cases shared mattresses. For most of them these living conditions would be better than the earth floor huts of their home villages.

"We'll take these in for review," she said.

Srikumar protested.

Hind held up her hand, a gesture her mother had used a thousand times to stop her arguing with her sister. "Before that, we need these contracts also in Arabic." She passed the file to Hanosh.

"But this will take days! Weeks." Srikumar mopped sweat from his brow. The man grimaced at Hanosh, who tilted his head again.

"This is the procedure," Hind said for the hundredth time. If they'd told her that embassy work involved disappointing people, lots of people, she might have stayed where she was.

"We need this to start on a high priority project." He held a small brown envelope in his hand. "Very important."

Hanosh stared at the envelope dangling between them.

"That's illegal," Hind said sharply. If the project had been close to any of the top holdings back home she would have known about it, because the sheikh in charge at the Gulf end would have his man calling daily for updates. She rapped her knuckles on the desk to indicate the conversation was over. "If you don't like it, appeal to the ambassador in Delhi."

"He doesn't take meetings." Srikumar gestured at her as if to say *this is how we found each other in the first place.* "This delay is not beneficial to me, or to the work the company will do for you."

Hind folded her arms. "You requested a meeting, and you have had one."

Srikumar looked at Hanosh, who handed him back the folder. Neither he nor Hind responded to the man's continued complaints as he was escorted from the room.

Hind checked her watch. Only four more hours to go. She wanted to ask Hanosh why he was so nonchalant about the bribe. But from Srikumar's attitude, and not for the first time, she had a sinking feeling that whoever had occupied this office previously had not shared her scruples.

"You're doing the right thing," Hanosh said quietly, his eyes round in surprise. "If you take money from him, word will spread. Then everyone will be down here on our head."

"Send in the next one," Hind replied. On her own, she was not going to change this tide already set in motion. If only she'd listened when they said an embassy was no place for a woman.

This time the applicant was a woman. Her beady eyes ate up everything in the room, including Hind's leather purse on the table in the corner. "Good morning, madam. I hope you like it here."

"Yes, fine," Hind stammered, taken aback by her forwardness. She took the docket Hanosh passed to her and flipped through the pages. "You're Nepali. Why are you applying here at the consulate in India instead of your home country?"

The woman folded her hands over an ample waist. "Well, I am expanding operations. You know, housemaids, your people need lots of help. Big, big families."

Hind looked through the flat stares of dozens of women in their passport-size photos. A stinging retort burned at the tip of her tongue. *Good thing, so you can make your money off us.* But there was no need for such agitation. The woman was only speaking the truth. "Well, Ms. ... Aisha, this is very unusual. I'll have to send it to the economic section in Delhi."

Aisha shifted in her seat. "Is that necessary? We can do business, can't we? As women?"

Irritation pricked Hind all over. She fidgeted with her headscarf like a teenager. "I'm sorry, but you'll have to translate all your company documents into Arabic, including the licenses."

"Ready." She thrust the papers across the desk to Hind; a blue stone twinkled from her pinky ring.

"I'll take a look at them," Hind said. "Please give Ms. Aisha an appointment for two weeks."

Hanosh scrawled a note on the notepad he kept in his pocket. "Yes, madam. Will do."

"Something from my side," Aisha said.

Hind pulled her attention away from the computer back to the woman, who was now pushing a box across the desk. "We have a no-gift policy——"

"Little, little." Aisha's chin wobbled in her eagerness. "You know, a sweet."

"Thank you, but no." Hind stood, pressing the box back into the woman's hands. She signaled to Hanosh to get Aisha out of the office. He came forward, his pencil-thin figure dwarfed by the buxom woman in her heels. Hind pretended to receive a call on her phone so they didn't see her laughing at his attempt to usher the woman out by her elbow.

"Seeing you soon," Aisha called before the door closed.

Not if I can help it. She pressed her fingers against the base of her neck. Three and a half more hours.

Hanosh returned. "Next person——"

"It can wait until you finish," Hind said.

Hanosh straightened, brushing crumbs from his shirt.

"You ate it?"

"She made me," he said, ducking his chin.

Now Hind did laugh, loudly, with a sound that filled the room like the whistle of a train.

"The next person——"

"Break." She stood.

"Madam?"

"Break." Hind walked to the window. Across the street two children stood on the sidewalk, watching cartoons playing on a television in a storefront. They looked like they needed something to eat.

Chapter Eight

Abdulla contemplated his brother at the foot of the dining table. *Was Saad ducking behind the tulip arrangement?* Abdulla shifted his angle as the maids placed a series of dishes across the middle of the table.

"This is like the Middle East meets Downton Abbey," Sangita said under her breath. "I've seen that chandelier on Pinterest." She took a seat next to Abdulla. "You didn't tell me no pants," she whispered. "They're all staring at me. This much silverware … we're staying for lunch and dinner." Her wide eyes took in all of it: the twelve-seat table, three plates placed at each setting, paisley weave chair covers.

"You're sitting down," he replied. "No one will notice."

He hadn't told her the aunts preferred skirts because he didn't know— at least on a conscious level, certainly not enough to tell her—or that everyone would continue to stare at her for a little while yet. His mother could no longer cling to the hope that he'd call it off, but she was still far from accepting the new family set-up.

Sangita pulled herself closer to the table, tucking her legs under as if they were weapons that needed to be concealed. The niceties that Sangita pointed out, the invisible lines she tripped over on a daily basis, were on the periphery of his experience of his own culture. If Abdulla admitted the truth, that he didn't know the ins and outs of women's behavior, she would launch into another of her lectures about male privilege. The other men in the family entered, giving their greetings to the room at large. With his father and uncle, plus a shaggy Khalid who wiped sleep from his eyes before slamming himself into a seat next to Saad, the table was full.

Abdulla brooded over his brother. Saad's collared shirt disguised the mischievous nature of the man-child who wore it. His hair brushed the back of his neck. Abdulla peered at the hair sprouting sporadically along the boy's chin, as if it couldn't decide whether or not it would spread. Saad passed a silver-edged plate to their mother as the extended family swapped serving bowls piled with rice and meat. His aunts nudged baskets of freshly baked bread toward their husbands and children, who piled meat alongside chopped parsley salad. Maryam spooned rice and chicken onto Saad's plate before serving herself.

"Everyone knows I'm the best," Khalid said, breaking the deadlock of Abdulla's staring game with Saad. Abdulla made a mental note to ask his nephew what he knew about the bullying episode at school.

Saad flicked Khalid in the cheek. "You are not."

"I am the best at Minecraft." Khalid responded with his own flick, which knocked over a bottle of water, sending a cascade into Noor's lap.

"Uff, why don't the children eat in the kitchen," Noor exclaimed, "if we insist on staying in for these Friday lunches." She pushed away from the table and dabbed at the spreading stain on her leg. The water created translucent splotches on her peach skirt. "We could go out like any other family."

"That was an accident," Khalid protested.

"See, see, I got the highest score." Saad waved his phone in his cousin's face.

"No electronics at the table." Grandfather Jassim tapped the table with his fist. A rattling cough interrupted the rest of the scolding.

The table went silent as he broke into a coughing fit.

"Sorry."

They ignored Saad's apology as Jassim worked to catch his breath. Mohammed rubbed the older man across the back. Maryam passed them some water.

"The time for these antics is over," Jassim wheezed. "You are becoming men now. When I was your age, I spent all day on a boat, diving five, ten times into the ocean."

"Good luck getting this lot to wake up before noon," Noor muttered.

Abdulla snorted in agreement. His mother tsked, probably chalking up his derision to teasing.

"Take on some responsibility." Jassim waved off the offers of water and suggestions to stretch his legs. He reached out a shaky hand for the yogurt. "In my day we ate meals like this cross-legged on the floor."

Abdulla frowned at Saad. All signs of contrition gone, he now eyed himself in the horizontal mirror that ran the length of the wall facing the table. Saad turned his head first one way then the other, examining the stretch of skin under his nose. *No, James should count himself lucky he had no family to keep track of.* His business partner could do as he pleased, whenever he wanted. Abdulla longed for the days when that had been true for him as well.

"Yes, *Yeddi,*" Khalid said.

His grandfather's words reminded him that Abdulla's carefree days were long ago, when he was Saad and Khalid's age.

His mother reached over and patted Saad on the hand. "They will make us proud."

"No more babying," Jassim warned.

Saad and Khalid sat up straighter as their grandfather continued to admonish them. Born a few months apart, most people mistook the boys for twins.

"As if we had rules for them," Luluwa muttered. "Or they would listen."

"I'm full." Jassim leaned back in his chair. His arms extended like sticks against the table.

Abdulla rose, but Mohammed and Saoud jumped up to help their father from the room and beat him to Jassim's side. Alarmed glances ricocheted between Abdulla and his father and uncle. Jassim, buoyed by the news of Abdulla's impending wedding, had blossomed in the past few months. His shirts had filled out, and rosiness had crept back into the ash-grey of his cheeks. But it was not a complete recovery. The trio made their way out of the dining room and into the *majlis.*

"That's enough, please. Let everyone eat without another tirade from Ms. Modern." His mother turned her attention away from the boys. "*Zein,* and then what?" Maryam gestured for her sister-in-law Wadha to pass her plate so she could pile on the *machboos.*

"And then I told them, 'No, she's studying, so it wouldn't work out.'" Wadha shrugged, nibbling at the chicken.

"Is that code for 'we're not interested'?" Sangita whispered.

"Huh," Abdulla said. The mixture of English and *khaleeji* dialect swirled in the conversation around him. His fiancée's elbow burrowing into his ribs gained her his full attention.

"More or less." Luluwa leaned over and nodded. "If they say a girl is studying, then it's a polite no. Good grasp of context."

Sangita flushed under the praise.

Abdulla winked at his cousin. "You're getting better," he murmured, squeezing Sangita's fingers under the table.

"It'd be smart to remember this. Because weddings will always be the context." Luluwa crossed her eyes.

Abdulla's aunt didn't give any details about the would-be groom behind this failed proposal, because the object of his desire, her younger daughter, Noor, sat at the other end of the table, oblivious to the machinations about her future.

"*Wa enti, tabeen?*" Wadha asked Sangita.

Abdulla chewed on his rice. The confusion on Sangita's face felt like a thorn in his heart. Asking his aunt to speak English would be an insult. Yet stepping in to translate would earn him no thanks from Sangita. They endured this painful lesson in Arabic dialect at least once a week.

"*Tabeen?*" Wadha shook the basket of bread.

"Um, *na'am, shukran.*" Sangita took the basket, placing a circle of baked bread on her plate.

"*Ma sha'allah,* such great Arabic!" Wadha said. "You could read the evening news."

"But not have a conversation with the people across from me," Sangita muttered.

"Don't be so hard on yourself," Abdulla whispered. "I couldn't do Hindu with your family."

"It's Hindi," Sangita hissed.

Oh, Allah, give me points for trying. "I know that." He tore a large piece of bread in half and passed it to her as a peace offering. "It's not like I want to be here either."

She shook her head.

Maryam held her phone at a slight angle and passed it forward and backward over the dishes.

"*Yema,* what are you doing?" Saad asked. "What happened to no phones at the table?"

"Shush, mind your plate," their mother said. "This is for Snapchat." The tip of her tongue caught between her teeth as she concentrated on the width of the table to capture all the dishes that made up their meal.

Saad covered his face with both his hands. "That's for people doing interesting things. Not eating *machboos.*"

"I have two thousand followers," Maryam retorted.

"Really?" Abdulla tapped his screen. His company account had only a few hundred. "That's a lot." *Of course, they weren't posting regularly yet. Only pans of meetings and James's fancy coffees, to hide the fact that they were still only at the concept stage and had pretty much no idea what they really wanted to do.* "When we open, will you send some snaps for us?"

"I have twenty thousand followers," Saad called from the other end of the table. "I'll send snaps if you give me a corporate discount."

"You'll get a family discount anyway," Khalid retorted.

"No one who can pay good money is getting discounts," Abdulla said. "It's a business, not a family charity."

"This is ruined," Noor announced. "I'll finish in my room." She left before anyone could protest, pockmarked skirt billowing around her.

His father and uncle re-emerged without comment. Mohammed clapped his hand on Abdulla's shoulder on the way back to his chair. Relief coursed through him that his father didn't press him, as the eldest son, to join in on the round of visits for tea with the neighbors, or sit through the long sessions of tea drinking in their own *majlis.* Within minutes, however, the men were gone again. The sight of Jassim's weakened condition diminished everyone's appetite. Wadha and Maryam dismissed themselves shortly after the men and went to enjoy their tea and gossip in the sitting room.

"It's hopeless," Sangita said, dropping her fork onto her plate with a clang.

"You're doing great," he said.

Luluwa nodded. "You understood her."

Abdulla reminded himself to get his young cousin a present, though he had no idea what she was into these days. Not male pop stars anymore, and she seemed to be over mauve.

"Newsflash, pep squad," Sangita said. "I can't speak. Not one sentence." She pushed away from the table.

"You said 'thank you,'" Luluwa began.

Sangita threw up her hands. "Almost two years of Arabic class at university level to be able to say yes and thank you at lunch time. What a waste of time. I should get a refund."

"You'll get the hang of it." Abdulla pulled her chair toward him. The leg caught in the carpet, halting her progress.

"I won't," she said. "Not sitting alone at home every day. Walls don't speak." She wrapped her arms around herself when he tried to rub them.

Anita came in to clear the dishes. "Ma'am, you finish?"

"Yes, yes," Luluwa said. There was enough food left on the table to feed another family. Anita hustled away the dishes, together with the new woman Abdulla's mother had hired as Sangita's dedicated helper. Much younger and darker than Anita, Sally watched everything the older woman did and copied her like a shadow. The two maids shuttled the dishes out of the communal dining room, back across the open courtyard and into Maryam's kitchen, where they would finally have their own lunch from the family's considerable leftovers. Maybe they would invite the drivers in if they weren't busy, or fighting.

"Coffee mornings," Luluwa said, snapping her fingers. "You should go to those coffee mornings expat ladies always have. You know, in a café. Meet some people."

Abdulla nodded. "That's a great idea."

"Oh, you two." Sangita stuck out her tongue at them. "Pat me on the head and send me to play with the boys, why don't you." Saad and Khalid, engaged in another heated dispute about who was better at crafting pickaxes and who had mined the most emeralds, looked up. "What'd we do?" Khalid asked, eyes rounded.

Luluwa laughed at their bewilderment. "Nothing. I think your video thingy is calling."

They didn't need to be told twice and bolted from the room like it was on fire.

Sangita went with them before either Abdulla or Luluwa could say a word.

"It's bad," Luluwa said, popping an abandoned strawberry into her mouth.

Abdulla ran his fingers through his hair. "Thanks, Captain Obvious."

"Go on your honeymoon," she said.

Abdulla groaned. "Not you too. I can't right now."

"You quit your job to be at home more."

"I quit my job to go into business for myself. That means I'm always working. We're starting from scratch with a gourmet grocery concept. Healthy eating."

"Grocery?" Luluwa picked up a discarded grape and checked it for blemishes. "I thought it was a restaurant."

"Never mind," Abdulla muttered.

His cousin shot him a sideways look. "You know what you're doing?"

"No," he said, snatching the grape out of her hand. "Neither do you." He left the house for some fresh air before Luluwa could come back with a rejoinder.

The palm fronds reached upwards like seeking hands along the fifteen-foot boundary wall blocking the view from the main street. They were ensconced in privacy here, a sheltering he had found stifling even before he decided to marry a stranger. Now, he found life in the family compound suffocating.

The slam of the Cadillac SUV's driver's side door jarred him from his thoughts. Saad was sitting behind the wheel, not in front of his gaming console.

"You're not going anywhere on your own," Abdulla called. "And for sure you're not driving."

"I forgot my backpack," Saad said, holding it out from the driver's side window. "Khalid got it for me."

"So you're going to do homework next?" Abdulla said.

"Yeah." Khalid popped out from the back of the SUV.

Are they trying to steal the car? Do boys still do that? At their age, as the family's only boy, eight long years before Khalid or Saad, Abdulla had spent most of his time with his mother's side of the family, whose boys were rough-and-tumble lads who borrowed their father's car to joyride through the neighborhood. Back then, the Nissan pickup truck in which they bumped through the dusty streets could barely make it out of the potholes. The SUVs in their courtyard now would flatten a grown man even at low speed. What had brought Abdulla around? His face hardened with memories of the military academy. Back then, a future for a man meant service in the military.

"I'm watching you two," Abdulla said. He heard again the echo of his father in this vague threat. He was watching them in whatever time he could take away from the business or helping Sangita. Which was next to never.

The boys slunk off together. They retreated into the side of Khalid's house, their heads close together, whispering, as they looked over their shoulders once, twice at the car.

Abdulla ground his teeth. That wasn't what he wanted to say—and not something they would listen to anyway. He came closer to the car, wondering if they'd tried to bribe the driver. This was a common tactic for teenagers when they realized they had more power than the men their families employed. There was no sign of either of the guys. Abdulla circled the car. An acrid smell filled the air. "Wait, you're not—" The telltale cigarette butts in the corner of the football pitch answered his question.

"Saad!" Abdulla called. He was the only one in the courtyard. If he kept on calling, everyone in the family would end up out here except for the boys he was after.

He didn't know how to interpret Saad and Khalid's fecklessness. Was it mere childishness, something they would grow out of as they became men?

Or was this the behavior of the spoiled generation his father grumbled about, with everything handed to them on a plate? Abdulla had received full funding to go abroad to Sandhurst and then to the London School of Economics. Yet he couldn't remember the last time he'd seen a school report for either his brother or their cousin. Surely someone was keeping check on them?

A cat rubbed itself against his leg and yowled. Abdulla shuddered. "Tet, tet," he said tersely and stumbled against the SUV's bumper, hoping to scare the creature away. Other than the malnourished animals from the *souq*, dyed baby chicks and an occasional red-eyed rabbit, they never had pets growing up. The orange cat yowled again in protest. Its tail swayed as it made its way closer. "Tet!" Abdulla raised his foot.

The cat bared its teeth, the fur along the ridge of its back rising. This set the hair on Abdulla's arms tingling. Normally the neighborhood cats scurried away when people approached. He would ask his mother to speak to Anita—maybe that new girl Sally didn't know that feeding cats in a country of strays was not a good idea.

Sangita crept out of the house and appeared at his elbow "Maybe the cat doesn't speak Arabic either," she whispered.

For the second time in minutes Abdulla jumped, clutching at the hood of the SUV for support. "Don't do that!"

She wore a black *abaya* and a *shayla* over her hair. "Shoo!" The cat sat on its haunches, licking a paw, and regarded them with a tilt of its head. "Leave the poor thing alone." Sangita leaned her head on his arm. "Let's get out of here for a little while."

Abdulla gathered himself, straightening. The cat had disappeared. "I'm going to change," he said.

"You look great in a *thobe*," Sangita protested. "I'm dressed."

"That'll come off in two minutes. I'll be right back." He jogged around the side of the house.

"Promise?" Sangita called after him.

Abdulla stripped down, relishing the anonymity of jeans and a long-sleeved shirt. They could be just another couple out to enjoy the day, without people staring at them, trying to recognize him, or to place Sangita. "There." He emerged, running his fingers through his hair. "Now." He slid into the driver's seat and flipped down the visor to get the keys. With most of the family living on the compound and five women who didn't drive—now six with Sangita—the drivers were always ready at a moment's notice so the keys stayed in the vehicles. With teenage boys around, Abdulla thought he should speak to the drivers about that.

"Okay, Clark Kent." Sangita peered closer to the mirror and adjusted her veil. The orange cat watched them from beneath a shrub.

"Is that the same cat or another one?" The cat licked its paw as if Abdulla were the one intruding. "Is there something strange about it?"

"Other than the fact that they roam free all over the streets, no one seems to do anything about them, yet everyone complains about litters of kittens?"

"Never mind." Abdulla reversed out the front gate.

"I mean in a place like this, getting the cats under control could be easy. You make a grid of the city, you assign weeks to each part of the city, then you go around doing the trap and neuter thing, and return them if neighborhoods want them."

He glanced at her from the corner of his eye.

"You're giving me the eyeball? This is a workable solution."

Abdulla shook his head. "Cats are not the priority."

"So much potential." Sangita drummed her fingers on the side of the door. "Seriously, remind me again whose bright idea it was to bring cats in to deal with the rat problem. How much do you think they charged for that piece of advice?"

The tightness in his chest eased. "I don't know." Abdulla laughed. "But it was definitely too much." His wife's reflection in the side mirror reminded Abdulla how people change. Saad would be fine. He was a boy from a good family.

Sangita winked.

"Where to, madam?" he teased, palming the steering wheel. Given the country's strict gender segregation, a car was one of the few places couples could be alone away from the prying eyes of chaperons and nosy onlookers.

"The movies," she said, settling back against the car seat.

"You know they're censored."

"So people in the rest of the world have it easy. Here, it's like a test of intelligence. Can you can still make sense of the story?"

"We'll end up watching action or horror," he warned.

Sangita grinned. "All the better to cling to the manly arm of the one you're with."

He laughed again. Yes, people changed, and, therefore, so could families. He hoped for both their sakes he was right.

Chapter Nine

Hind loosened the scarf she wore at work in case someone who knew someone in the family came through. The shadow of life at home could stretch out and reach her even here. She'd had a whole afternoon of the same pleading looks on a variety of brown faces, some wide, some narrow, some of their owners remarkably fat, and some with waists so slender that their pants were far too wide. She laughed mirthlessly at the thought that her aunties would recoil in horror to see Hind meeting with men—and so many of them—as the major part of her job. She now spent her days enjoying the freedom of a woman living on her own away from the social dictates to which she'd been raised, yet the cooler temperatures of the monsoon season brought a stickiness similar to the humidity at home.

Hind pressed her head back on the chair and swiveled round to look out the window. The petitions for visas had gone on and on; against Hanosh's advice she'd also seen the walk-ins. The rain now pinned her in the office. No one on any of the other desks worried about getting drenched. Back home the desert winters brought only a light drizzle. Once every ten years the streets flooded. Hind jostled her mouse. *Better to wait this out.* The newly wed Hanosh scurried home, his wife's dinner likely waiting for him.

"We're closed," Hind called out when the security guard knocked on her door.

"He says he knows you, madam," the guard said.

"Well, tell him to make—" Her words stopped in her throat. There in the doorway stood the man she'd forced herself not to think about since she last saw him—with the result that she had, therefore, thought of little else.

Ravi shouldered past the smaller man and into her office. "I'll only be a minute."

"It's fine," she told the man as she rose from her chair, her *shayla* falling onto her shoulders.

The guard shrugged. It wouldn't be on his head if anything went wrong. His dark fingers pulled on the doorknob.

"Leave the door open."

The guard looked from one drawn face to the other and marched back downstairs.

"Still can't trust yourself alone with me?" Ravi said in a low tone. He studied the framed geometric patterns along the wall.

"Still can't leave me alone?" she retorted. Hind held on to the edge of the desk.

The intervening months had been kind to him, softening the sharp angles of his face with a few more laugh lines, wrinkles at the corners of his lips and eyes. He hadn't changed much. Perhaps a little thinner, maybe a touch less hair on the crown of his head. He wore it closely cropped now so that he almost looked bald. A rumpled cream linen blazer hung from his broad shoulders.

He exhaled. "Sorry, I didn't mean to start on that note."

Hind sank back into her chair, the fight draining out of her at the sight of his stooped shoulders. She indicated that he could sit across from her.

"I'm here on family business."

As he drew closer, she became aware of the blood rushing through her ears, the pulse pounding at her throat. *He's here on business.* "Everyone's gone for the day." Hind pushed a bottle of water across to Ravi. He drank half the bottle in one gulp while rain pelted outside. "We don't give charitable donations, if this is for the orphanage."

"No." He twisted the cap back on. "This is about the upcoming exhibition. The dhows."

"Well, start from the beginning." She flushed at finding herself in the dark. What was he talking about?

He placed a binder on her desk.

Commemorative Exhibition on the Maritime Trade of the Indian Ocean, she read. Hind flipped past the black and white image of a wooden ship, like the ones that nowadays took tourists out for swim cruises or fishing off the Gulf coast. The next few pages contained more images, four to a page, black and white, of sailors in white cotton gowns, staring straight into the camera.

"We're a small staff." She turned another page. "We don't have a cultural attaché, so I don't see how we could help."

Her fingers rested on a full-page spread of a ship's crew gazing at one man who held a pearl high above his head, a triumphant smile splitting his face. There was something familiar about the twinkle in the man's eye, about the boat, the array of men.

"That's your grandfather," Ravi said.

Hind's gaze jerked from the page to Ravi's eyes, then away again when she saw how close he was as he leaned in to view the book through her eyes. "How would you know that?"

He tapped an inscription at the bottom of the page: *Merchant and diver Jassim bin Mohammed 1970, Mumbai, the Pearl of Great Price.*

"But how? When?" Questions swirled on the tip of her tongue as she took in the image of the man again, noting the familiar angle of his nose, the same as on the faces of her father and uncles.

Ravi leaned his elbows on the desk. "I started a management company, and they brought us in to do some reputation enhancement. They selected me because my sister …"

"Is married to a Qatari." Hind finished the awkward sentence. *Married to my ex-fiancé. My cousin.*

Ravi cleared his throat. "They thought I might have some inside knowledge of the culture. We put together a package suggesting they have a look at maritime history, sailing, trade, etcetera, and," his hand swirled above his head, "they liked it. Thought it an easy sell."

"Smart." She browsed through his tables of ships' names, captains' names, and the cargo they sailed with.

"Sangita did this?"

"I did it," he said. "She put me on the right track."

Consultant profile: Ravi Patel MBA. She looked up in surprise. "You went back to school?"

He shrugged. "We all have to grow up some time."

"The orphanage?"

"Still there; I check on it now and then. Most of the girls are old enough to be married now. And the boys, we're putting the last ones through school."

Hind closed the folder. *So the idealist Ravi has become a businessman—though still a philanthropic one.* "Thank you for telling me about this," she said. "I'll let *Yeddo* know next time we speak."

Ravi leaned forward. "We need your help."

"Seems like you've got it all planned out."

"Your grandfather's ship; we want it to be part of the exhibition."

"It was destroyed," she said. "It's at the bottom of the Indian Ocean."

"Covered in silt." Ravi rubbed his hands together.

"Exactly. A wooden boat, underwater for more than forty years. There was a storm, he was lucky to have survived."

"Sand is a preserver." Ravi opened the binder again and tapped at a double spread of pages she'd overlooked. "Sonic scans have shown that much of that boat is still intact."

Hind peered at a grainy underwater image showing the tip of the ship's prow peeking out from a hill of sand. "Not possible."

"One way to find out," Ravi said.

She ran her fingers over the image, hearing her grandfather's voice in her ears, telling them stories of pirates, the British fleet, the need to get pearls to market ahead of their rivals, the livestock and spices they had to transport in the slower months to make ends meet. These were the tales of her childhood, the memories of her grandmother waiting and waiting, most often pregnant, wondering if her husband would return from his latest voyage.

"Even if it were possible," Hind tapped the image one final time, "it would cost a fortune to raise it."

Ravi turned the page and showed her an itemized budget. She raced past the technical details about assessment, excavation and dredging, and homed in on the final figure. "No way would anyone agree to that."

He reached across the desk and pointed to the official state seal granting government authorization for the spending.

"Wow."

"So the easy part is done," he said.

"Easy?"

He nodded, the joking tone replaced by a new seriousness. "All that remains is the hard part."

Hind spread her hands, palms upward, at a loss for words. They'd a found a ship, her grandfather's ship; most of it was intact, and they'd secured the funds to raise it. "I can't imagine what's left to do."

"The owner, as he is alive, has to give permission."

"*Yeddo?*"

Ravi nodded. "We … you … have to ask him if we can raise this ship."

Hind pulled at the necklace at her throat, the one that said her name in Arabic. "But his men …" Slowly the realization crept over her. *Jassim had been the only one to survive the fatal sinking.* All of the crew and the cargo had sunk, including the "pearl of great price".

"Human remains decay in moisture," Ravi said. "The bodies are likely gone. The most we'll find are bones."

She now understood why this was the hard part. In all the bedtime stories their grandfather had told them, he'd never spoken of the ship capsizing and killing every one of his companions. Would he ever agree to foreigners hauling up his long-lost dhow, filled with so many memories?

Chapter Ten

Their previously animated extended family life became a game of avoiding the new girl. The uncles and aunts stayed in their houses rather than congregate in Grandfather Jassim's *majlis* or the courtyard. No one knew quite what to say to the couple, so they didn't say anything at all. The women smiled at a distance, from across the room during family lunch on Friday afternoons. Luluwa sat next to Sangita for as long as the American could manage to stay at the table. Noor floated in and out of these family lunches, still unsure of her loyalties, given Sangita's marriage to her sister's former fiancé.

Are you coming? I'm leaving now. The vibration of Noor's incoming text shook Luluwa's phone, as if in irritation.

Luluwa glanced into the courtyard from the window of her room in her grandfather's house. No sign of Noor's imminent departure as threatened. Her eyes strayed to the upstairs bedroom of the opposite house, where her parents had spent most of their lives, certainly since before she was born. *I should go see her.* The curtains of the room were closed. Not unusual for a house where a woman wanted to avoid the gaze of any male passersby, even inside the boundary wall, like gardeners or visitors' drivers. But she suspected that rather than modesty, the reason those curtains were closed against the persistent desert sunlight was that Sangita slept most of the day away. Abdulla left for the office before the rest of the family awakened. Deliberations over the right business to pursue, and therefore the course of their future, meant a permanently delayed honeymoon.

Her phone's shrill ringtone announced her first task of the day: *9:00 a.m. physics exam.* Reading the words put Luluwa's stomach in knots. She pulled on her *abaya.* Luluwa wanted to move in with Abdulla and Sangita and give the woman who was now her cousin-in-law some company. After the wedding, her aunts had insisted that they give the couple their privacy. They'd lowered their voices around the word, making Luluwa blush. She couldn't protest, even as she held Sangita's trembling hand at the airport while her mother walked away through the security screening.

They'd returned to an empty house, the one abandoned by Luluwa's parents when they'd divorced. Her father had departed from the family compound to start life with his new wife, and Luluwa's mother, shunted into exile from the family and with nowhere else to go, had been forced to move in as part of her married brother's household on the other side of town. Rattling around the family compound would be the non-glamorous status quo for the newlyweds until the renovation of Abdulla's apartment on The Pearl was finished. The water damage from the burst pipe in the apartment above had drenched the entire side of their building.

Luluwa's phone buzzed with a second reminder. Academic calendars had no regard for family dramas. She ran across the hallway, past her aunt chatting on the phone—something about the cheap paper someone had used for their wedding invitations?—and down the steps, clutching the banister for support. Her shoes screeched against the marble.

"Slowly, slowly." Jassim looked up from his newspaper in the living room. He swiveled in his armchair. "If you are late, you are late."

She slowed her gait, skipped up the few steps into the room, and pressed a kiss on his forehead as a sign of the respect due to elders like her grandfather. "Ah, *Yeddi,* life isn't what it used to be."

"Did we give you too much responsibility, sending you to university early?" He took her hand, surprising her with the strength of his grip.

"No," she said. Being one of the youngest in her class didn't bother her as much as it did everyone else in the family. Another reason she couldn't let on that things were other than she hoped. "You're right. Life is what it has always been. Full of opportunity and challenges."

His eyes swept past her and out the arched front windows to where the desert sun shone as it had the day before and would in the days to come.

"You're sad." She clutched his hand in return. Blue-green veins criss-crossed the leathery skin between his wrist and knuckles, more of them than normal. She vowed to take him to his doctor soon. Abdulla and Jassim were the only two in the family who saw her as she was, rather than trying to mold her into their ideal version of a young woman.

Jassim smiled at her, not dismissing her insight. "I am thinking of the past," he said. "Not sad, exactly—"

"Nostalgic?"

He changed his grip to stroke the back of her hand. "*Ma sha'allah*, you're the smart one. With books, and also you see with your heart."

"The numbers come easy to me," she said with a blush. "I don't work for them."

"Then this is a gift. I used to dive like it was nothing," he said. "Down past all the other men."

Her phone beeped. It was Noor, sending her a warning. *Leaving now. Not kidding.*

"If I didn't have that talent, my life, nothing in our lives, would be the way it is now."

"You would have stayed in India," she joked.

He smiled at her. "We lived from one trip to another, but we were alive on the sea. She could give, and she could take, like a jealous woman."

She ran her fingers over the curved gilt arm of the chair. "You could do what you wanted," she ventured. "Out on the sea."

"Not that simple. Your great-grandfather risked everything for our boat and the sailors. A single voyage could take months and months to pay off. And life on the land, the land calls you back—" he broke off in a cough.

Luluwa crouched down and grasped his hand again until the rattle in his chest subsided. "Are you …?"

"I'm fine. This," he gestured toward his chest, "this is a morning thing." He waved off her concern. "Life on the land was made easy when the liquid gold came bubbling out of the ground."

"That sounds worse," she said, tilting her head.

"You're not the doctor; you're the mathematician. Prepare for the future. This liquid money will soon be gone too."

I want to be a designer, but there's probably no money in that.

"My father, *Allah yerhamho*, he knew the land would yield something, even if not food. Since the foreigners were crawling all over our dunes like ants, he made me stay here to see what it was."

The phone pinged like a tiny submarine in her back pocket.

"Going somewhere?"

"Yes." Luluwa rose. She gathered her bag and adjusted her headscarf. "I've got classes today."

He gave her a slow smile. Another cough started.

"If you want me to take you to the doctor …"

"One of your uncles will do it. Go on to class."

"I'll be back. *Ma'a salaama*." She backed away and gave a last wave before dashing through the kitchen and out the side door into the car park, her *shayla* slipping down onto her shoulders. *And I'll ask Uncle Mohammed what the latest is with Yeddo's checkups,* she promised herself.

The white Cadillac SUV used by Noor and her mother headed round the circular driveway toward the gate. Luluwa waved frantically. Noor either didn't see her or was too irritated with her to stop.

Luluwa stopped waving. Her hand dropped to her side limp as a flag. What a shame. She needed the ride, and a friendly debrief chat with her cousin. Luluwa fumed. *Why can't my parents give me a car? Or at least let me drive.* A useless line of questioning. She wiggled her phone out of the back pocket of her jeans to beg Noor to come back.

Aunt Maryam's driver Naren, all arms and legs, his belt winding twice around his waist, was polishing the side mirrors of the cream SUV.

"Naren, we have to go now," she said.

The driver leaned against the car and typed a message into his phone. "But Khalid and Saad," he said. "I am the one taking them to school."

"Come back for them. I'm going to be late for class." She made a beeline for the SUV parked to one side of the courtyard, wedged between her father's and grandfather's houses. In the second-story window she saw the crown of Jassim's head and a leathery hand waving as if he'd heard her. She smiled and reminded herself to go and see him again later today—if she wasn't too late coming back from university.

No one in the family understood what she did for long hours in the labs on campus. Or more accurately, no one understood *why* she put in the hours it took to stay on the dean's list. Her family met her demonstrations of working circuit boards and models of molecules with murmurs of feigned admiration or bemused silence, as if to say, "What's it all for?" She wasn't, in the end, going to don the coveralls of a petroleum engineer and board an oil rig, or climb inside some power generating plant, was she? No, she would take a more "appropriate" desk job, like hundreds of female engineering graduates before her, and be content with filing reports from a glass tower in the business district. Except none of it interested her. She didn't want to be in the field, and she didn't want to be in the office.

Luluwa didn't let on to anyone that she found the multicolored stalls in the fabric *souq* of infinite interest. If anyone knew she secretly wanted to be a fashion designer that would be the end of life as an engineer and any hope of financial independence from a husband.

She rounded the boot of the car and was reaching for the handle of the back door when the sight of a bare-chested man wearing black tattered trousers brought her up short. She blushed, although the stranger was the intruder. None of her uncles wandered around the compound shirtless. None of them had muscles that bulged in their arms. Even Abdulla's whipcord limbs showed signs of softness under the onslaught of marriage.

He stared at her without blinking, the bold intensity of his gaze rendering her speechless. His laser-like focus dispelled the reproaches hovering at her lips. Black hair, longer than even her cousins would have worn it under their *ghutras*, swept across a wide forehead, the ends curling around the nape of his neck. His lips moved, but she couldn't hear the words and only felt a rush of hot air, as if she were standing in front of the sliding glass doors at the mall, blasted by the heat outside. He reached out for her; the ends of his fingers tapered to a point. *This is how assaults begin,* she warned herself. Yet no matter how hard she tried, she couldn't escape the magnetic pull of those eyes.

"Madam, they're coming now," Naren said.

Luluwa whirled round to find the spindly driver opening the door behind her. She quickly turned back, but the stranger was gone. She shivered in the cooler air coming from the car. "Did you see him?"

Naren looked from her to the inside of the vehicle. "They are coming now, madam," he said. "You enter."

"You didn't see that man?"

Naren glanced around. He squinted at her with the look everyone in the family gave her when she said she supported some modern idea, like women driving.

"Never mind," she muttered. Pulling up her *abaya*, she stepped onto the running board, then slid onto the leather seat of the SUV. Khalid and Saad slugged their way forward.

"Let's go," Luluwa said. "We're late."

Saad climbed into the front seat. "Let me drive." He made a grab for the steering wheel.

Naren made a tsking sound and shooed his hand away.

"That's not going to happen," Luluwa snapped. "If anyone is driving, it's going to be me. Put on your seatbelt."

Saad leaned forward and clicked the belt into place behind him.

"Properly," she said. "I can't believe I'm seeing this after ..."

"*Allah yerhamha,*" Saad said. For a moment their bickering stopped as they remembered Fatima, the sister Luluwa had lost in a car accident. "I don't want to mess up my *thobe*."

"You're going to school, not the mall," Luluwa retorted.

"You're in a bad mood," Khalid said, getting in on the opposite passenger side. The car gave a series of beeps as it rolled forward.

"You guys should have left hours ago. Doesn't the bell ring at seven-forty?"

"Five past eight," Khalid grumbled. "We're not that late."

The numbers on the dash glowed 8:10.

"Besides, why didn't you ride with Noor? Stay out of our business."

"I wasn't fast enough for her." Luluwa wrapped her *shayla* around her head. "Did you see that random guy in the compound this morning?" she added to avoid any further scrutiny.

Saad listened with a lean of his head that reminded her of his older brother, Abdulla. His right ear tilted toward her, an arm across the top of the back seat. After all that, neither of the boys wore a seatbelt.

"Did you see him?"

"No." He sat up straighter. "But if someone is harassing you, even more reason you shouldn't be driving. You know they like to follow girls home."

"Never mind."

Saad shrugged as Khalid turned up the volume on one of the latest *khaleeji* ballads on the car's audio system. He leaned over to honk when a red truck inched in front of them, barring their vehicle from entering the slip road in front of the compound.

"How are we supposed to get out of here, *hamar?*" Saad called through the windshield.

Construction work on the main road made impatient drivers cut through the neighborhood lane in front of the exit to their house.

"Patience," Naren said, pinching all five fingers of one hand together in the familiar local gesture.

"Too nice," Saad grumbled. "We'll be waiting all morning."

Naren inched further out into the double stream of cars, which were making lanes where none existed. The aquamarine city bus braked, letting them slip into the traffic like a fish into a brook. Naren expertly merged onto the main road, hitting the gas before the light turned red, only to be caught by the next signal a few meters down.

The city crawled by, the gridlocked traffic slowing their progress. Sunlight shimmered across the glass front of a three-story hypermarket. Luluwa slipped in her earphones. A man in a yellow coat and brown pants walked the lanes of immobile cars, peddling Arabic-language newspapers. They waited three cycles of the lights to make a U-turn. Though the boys' school was only ten minutes from the family compound, it took them more than twenty to get there; the other drivers honked, cut each other off, and exchanged angry glances—some even gestured aggressively.

"Will you come tonight?" Khalid asked as they pulled into the dirt lot opposite the school entrance. Despite it being twenty-five minutes into the school day, cars still filled the area. Traffic was terrible throughout the city.

Luluwa slipped out one of the ear buds. "To what?"

"We made a Ouija board," he whispered so Naren wouldn't hear. "And we're trying to use it."

"What do you know about Ouija?" Luluwa couldn't help but smile. There was never any predicting what these two would get up to.

"We called someone," Saad insisted. "You'll see."

She waved the boys away as they stepped out of the car. "I have real work to do."

Naren rumbled the car across the dirt lot, over stones and dust, toward a clogged artery where two roads merged at the entrance to the main road. Relieved of their young charges, the other drivers now vied to be first to the next traffic signal.

"Don't play it with them," Naren said. His eyes met hers in the mirror.

Luluwa didn't know how to handle this unaccustomed advice. Despite the years they'd known each other, they rarely talked in the car, partly because they were rarely in the car alone. Most often Naren shuttled the women of the family around—Aunt Maryam on a round of family visits, or Luluwa with her cousin to the mall. She should really have a maid with her, like Noor, who traveled everywhere with Anita. Luluwa's mother had taken their maid to her brother's house, and so here was Luluwa alone with a driver. *Unthinkable in some families.* Yet neither Abdulla nor her grandfather was as strict as they could've been about these things. Luluwa was not going to volunteer that she, who would be exploring her independence in many countries, needed two chaperons. Wasn't it enough that the driver knew her every movement?

"Why not?" Luluwa asked, amused by his concern. "They're kids. It's a game."

"The Ouija is dark magic." Naren's eyes returned to the road. "You shouldn't let them play with it. They may call something. Something bad."

Luluwa suppressed a giggle. She schooled her features to keep from laughing at Naren's furrowed brow and serious tone. "I'll speak to them," she said, slipping the right ear bud back in.

* * *

The jinni jumped onto the former fishing boat with the litheness given to him by his four-footed form. Fresh fish, a stench he would have run from in days past, called to his rumbling stomach. All work had halted on the dock as the confounded humans revisited their technological plans. Khaldoon could afford to let himself wander a little further, like in the old days before they had these foolish notions of excavation.

"Eh—shoo!" A man in rolled-up pants with a broom gestured in his direction.

The jinni bared his teeth and sank his claws into a piece of white fish dangling from the edge of the trash can. He dragged it with him, moving backwards.

"Get that cat off here. We're leaving," bellowed a man in uniform from the top of the gangway.

The man sweeping the deck threw up his hands. "I tried. Stupid creature."

The jinni hissed, not so much at the words as at the sight of the shoreline receding over the stern of the ship. Sharp, metallic, the blood of the fish filled his mouth, even as dread overtook him with the rocking movements of the ship.

"No stopping until Dubai," the uniformed man shouted over a resounding horn.

"Come here." The deckhand put down his broom and reached for the jinni with both hands.

Khaldoon bared his teeth once more. A human touch would release him from this feline form, the very thing that had trapped him in it all those years ago. Now he needed his cat's body—any physical body—more than ever, if he was to be able to alert his human savior to the coming danger. Humans didn't understand cats, so communicating and convincing the old man was going to be difficult. But at least in cat form people could see him. In his pure, elemental form the jinni was almost always invisible to humans.

"A kitty!" A young girl with blonde curls squealed from the deck above them. "Look, Mum, a kitty."

The man paused for a moment and put on a bright smile for the passengers: the girl and her mom peering from the deck above. A clattering of steps marked their descent while the jinni spat out a few bones.

"Is that your cat? Could my daughter pet it, just once?" Because of her slow drawl, the mother's words took a moment for them to understand. Not Indian, not Arab, not British. How did humans achieve such diversity even though they were such a limited species?

The deckhand shrugged, the sheepish grin still on his face. "Not mine."

"Here, kitty." Unlike the diver earlier, the child moved with the speed of a bee. She had her bare hands around the jinni's trunk before he could spring away.

"Careful, we don't know if he's had his shots."The mother hovered over her shoulder, pushing up a pair of dark glasses that magnified her worried gaze.

"Oh, can we keep him, Mum? Can we?"The girl squeezed hard, too hard, thoughtlessly hard in her excitement."I wish he was mine!"

Before Khaldoon could protest with a scratch or a yowl to scare the child away, her touch went like an injection of ice straight to the center of his being. He popped out of the cat's body like soda bursting from a can. Free, free, free! He floated in the air, unable to believe his luck.The cat was not so fortunate.Without the jinni's power to prolong its life, already extended well beyond the normal twelve or so years for a cat, its heart instantly stopped beating.

"Something's wrong. Mum? Mum!"

The jinni soared above them all, away from the girl's hysterical cries at the now dead animal cradled in her arms and the commotion of crewmembers coming to their aid.The girl's tight embrace had set him free as easily as a touch had trapped him in the cat's body decades ago.With no other force, or element, or body, to imprison him, she could not claim him as her own. At long last he was free.

A ripple on the waves reminded him of what lurked in the depths below. He had to get to Jassim to warn him. Though his job was now considerably harder. How could he convince someone who hadn't seen him in decades? A creature whose thought processes, as with most humans, relied entirely on language would hardly be persuaded by Khaldoon in his elemental form. He would have to search out someone open to the mystical side of existence.

Chapter Eleven

James tapped on Abdulla's computer screen. Abdulla started, his eyes suddenly relaxing after hours of looking at financial projections in Excel. "How long have you been standing there?" he said, rubbing at his eyes.

"A few minutes." James' brown-blonde hair stood on end, adding a few inches to his five-foot-five frame. He peered at Abdulla over half-rim glasses. "You okay?"

"We need a window in this room." Abdulla pushed back from the table and took off his *agal* and *ghutra*. "I don't know if this is the right direction to go," he admitted.

James was the only person he could say this to out loud. His father already thought Abdulla was being reckless, giving up his secure government job to strike out on his own. The fact that someone in the family had let them use this space, a cube of a room in a building that housed a construction company and a book printer, summed up their inglorious beginning. Now that the grocery concept was on hold, there were no more meetings at the Four Seasons. No more exasperated architects breathing down their necks. This release, and all of the possibilities ahead, should have been liberating. Instead, Abdulla felt the walls closing in on him, the industrial grey carpet blurring his vision.

James took out his phone. "I have an idea." His blunt fingers tapped on the screen, pulling up a video.

Abdulla watched thirty seconds of the camera panning over a spread like the sort of thing he would eat with his family on a Friday. The mole on the side of the woman's face in the corner of the screen gave him a start. He peered closer. Light glimmered on the silver edges of the bowls. "That's my mom's table!"

"Really?" James glanced at the screen before playing it again. "See how many views."

"Fifty thousand," Abdulla said. He took his friend's phone and tapped at the screen. "Why would any locals watch this? They probably eat much fancier things at their meals."

"Expats," James said with a snap of his fingers. He sat in the chair across from Abdulla's desk. "Expats want an authentic local restaurant. When their friends come to visit, when they have a business meal with an international partner, when they can't get into a local's house, they want the next best thing." His Adam's apple bobbed up and down with excitement.

"Hm." Abdulla brought the Snapchat video up on his own phone, scrolling through the comments.

Don't know anyone who's ever been in a local's house. So guess we'll never get the pleasure.

Looks delicious. Someone post a recipe!

Does this taste different from biryani? Looks the same.

"New concept," James said. His green eyes shimmered. "Make it like a house, a traditional house. Waitresses wearing—what do women wear at home?"

"Anything they want," Abdulla said. "They're at home. I don't think I want to exoticize —"

"Hear me out," James said. "See, no one knows that. No one knows what you all do when you're home."

"James, we're humans," Abdulla protested. "Not like an endangered species."

"Well, what about when they have guests over?"

Abdulla looked at him blankly. "I don't know. Men aren't usually invited."

James sighed, rapping his knuckles on the desk. "Fine, if you don't want to go this route, let's do Biryani Hut."

Abdulla laughed. "Okay, you're losing it. We know nothing about biryani."

"But your wife is Indian, right?" He gave Abdulla a sideways glance, the kind they used to exchange in commiseration at a particularly dull lecture.

"More American than anything," Abdulla mumbled. "Plus, she doesn't cook." Memories of Sangita's empty refrigerator in England raised the ghost of a smile.

"You've got to take this seriously," James said. "We're supposed to be operational in six months, and all we have is an empty shell space that used to house a fancy jewelry store."

"I know," Abdulla said. "I know." All signs of mirth vanished, leaving his mouth a thin, straight line.

James hopped up from the chair. He strode back and forth like an athlete on the sidelines. Abdulla watched. Neither of them had been particularly good at rugby, and neither had the bulk for it. *Which is why we're here in this office.* With a modicum of talent, he could have made the national football team and begun raking in the benefits of the coming World Cup.

"What about a focus group? Expat women. Ladies who lunch; that kind of thing." James fired suggestions with the same persistence as when he'd quizzed Abdulla on macroeconomics.

"Sure, let's get some people together and talk about it," Abdulla said. His friend's pinched lips gave him a pang of guilt. "I'll make it work; don't worry, James. No one is going to think of your coming out here as a boondoggle."

"Okay, yes, sure. Good. Talk." James forced a smile that didn't reach his eyes. They both knew his parents had protested at his leaving a lucrative career in investment banking to join Abdulla at what they felt was the edge of the world. The ding of James's phone caught his attention. "Going to meet with potential vendors for the booths, etcetera. You coming?"

"I've got to get my mom's car re-tired."

"Seriously?" James said, looking at him. "You've got to be joking."

"I know. One driver is on holiday, and the other one is out with my aunt. My dad is traveling. One uncle's at work; the other's a loser—I'm everyone's favorite guy. Update me."

James shrugged as if to say, "Pissing away your fortune is on you."

Abdulla stretched, reassembling his headdress. *Family, new enterprise, family.* Maybe a government job wasn't so bad. He felt like a child being told he could now color outside the lines. Only the paper was so big he couldn't get started. He climbed into the Cadillac and stopped and started through traffic on his way to the Industrial Area. The city receded behind him in an orange haze as dust swirled across the highway. He took the curve of the overpass faster than usual, peeling the tires like a teenager. Out here the semi-order of the city, the wide streets and multistory buildings gave way to a crisscross series of impromptu streets. Potholes big enough to break your axle scarred the landscape. Abdulla maneuvered around Indian men in long cotton skirts and past rows of smashed vehicles, dust caking their shattered windscreens like too much makeup. Garages or gatherings of forklifts, cement trucks and other construction equipment stretched as far as the eye could see. He pulled into the Cadillac service center with relief.

At the shop the Indian mechanic, customer service manager, and all-round handyman scurried forward and indicated that Abdulla could sit in the waiting area. Abdulla prepared to make a series of phone calls, beginning by dealing with whatever complaints Sangita wanted to pour into his ear. If she was feeling herself, the biryani idea would make her laugh. If not—

"*As-salaam alaikum.*" A man in traditional dress blocked the light streaming in from the front of the shop.

"*Alaikum as-salaam,*" the mechanic replied automatically, as he would to anyone entering.

Abdulla started at the familiar rumbling voice. He snuck a peek at the man. Sure enough, he recognized the enormous feet, some of the biggest he had ever seen, from his days at the British military academy. Abdulla stood and held out his hand to Ali, his classmate from Sandhurst.

"When did you get back?" He allowed the larger man to envelop him in a hug. "Bin Youssef. It's good to see you."

At the sound of the old nickname Ali squeezed, cracking Abdulla's back. Men were often called by their father's names, and Bin Youssef suited his friend, particularly after the early passing of Ali's father.

Abdulla had had no aspiration to go into politics or the intelligence community, and so he'd headed straight into graduate school, throwing himself into a number-crunching master's degree at the London School of Economics. He left his friend at the military academy and lost track of him over the years. But intelligence had been the only career destination on Ali's list when they graduated. While Abdulla took the business route, the other man stayed on to do special courses for the elite forces.

Ali laughed, his meaty hands resting on Abdulla's shoulders. They embraced again as friends who'd been separated by the years, then stepped apart to touch noses together in the customary way of close relatives. They were related, Abdulla couldn't remember how, in some way or other on his father's side through a web of cousins and marriages.

"I've been back a couple of years," Bin Youssef admitted.

"Wow." Abdulla took in the police officer uniform, the two stars on the shoulders. "You're doing it." While other men from elite families had simply whiled away their time at Sandhurst, Bin Youssef took the training to heart, reading up on the texts and garnering distinctions in the extra courses.

"*Hamdullah,*" Bin Youssef said. "Getting there."

They sat on the grey sofas in the service center waiting room while the television blared a Western movie dubbed in Arabic. Abdulla's silver ring shimmered in the overhead light.

"And married," Bin Youssef noted. He gave his friend a smile and clapped him on the back.

"*Hamdullah.*" Abdulla ducked his head, crossing his arms so that the ring hand was folded away. "Only a few months." Most local men and women didn't wear rings, but Sangita had insisted, as a way to solidify their union amidst the turmoil of the family. Such a simple thing, he couldn't say no. Now, in the cold light of day, sitting next to his friend, the gesture seemed silly.

"Me, too." Bin Youssef held up his hand with a grin. "These women. What can you do? Everyone's wearing rings these days."

They contemplated the scene in the movie for a moment: a group of women at a counter eating ice cream. The subtitles said they were all wives of the same man—well, an ex-wife, a wife, and a girlfriend.

"Foreigners," Bin Youssef muttered. "Their lives are so easy."

Abdulla read the lines as the women plotted their revenge on their ex/husband/boyfriend. "Doesn't seem like this guy has it easy."

"This is just silliness," Bin Youssef said, waving his hand. "For the movies. Everyone knows they're not that crazy."

"Hm." Abdulla was struck by the half-hearted defense of foreigners from a conservative man like his friend.

"We're the people who have real complications."

"Yes," Abdulla agreed, thinking of Sangita. There was no telling how Bin Youssef would react to him marrying outside of their nationality. Most men would congratulate you with a sly wink—Lebanese or Syrian? His stomach turned at the hierarchy of women who were second wives. Part of the reason his cousin Hind could no longer be friends with her former bestie was that women saw men marrying foreigners as a betrayal, since their sisters and cousins were barred by law from marrying foreign men.

"Like this social media. Do you let your wife post on Instagram and things?"

"Excuse me?" Jolted out of his train of thought, Abdulla gazed at the man sitting next to him.

Bin Youssef leaned over, lowering his voice. "Mine is on all the social media. Twitter, Snapchat, Insta. She's always posting this and that and—"

"You can't tell her not to," Abdulla declared before he could stop himself. He inwardly cringed. Too much time spent listening to Sangita's complaints against patriarchy.

Bin Youssef arched an eyebrow at him.

"I mean, of course you can," he corrected himself. "But what is she posting? Her outfits and her hair—her face?"

Bin Youssef slipped out his phone. "Nothing like that." He let Abdulla scroll through the feed. Most of the pictures were grainy images of men in blue overalls sitting or squatting in various parts of the city. The captions included a string of hashtags about perspective, migrant workers, and the location.

"Oh, that's fine." Abdulla passed the phone back to him. "This is the thing now. Girls are into community service." He thought of Luluwa and her knack for numbers. "Science, even. They want to work."

"My sisters aren't like that," Bin Youssef said in a gruff voice. "I mean the older one, no. The younger one—too soon to tell."

Though the only two in the waiting area, Abdulla's friend shifted closer to him. One did not talk about wives in public. Mothers, sisters, cousins, maybe. But young wives? And certainly not to anyone who wasn't her brother or father or uncle.

"Well, better that than bags and clothes," Abdulla said. His other cousin, Luluwa's best friend Noor, came to mind. "No, she's interested in the country. You want to serve the country. You two are perfect for each other, *ma sha'allah*." He punched him in the shoulder.

Ali grunted. "That's what she says. Sorry to talk about these things. You know my father—"

"*Allah yerhamho*," Abdulla said. Ali's father had died from cancer while they were still kids. He cleared his throat, wishing for a way to ease his friend's embarrassment. "My wife is American," he admitted.

"*Wallah?*" Bin Youssef said, incredulous.

Abdulla nodded solemnly.

"So no, you can't tell her not to!" Bin Youssef chortled.

"Indian-American. It's complicated. You should come for dinner. Both of you. Once we're settled in our own place."

Bin Youssef regarded him. "You really have changed."

Abdulla shrugged. "Hasn't everything?"

"Your car ready, sir." The Indian mechanic wrung a spotted towel through his hands.

"But he came first. His car ready first," Bin Youssef protested.

The Indian man's belly quivered at the rumbling voice. "He change all four tires, sir. This take time. You change only one."

"Don't worry about me," Abdulla said. "I've got tons of work to keep me busy."

"Okay. They're expecting me at the station." Bin Youssef shoved up off the sofa, rocking the entire piece of furniture with the force of his movement. "I'm working on something—"

"Big?" Abdulla said. Despite himself, he felt a pang of envy. Here was his friend serving the country, and Abdulla couldn't decide whether he wanted to go into groceries or menus.

"Can't say much," Bin Youssef said. "You have my number?" He gave Abdulla a missed call. "Need anything, give me a buzz." His lips disappeared into his beard. "*Ma'a salaama.*"

Abdulla stood in farewell and sank back onto the sofa as his friend climbed into a red police car emblazoned with the livery of the intelligence services. He imagined recounting their meeting to Sangita. The bit about Instagram would not go down well. A twinge of guilt pricked him as he remembered his strict rules about her blog. He hadn't been entirely honest with Ali about his stance on social media.

With a wave, Ali pulled into the traffic. His taillights receded up the ramp to the highway. Abdulla wished the answers for his own romance were as clear-cut as his own advice to Ali.

Chapter Twelve

Hind settled into the sofa. The strains of a Bollywood movie filled her apartment. She wanted to be transported into a world of rapturous love where the villain always lost and the heroine changed outfits at a dizzying rate. But Ravi's binder beckoned to her from the edge of the coffee table.

Their conversation had disintegrated when she'd refused to call the family to see if her grandfather would be willing to consider the possibility of dredging up the boat. Instead she promised to think about it.

"That's a polite way of saying no," Ravi had said. "I've heard it before."

That had been her exit line from their relationship that never was. Hearing their raised voices, the guard had reappeared and escorted Ravi out.

"One week," Ravi had said. "We have a week to begin excavation before the cyclone season or we'll miss it. Another storm like the one that took down the ship and it'll be lost to us forever."

The Bollywood heroine was resisting the hero, a likeable guy who was chasing her around their college campus asking for her name. She giggled and ducked behind her notebooks while her girlfriends crowded around her.

An incoming Skype call jolted Hind out of her thoughts. The face of Jessica Alba, Noor's American lookalike, popped up as the profile photo. Hind groaned when her sister's face filled the screen. She'd accidentally hit the *Accept* button.

Noor was fully made up, sweeping eyelashes giving her a startled look as she peered over the feathered shoulders of a shimmering black dress. "What do you think? Too much for a winter wedding?"

"Cute," Hind said automatically.

Noor pouted.

"Hot," Hind corrected.

Noor perked up. "What's wrong?"

"Nothing." Hind faked a yawn, hoping a show of sleepiness would put a quick end to the conversation.

"Bollywood again?" Noor tapped the screen where Hind's blue sleep shirt filled the box.

"It's raining," Hind protested.

"Go dance." Noor twirled around, arms outspread; the bell of the skirt gathered around her ankles.

"That is a nice dress." Hind sat up. "Whose wedding did you say you're going to?"

"Ah, someone's cousin from uni."

"Save some of your money," Hind said. Her sister was slipping into a pair of stilt-like red lacquered heels. "Another new pair of Louies?"

"*Ummi* gave me some money. I did well this semester."

Hind readied for a volley of questions. If their parents—their mother—was spending this much on Noor to go to weddings, the underlying rationale could not be good. At least in Hind's view.

At this point Luluwa entered the frame. She waved hello to Hind. Hind smiled in return, taken aback by the changes hair styling and makeup could effect on a teenage girl. Luluwa's azure blue gown was more traditional than Noor's feathered bolero-style dress, but the high waist emphasized her slender build. Waves of curled hair cascaded over her shoulders to her waist. The girl could have been an Arab Rapunzel.

"Lulu," Hind said, "how are you?"

Her cousin took a step back, her face registering surprise that Hind was addressing her directly. They hadn't spoken since Abdulla and Sangita's engagement.

"Hi." Luluwa peered back at Hind; soft waves framed her face.

"How's everything?"

Noor, putting the finishing touches on her makeup, doused herself with a mist of perfume.

"Good," Luluwa said. Her eyes darted around the room, rather than at the screen. Hind saw in her own Skype window the intensity with which she regarded the girl.

"How's *Yeddo*?"

Luluwa's eyes came back to meet Hind's gaze. The question jolted her into words. "He seems fine," Luluwa said.

"Yeah?"

"He … seems troubled by the past," Luluwa admitted. A shadow crossed her face.

Hind tapped the screen to see if it had frozen. Luluwa's lips moved as if she were muttering to herself or praying. "I don't know how much longer he can go on."

Was it the light, or was that sweat glistening along her cousin's collarbone? She flinched, as if someone had struck a match.

"We have to go," Noor sang out behind them, "if we want to get in before the bride arrives."

"Maybe get him to talk more about his boat?" Hind sat up.

"The boat leads to memories of India," Luluwa said. "His lost family—it's not pleasant."

"Speaking of going …" Noor loomed behind Luluwa. "Gotta run. Talk to you soon. And get out of the house already. You look pale."

The screen went blank before Hind could say another word. She turned on the camera to assess the seriousness of her sister's claim. Yes, there were shadows under her eyes, appearing even darker thanks to the pallor of the rest of her face. Was it the light or was her skin a yellowish color?

She threw the phone on the sofa as she thought about Noor's evening. Nothing could be worse than going to yet another wedding. She and Abdulla called off their marriage before the ostentatious wedding reception, but Hind had spent several years going to these elaborate affairs, having to order dresses from abroad months in advance so that her mother could show her off discreetly. From beauty salon to hotel back to the salon: you could spend your whole life —and income—bustling between parties. *Now it's home, office, home,* she thought, picking at the dry skin on her fingernails. *Not exactly anything to text anyone about.* She fell onto the cushions, thankful no one could witness her boredom. Back to the comedy club? Being around so many people having a good time had made her feel more lonely, not less. Her phone buzzed under her hip.

Sale on all brand and off-brand names on Fashion Street. Up to 70% off! Shop now to avoid disappointment.

Plan your social life by spam text. That was an option probably not listed in any expat survival guide. She deleted the message.

At least go to the gym, Noor wrote in WhatsApp. *Don't let yourself go.*

Hind snapped a photo of the stack of soda cans in the kitchen. She wanted to be angry at her sister, tell her she was busy with so many things in her new life that she didn't need advice. But Noor would be observant enough to know that wasn't true.

"Fashion Street, here we come," Hind muttered.

She pulled on jeans and a t-shirt before heading out into the street to catch a taxi. The driver's eyes flicked over her outfit when she gave the destination. Hind sat sulkily in the corner of the taxi with her arms folded. Was she not hip enough even for the taxi drivers in Mumbai? An Indian man would never have given her the once-over back home. They were terrified of offending someone in an *abaya* and being deported.

"You're from where, madam?" he asked as they inched along in the nighttime traffic.

"Guess," she said. Claiming your Gulf roots abroad invited others to take advantage of you by hiking up prices. Everyone thought they had oil wells in their backyards and money growing on palm trees.

He spoke a few words of Hindi that sounded like a song made up of consonants. She shook her head. "I don't speak Hindi, sorry."

"America," he ventured, after another serious assessment of her hair sweeping over her shoulders.

She laughed, loosening her stiff pose. "Yes."

"I can always tell by the accent," he said in his lilting one.

"Right." She smiled out the window.

"Be sure to bargain at these places. They price gouge foreigners." The vehicle slowed in an area lined with small stores that opened onto the street. Clothes dangled on hangers out front, as pedestrians competed with shelves full of shoes for space on the sidewalks.

"Thanks." She handed him several rupee notes, crisp as the day she got them from the ATM. With most expenses paid for, and no social life, she had little need for cash.

A mother and her teenage daughter waited on the other side of the car for Hind to exit before climbing in and haggling with the driver about their fare home. Hind stepped into a melee of sound, color and smell. *Should have maybe done a bit more research,* she thought as a group of grungy teenagers moved past her, one so close he knocked her bag off her shoulder.

Clothing filled the street as far as the eye could see. Across and to the left, bangles glittered in the fluorescent overhead lighting. *Noor would have a field day in a place like this.* Her older sister, however, stood rooted to the spot. Her taxi was taken. She would have to walk to the other side to try to get another cab going in the opposite direction. If she wanted to get home she had to run the gauntlet of shopkeepers' cries. Speakers blared Hindi film songs. The air was pungent with the smell of frying spices. She breathed deeply as shopkeepers called her in to look at their particular wares.

"I'll give you a good price," a man called, his bald spot sweating in the night heat.

Hind made her way among couples out for a stroll and past young parents hauling along a sleeping baby; the child's head jostled on the father's shoulder with each step. Okay, she might not buy anything tonight, but it seemed like other people were out for the same thing. A reason to leave the house.

Chapter Thirteen

She arrived a few minutes before class started. "If you're on time, you're five minutes late," was one of the professor's favorite catchphrases. Luluwa climbed the steps of the auditorium. Each of the concentric semicircles featured a single long, curved desk split by a middle set of stairs. In front of each black chair rose the slender neck of a microphone. Blackout curtains were drawn against the floor-to-ceiling windows. She took her place on the third tier of seats just seconds before Dr. Roberts, their professor of physics, walked in at ground level.

One of the guys on the tier below her whispered in dialect to the student sitting next to him, "Let me see the card." His co-conspirator Abdulaziz complied, pushing a jumbo index card across the table.

"If you don't know it by now, gentlemen, it's too late," Dr. Roberts chided, his gleaming bald head wagging.

"Yes, sir," the recipient of the card, Hamad, mumbled.

"Ready?" His dark eyes swept the room, rewarded by a series of nervous nods. "Alphabetical this time," he said.

Luluwa groaned inwardly. In a class full of Abdulazizes, Abdulrahmans, Ahmeds and Hamads, this meant she would be among the last to begin. Fluorescent lights glared down on the fifty or so students taking this required class. She fiddled with the microphone on her desk, turning the power button for the laptop outlet on and off. Nothing but state of the art for the government's once-flagship project, the American university branch campuses.

"Abdulaziz." Dr. Roberts intoned each name as if pronouncing a prison sentence or announcing a nominee for an award.

The student rushed to the front and returned to his seat with the printed exam paper fluttering in his grip. One by one the class came forward to collect their papers.

One of the guys—was it Mustafa? —sat with his arms folded in his lap. On the way back to her desk, Luluwa tripped and caught herself against the edge of the guy's desk. As she stood up, she noticed writing on the inside of his wrist—formulas, she was sure of it. She continued up the stairs and took out her pencil and calculator, her mind whirring with possible scenarios. She could go back down to Dr. Roberts's desk and whisper to the professor that she needed to talk to him. Then everyone would know that she'd been the snitch.

"Thirty minutes," Dr. Roberts said to the room at large.

Get on with the test. Luluwa reached for her pencil and worked through the problem sets even as the larger dilemma loomed in her mind.

* * *

"Go to the last page if you haven't started it yet," Dr. Roberts said. His phone gave a buzz that echoed to the concave ceiling.

Mustafa rose, went forward and handed in his exam paper.

"So soon?" Dr. Roberts' gaze swiveled across the first page of Mustafa's test. "Well done."

Well done? Luluwa chewed the inside of her lip. She clenched and unclenched her hands, willing herself to have the nerve to say what she'd seen. A quick glance around—Hamad was smirking, and the remaining students were bent over their papers, scribbling to finish. Luluwa's cheeks burned. She sat through the spectacle of five other students turning in their exams while hers remained pinned under her trembling elbow. She wished for the umpteenth time for a friend in the class. Most of the girls in this university had been to government schools, not private international schools like Luluwa and her cousins. They tended to hang around together, eyeing new girls with suspicion.

"Fifteen minutes," Dr. Roberts said.

Sweat trickled down the back of Luluwa's t-shirt under her *abaya*.

"When you've finished with the exam, please begin reading section five."

More and more chairs rolled back as students reached for their bags, tucked underneath the desks. She gnawed at her pencil. Abdulaziz was fidgeting with his *ghutra* and *agal,* fussing with the placement of his headdress on the crown of his head. She, meanwhile, left her headscarf alone, draped loosely around her head just once, the ends flung over her shoulders. She wouldn't keep touching it like girls did in some other classes, adjusting, rearranging—a constant game of hide and seek with hair that was not supposed to be seen but showed all the same. *Focus,* she thought. *Finish your paper first, then deal with him.*

"Luluwa," Dr. Roberts said. "That's all we have time for."

Luluwa descended the tiered steps, down, down, toward the front of the room, ignoring the pleased grin Mustafa wore. She placed her exam on the table, not trusting herself to speak. Unlike everyone else, who whispered to Dr. Roberts about how many hours they'd spent studying for the exam in the hope of influencing his opinion in their favor, she simply went back to her desk.

"Good to be thorough," Dr. Roberts said, coming to the front of the room. "Doesn't matter how long or how little time it takes. It's about how well you know the material. This paper," he waved one of the last exams to be submitted, likely hers, "may contain as many correct answers as this." He picked up the first one and waved it like a flag. "On with your day, everyone. Keep reading. Let's see how far you get with the sample set."

Luluwa gritted her teeth as the remaining students scattered to their next class or lunch.

"First or last," Mustafa said as he pulled on his messenger bag. He ambled alongside her. "We may get the same grade."

She pushed at the metal crash bar to open the double doors. "You were looking at the answers," Luluwa hissed.

Mustafa paused in the marble hallway, tugging the strap of his bag to make sure it wasn't wrinkling his *thobe*. "You don't have proof."

"If I pull up your sleeve, I'll have all the proof I need." She pointed her pencil toward his forearm. This was a lost proposition. She couldn't touch him in public, and his grin said he knew it.

Several bearded men in jeans and worn t-shirts walked down the hallway toward the lab on the other side of the auditorium. Their approach forced Luluwa closer to the red marble wall.

"What were you doing looking at my arm?" Mustafa stared at her, unblinking. "You're not making sense."

"And you cheated," Luluwa said, her voice rising. "You'll make the curve impossible for everyone." She threw up her hands in exasperation.

"See you next week." Dr. Roberts emerged from the classroom; exam papers peeked from the top of his leather briefcase. He looked to Mustafa for confirmation.

Luluwa's eyes snapped sparks at the professor for his cluelessness.

"Luluwa was asking me how I solved one of the problems," Mustafa said.

Dr. Roberts chuckled. "We can talk about that next class, you two. Take a break for now. I know this one kept everyone up all night."

She had a hundred things she wanted to say to both of them but couldn't find a way to start. Dr. Roberts waved a goodbye before carrying on around the corner.

"You're a cheater, and that means you should fail the class. The honor code," she said to Mustafa.

He stepped away from her, toward the floor-to-ceiling windows across the hallway. "Prove it," he said, drawing his arms across his chest.

"Come here, then." She reached for his sleeve.

"Don't you know better than to try to touch me? What kind of behavior did they allow at that international school of yours?"

"I wasn't—your arm—" Luluwa sputtered in protest.

"I won't meet you in the lab tonight. Find a girl to help you," Mustafa said in a voice that carried down the hall. Sarah, Maryam, and several of the other girls in mechanical engineering glanced up from where they sat hunched on a corner bench.

"I don't need your help." Luluwa backed away from him and that wide smirk she wanted to slap off his face. Another group of first year girls joined those standing at the window swapping notebooks and taking last-minute gulps of tea.

"You'll be fine," Mustafa shouted as if to comfort her. "I'll call you later."

Luluwa's cheeks burned at this implied familiarity. While some of the older girls did share their phone numbers with male classmates and would sit next to them or work with them in groups, most of the students preferred to stick to their own gender.

"She has no man in her house," one of the girls on the bench whispered as Luluwa passed them.

"Really?"

"Yes, I heard her father got a new wife."

"No wonder she can stay out all night."

Luluwa trembled from head to toe. No telling which of the ten girls in the corner had said what. This was the ultimate insult for a woman—to suggest that her virtue was unguarded, she had no male protector. She slunk away before Mustafa could insult her again.

* * *

Luluwa fumed through Literature and the Other Arts, her other class of the day. She sat brooding like a storm cloud at the end of the table, while the florid American professor's chin wobbled in excitement as she explained the intricacies of literary analysis. All the discipline she brought to the major Luluwa let slide in the electives. Dark thoughts followed her home like an enveloping fog. In the living room dusk filtered light around the furniture and cast amorphous shadows across the silk rug. She tripped into the settee, swearing as a sharp pain radiated across her shin.

"Damn it," she spat out, grabbing her leg.

"Eeek!" Khalid popped up from behind the small sofa.

They squealed in unison at the sight of each other.

"You scared me to death," Khalid said.

"Me?" Luluwa sat down and rubbed her leg. "What are you doing here in the dark?"

Saad emerged from around the other end of the sofa.

Luluwa took in their downcast eyes and rumpled clothing. She'd heard rumors of this kind of thing and Sangita's dire warnings about the drawbacks of segregated living. "What are you doing?" she asked again in a louder voice. Unsure of herself, she retreated into her grandfather's sternness.

"Don't tell anyone," Khalid pleaded.

A growing sense of dread washed over Luluwa, quite apart from the dull ache in her leg. She was thankful to be sitting down.

Saad bent down and picked up a small saucer with an overturned thimble-sized coffee cup on it. Beside him chalked symbols and shapes in different colors marked the marble tiles. Crumbled purple, blue, and orange chalk littered the floor and stained the knees of the boys' *thobes*.

"You were in my art supplies again?" She peered more closely. The writing wasn't in Arabic or English. She crawled onto the floor, leaning gingerly on the leg that still smarted.

"What is this?" Her fingers hovered above a five-pointed star.

"Ouija," Saad said. "We made it ourselves."

"I thought you were kidding about that." Luluwa sat back on her heels.

Dusk obscured their boyishness, and their silhouettes hinted at the men they would become, broad-shouldered like their fathers and uncles.

"Whatever gave you this idea?" she asked.

"We're bored," Khalid exclaimed. "*Ubooy* won't let us play video games during the week, and *Ummi* thinks we can spend all our time riding bikes like kids."

Luluwa gestured toward the mysterious paraphernalia. "Did you feel anything?" Reprimands should've been forthcoming, but curiosity got the better of her. Naren's warnings that morning had piqued her interest.

Their pupils suddenly constricted as the overhead lights snapped on.

"Ouch," Luluwa said.

Their grandfather stood frowning over them, arms crossed, his tightly pursed lips disappearing into his beard. "What is this stuff and nonsense?" Jassim blustered. "Playing on the floor like children. You should all be doing your homework." Wiry white hairs poked out from the slits in the unbuttoned sleeves of his *thobe*.

"*Yeddi.*" The boys sprang up, like puppets on a string.

Luluwa pulled herself into a standing position.

"Where do you think you are, the fish market?" Jassim tugged at the rumpled collars of each of their *thobes*. "Get changed. Your Arabic tutor will be here soon."

"Yes, *Yeddi,*" they said.

"And get someone in to clean up this mess." Jassim lifted his foot; orange stained his sole. "What is this scribbling? You boys are close to being men now. Stop drawing on everything like children."

Khalid and Saad's eyes pleaded with Luluwa not to reveal their secret. She shook her head in reassurance. She wouldn't say anything.

"I'll come check on you," Luluwa said.

The boys scurried off in relief, reminding her of earlier years when she chased them through the house pretending to be Um Hamar, the donkey lady who frightened children. Their squeals rose to the ceiling, begging her to stop.

Irritation filled her grandfather's frame with strength. Gone was the frail man she'd left coughing this morning. Before her stood Jassim as he would've been in his younger days, alert and watchful. "Rascals," he said, shaking his head. "Make sure they do their homework." His eyes twinkled. "You can't be too indulgent with boys; you spoil them."

"I will." Luluwa said nothing about the game they'd been playing, a game that most people would consider *haram,* forbidden, or unIslamic. Some lines even her progressive grandfather wouldn't cross.

"Good, I know you will." He gave her a wink before continuing up the stairs one step at a time.

She watched his halting progress. Any attempts to force him to the doctor now, when he was making jokes and walking around the house like the rest of them, would be met with derision.

As the only other child—though she resisted this designation whole-heartedly—left in the compound, it was her job to check up on the boys. Aunt Maryam had enough on her plate with the foreign daughter-in-law. Luluwa watched them run across the courtyard, wondering if she was protecting the very seeds that when they grew would turn them into men like Mustafa.

Chapter Fourteen

If you'd told a younger Abdulla that baby-making was hard, foolishly optimistic about what life had to offer, he would've laughed at you. After all, his first-conceived child had been an afterthought of newlywed life created in an awkward fumble of clothing and sheets. In order to procreate, Abdulla and Fatima, selected as mates for life by their parents and just getting to know each other, had to let go of lifelong inhibitions—and perhaps steal some of those moments promised to them by Hollywood images of love-making.

Was it his age or the pressure of trying to start a business that made intimacy so much harder the second time around? He couldn't fault Sangita. However she felt, she always came to bed smelling like night-blooming jasmine and looking even better. If her heart wasn't in it, he couldn't tell.

"I'm tired," he said that morning when she climbed into the shower with him.

She laughed—but was it to cover up her hurt? He couldn't tell, because he had no frame of reference for reading the signals from a foreign wife. An Arab wife would have immediately suspected he had another woman and gone through his phone and wallet—like his aunts reported that their friends did, only to find the husband had a secret family or was in the process of wooing one.

No other woman here. Unless the business counted. And if so, she was a demanding bitch.

"Can you sign this?"

Abdulla snapped back to attention and gazed at the top item on a pile of paperwork James was pushing in front of him. "An exit permit?"

"Got a couple of friends who are in Dubai for the weekend." James flashed him a grin. "Don't worry, won't do a runner on you."

Abdulla swiveled around in his chair and stared at the grey office wall. "Wouldn't blame you if you did," he muttered. He signed the document that gave James, his employee, permission to leave the country.

"Think I could get a multiple permit? Then I don't have to ask you each time." James took the paper and slipped it into his briefcase.

"Yes," Abdulla mused. "The fewer people I'm responsible for, the better all round."

"It's pricey, five hundred, but probably worth it." James clapped him on the back. "You need to blow off some steam. Why don't you come along? It's some of the younger guys from the program. You know, Kevin and that lot."

Abdulla shuffled through the rest of the paperwork, most of it a multipage contract for the retail lease. As good as a weekend in Dubai sounded, he couldn't leave Sangita alone with the family. And bringing her would defeat the purpose. Plus, what was he going to do when the guys went to places like the innocent-sounding Peppermint nightclub? "I need this to get off the ground," he said.

James gave him another slap on the back before grabbing his jacket. "Will see you on Sunday. Unless you want a blow-by-blow account from Sin City."

"Go, someone has to have all the fun." Abdulla shooed him out of their shared space. "And no, thank you, to texts full of wide-eyed wonder," he called after him. Expats loved the glitz and glamour of Dubai, a cross between Las Vegas and New York. A city built to be a marketplace and playground for the world, unlike most of the other Gulf emirates, which used their oil wealth in more sober, inward-looking ways with their own citizens in mind. *Maybe Sangita would be happier in Dubai.* As quickly as the thought came, he dismissed it. His family couldn't do with them being that far away, even if it was better for their relationship. He needed to be here to keep an eye on Saad. And the business. Lulu was acting strangely as well. Basically everything.

The bounce in James's step made him even more envious. No wayward brother, no lonely wife. No family expectations. He better be careful or he'd start feeling really sorry for himself. *Going to see friends.* Why couldn't he see a friend, too? There must be someone he could call. Maybe they'd end up like those guys who hung out at Starbucks, drinking coffee in the middle of the day. Ali's phone rang, unanswered. A few seconds later, *Who is this?* popped up in the text box.

Abdulla, he typed back. *Want to have a coffee at Landmark?* He stared at the screen, like a teenage girl, waiting for the reply.

Can't.Working a case. Maybe in a few weeks.

He dropped the phone on the table in disgust. Everyone had more important things to do. He tidied up the files and papers on his desk with a sigh. There was nowhere left to go but home.

* * *

He arrived at the house to find no lights on and not even the maid hovering around. A sticky note from Sangita on the dresser mirror said *Gym*. He changed out of his *thobe* into sweat pants and a t-shirt from last year's National Sport Day, then roamed around downstairs, trying out various locations as work stations. First the dining room, then the living room sofa, lastly the kitchen table. What did two people need so much furniture for? He skipped away from the thought before his mother's ruminations about grandchildren filled his mind.

"Abdulla, turn on the lights." His grandfather made his way to the switches on the wall.

"Sorry, *Yeddi,* was watching TV," he lied to cover up the strangeness of sitting alone in a dark room.

"Ah, you know we used to sing to each other for entertainment," Jassim said. His laugh rattled into a chuckle.

Ordinarily these stories made Abdulla groan inwardly, but tonight the silence of the house, and the emptiness in his heart, made him receptive to his grandfather's home-spun wisdom. "Songs about what?"

A smile hovered in the grooves of Jassim's face. "Imagine what it was like, hours and hours on the sea, no land in sight. We sang about everything: those who had gone before us; their bravery; the women who were waiting for us at home; the dangers of the spirits lurking in the deep." Jassim sat in the armchair across from him, a heap of skin and bones.

Abdulla shook the weariness from his mind and saw his grandfather clearly for the first time in months. The old man, the family patriarch, was the reason why the other adults in the family gave him and his new wife sidewise glances. Some wished they would get on with it, seal the family genes, as mixed as they would be now with a foreigner, and produce Jassim's legacy. Others probably wished the foreign wife away so that Abdulla could start yet again, for a third time, with a woman of Arabian blood.

"Spirits," Abdulla repeated.

"This isn't all there is to the world," Jassim cautioned. He pinched the skin on the back of his hand. "We are affected by that which we cannot see."

His grandfather's words echoed in his mind, calling back the time when an invisible tide had pulled Abdulla away from everyone he knew. The doctor had called it depression. After his first wife's death, Abdulla had been uninterested in going on with life. So had her younger sister. Luluwa's wan features, the circles under her eyes flashed before him. Studying had brought her back to life—or at least given meaning to it. But lately, something seemed off. You couldn't tell with teenagers what was moodiness and what might be too much responsibility too soon. He rubbed the bridge of his nose, unable to share his burdens, unwilling to accelerate his grandfather's decline.

"You know, Abu Derya, the master of the seas. He called forth whales, typhoons, jellyfish, anything and everything to thwart us." Jassim ran his fingers along the brocade of the armchair as if stroking the waves.

"It was good work." Abdulla doubted he could dive ten feet, much less the forty his grandfather had done month after month with a rope in his mouth and a basket around his neck in search of pearls.

"It was hard work," Jassim corrected. His eyes clouded over with memories. "The sea asked too high a price. She claimed many lives. Mine wasn't good enough." The last said on the breath of a whisper so that Abdulla nearly missed it.

"*Yeddi*," he said in surprise. "You can't blame yourself for the boat sinking."

"The boat." Jassim batted away the word as if it were sailing toward him on the air. "The men," he said. "They never had proper burials."

Abdulla sat in the gloom of the living room; his grandfather's grief hung round them like a shroud. This was true responsibility. To know that you lived on while others perished, always wondering if your life was worth the price. Wandering from house to house on the family compound in search of someone who would listen to your tales, yearning for one of the seven grandchildren to keep you company because your own sons were too busy and their wives were out with friends.

"But look at you now," Abdulla said, injecting as much joviality into his voice as he could manage. "All of this. Learning English. Breaking rules." He gave his grandfather a wink, hoping to lighten the mood.

Jassim coughed; the rattling sound set off alarm bells for Abdulla. "You are a good man. You remember the years we worked hard, when you were a child. But your brother, your cousins …" Jassim trailed off. "If only there were a ship we could send them to work on. As apprentices. You know how many years I was a *tabaaba* making tea and hauling ropes before I could dive on my own?"

"I don't," Abdulla said. "Tell me."

His grandfather's eyes grew misty. Instead of unfolding more of his story, his chin dipped towards his chest and he dozed off.

I should be so lucky. Abdulla broke into a smile for the first time in weeks. *To have memories of better days and someone to pass them on to.* Though first, he also realized, he had to father a son—or daughter—of his own.

Chapter Fifteen

Hind pressed on her tired eyelids, then focused again on the documents in front of her. She drank more coffee to focus, but the words still swam across the pages strewn along the desk.

Since her first two excursions out into the city, she'd taken to riding trains. You could blend in, sit near people, each lost in their own thoughts, without standing on top of them—if you timed it right—and get pulled into the rhythm of the city. Instead of crawling through town in the traffic, she could sit on a metal bench or stand, holding onto a steel grip, swaying with the track. Her mother would be mystified to think her daughter found trains entertaining. *Go to the ladies' gatherings. Make some friends.* Hind could almost hear her.

She'd managed to stomach one such gathering early on in her time in the city. She'd been requested to make an appearance on behalf of the consulate when the other Gulf ambassadors' wives came to Mumbai for a shopping trip. At first, hearing Arabic again had buoyed her spirits. But soon the sniping had started—was that last year's Gucci bag? And those earrings couldn't be real—even if she said the stones were from Jaipur.

No, the city was like a new friend, showing her the sights little by little. All the color and vibrancy she could want was out there on the street— even if she had to explore it alone. People from the Gulf had been exploring the waters off the shores of Mumbai for decades.

The Pearl of Great Price, Hind now read, *was found by an Arab diver in the 1970s in a giant clam in the Indian Ocean. Rumors surround its discovery and subsequent loss. The boat from which the pearl was found capsized in a cyclone, the worst in decades, taking all sailors and the pearl with it to the bottom of the ocean, and leaving the Pearl of Lao Tzu unchallenged as the world's largest pearl. The checkered past of the Lao Tzu Pearl includes murder, carbon dating and—*

"Good morning, madam."

Hind jerked up from the computer screen. Hanosh filled the doorway. Her aide's skittishness suggested he was on high alert today; his right hand shook against his leg.

"Good morning."

"The ambassador wants to speak to you." Hanosh's voice cracked.

"He does?" Hind's voice was steady, though a tremor went through her. Did he know she'd seen Ravi in her office without anyone else present? That would be enough to get her fired. The ministry gladly found any excuse to remove women from the Foreign Service. *The second largest pearl is the Palwan Princess* ... Hind swiveled away from the computer. Time to face the music.

"All right," she said.

"Phone."

"Excuse me?"

"He's on the phone, madam."

The red light on the base unit of her Cisco phone was blinking. "Thank you."

Hanosh scuttled away without her having to say another word. He knew as much as anyone how unusual a phone call like this was.

"*As-salaam alaikum,*" Hind said.

"*Wa alaikum as-salaam,*" came the gruff reply.

"Your Excellency."

He issued instructions to someone in the background on how he wanted his coffee. "Yes. Good that you're in the office." The phone magnified his awkwardness. Dealing with young female staff wasn't part of the Ministry of Foreign Affairs training, since most of the female diplomatic corps served as undersecretaries in the ministry back home. "Is everything going well?"

Hind fidgeted with a piece of hair on her cheek. "Yes," she said, eyeing the towering stack of labor contracts on the corner of her desk. "I'm waiting for legal counsel to come in and review—"

"Yes, yes." His sonorous tone suggested he had even more weighty matters on his mind than the mountain of work ahead of her. "There's a consultant we've been talking to who's coming in to see you. He has a proposal for an exhibit, an art, cultural thing. Would be good. Get us some good publicity about longstanding ties between the countries. Offset the whole labor issue, human rights, that sort of thing."

"Yes, Your Excellency."

"He's coming over. Your office manager has the details. He'll attend the meeting with you. High-level. Like you wanted."

Hind clutched the phone cord.

"I understand this project has some connection with your family." He cleared his throat meaningfully. "You'll make sure this works out, right?"

"Sir." Where should she begin to list the ways in which this project was over her head? Should she tell him about the pearl? Did he know about the pearl?

"I could ask your father, you know, if you don't think you can make this happen."

Hind sat up straighter. "No, sir, I'll see to it."

With a grunt of satisfaction, he disconnected the line.

Hind switched to her mobile phone and dialed her young cousin.

"Hello?" Luluwa's voice was a whisper.

"Lulu, it's me, Hind. I'm checking on *Yeddo*."

"I'm in class," Luluwa said in a low tone.

"Oh, God, sorry." Hind flushed, remembering her college days. "Send me an update when you can," she said also in a whisper.

"Okay."

Today must be the day of people hanging up on me, Hind thought, as once again she found herself listening to the dial tone.

Hanosh returned.

She looked up. "Mystery guest is here already?"

His forehead creased. "Madam, it's time for the legal meeting for this docket of contracts."

"Right." Hind resisted the urge to sigh. *You were the one who wanted to work in an embassy.* Her sister would chide her if she confessed to being bored. Hind might as well have stayed home if she knew so much of it was going to be desk work.

* * *

Hours later, shoes off, sticky notes covering the east wall of her office, Hind had mapped out the lawyer's recommendations. He wanted to see a specific set of changes inserted into every contract, and now she had to mark up all the revisions from his master list. Hind streamed classical music on her laptop, humming along with *Für Elise,* the one piece she'd mastered before quitting piano. "You will regret this one day," her mother had insisted when Hind said she'd rather take up swimming than continue with piano.

Oh, how right her mother had been. Hind paused in her repetitive task of outlining the set of new conditions. A covered woman could only swim in so many places, and most of those were indoors.

The pinging of her phone brought her back to reality. Luluwa, true to her word, had WhatsApped her a few lines about their grandfather: *Not sleeping much, persistent cough, bags under his eyes. Still talking about the old days.* Maybe the girl should be studying medicine.

"Madam, our special meeting is here." Hanosh skidded to a stop.

Hind fixed her *shayla* while slipping her feet back into her shoes. "We'll meet in the conference room." She waved her hand at the mess.

Hanosh nodded, doing an about-face.

"Oh, and what's his name?"

His Adam's apple bobbed like a cork.

Hind's heartbeat thudded in her ears. She felt out of her depth and longed for someone she could trust.

"Vimal Bose."

"Get Ravi Patel on the phone," she snapped. At Hanosh's blank stare, she tossed him the binder. "The consultant. Page 12. Get him to brief me on this Vimal Bose. And tell him to get here as soon as he can. Stall the other guy."

Another blank stare.

"Tell Bose I'm in a meeting. Until Ravi Patel can get here."

"Madam, Mr. Bose is already here, waiting," Hanosh stuttered.

"Keep him downstairs," Hind repeated, shooing him away. "Tell the guard to bring Ravi straight up." Her grandfather's favorite saying rang in her ears: *Better the devil you know than the devil you don't.* They had to get to the bottom of this for his sake.

Chapter Sixteen

Luluwa drummed her fingers on the calculator. She pressed the black buttons, and numbers popped up on the LCD screen. Her nails clacked away, the only sound in the library study room. Past the railing, girls had their hands curled around paper cups of coffee, their *abayas* gaping open, shoes off, everyone relaxed at the end of the university day. The mostly female clientele of the university library meant *shaylas* were off, either hanging on shoulders or stuffed into bags. The fluorescent lights buzzed overhead, a dull, constant sound, as the winter sunlight dimmed. In an hour or so it would be totally dark outside.

She fidgeted with her phone, replaying in her mind the scene from yesterday's exam. Just then a high-pitched laugh sent a wave of irritation through Luluwa. She pushed away her textbook and calculator, and the stack of pencils sharp enough to rip paper or poke out an eye. Gone now were the days of temptation when she would've slipped a sharpened pencil into the sleeve of her *abaya* and then into her handbag, to use at home when she couldn't keep the loneliness at bay in the yawning darkness that followed her sister's death. Pencils, pens, tweezers, nail files—anything to push against her cuticles until they bled.

University had rescued her from the cycle of self-mutilation. Now she wanted to press one of these pencils against Mustafa's throat until he confessed. The girls' giggles ricocheted off the marble walls of the library, magnifying their mirth. She straightened the edges of her homework sheet for the roads class. No one else in the major was working on anything like highway construction, because they all preferred to follow the safe path for local engineers: a major in petroleum engineering meant high-paying jobs in the private sector, at Shell or the national Exxon subsidiary. Luluwa would rather stab herself in the eye with a pencil than listen to one more technical-writing presentation by a student wanting to use their skills to become a manager.

I'm coming to get you, everyone else is out. Sangita's message jarred her from the dark bend of her thoughts. *Be there in twenty.*

The sinking sun cast an orange glow through the rectangular room, no longer offering much competition to the humming fluorescent lights. People trickled out of the study rooms like water draining from a bathtub until only Luluwa was left upstairs. She sat back in the metal chair, surveying her workstation: an island free of clutter amid the sea of abandoned papers, water bottles, pens, and stationery supplies strewn across every other desk in the room. Students left them helter-skelter because, like at home, someone else would pick up after them. She felt satisfaction in sweeping all the debris into the trashcan with one hand. If only she could disappear as easily as her garbage.

Twenty minutes was not long enough to get started on the new section but too long to lurk around downstairs.

A blank piece of paper fluttered to the floor. She put it back on the table, and then quickly, before restraint set in, she divided the page into quarters by drawing two lines, one down the middle and one straight across. She then sketched from memory, penciling lines here and there, draping fabric on an imaginary figure, tall like Sangita, with angular features. Luluwa created designs that she would actually wear at weddings, instead of sequins, if only her mother didn't care what her daughter looked like. She worked until all four boxes were filled, using highlighters to fill in the borders of the garments. As she worked, her irritation over Mustafa's rudeness abated, and the sting of the injustice of his cheating ceased to matter.

As she descended the stairs, she saw Amna, one of Noor's friends from the fashion department, among the group of girls taking turns posing for Snapchat. She prattled on about how her cousins loved the dress designs she showed them and would have them made in pastels for a wedding, and her aunt had connections to the best showrooms in London.

"Harrods," Amna said. "Imagine, everyone will see them then." Her red lacquer fingernails stroked the brocade on the sleeve of her *abaya*. "Just imagine, Kate Middleton wears one of my gowns, and I'll be the first famous *khaleeji* designer." Amna had a misty look in her eyes, the look high schoolers used to have when their engagements were announced.

"That doesn't mean anyone will buy them," Luluwa muttered under her breath. The hum of the air conditioning swept up her words. Not that Amna was paying attention. She was showing the others photographs of herself posing in front of a mannequin draped with the fabric destined to become one of the dresses of her dreams. Luluwa wasn't sure who was going to make these dresses, since Amna could barely draw a straight line. Maybe she could hire the mice from Cinderella.

Amna's phone rang, belting out a pop rhythm. She took it to the corner of the room, turning away from the frowning librarian. She then spent several minutes talking to someone while twisting her hair into thin ropes and admiring her reflection in the window.

"You dropped this." Mary walked up beside her, holding the crumpled sheet of sketches Luluwa had made in the library. She smoothed out the sides with her blunt fingernails while her inquisitive gaze took in all aspects of the sketches. Luluwa had designed a fuchsia paisley border on a black nylon robe with wide sleeves etched in the same trim. Finally Mary handed the sheet to Luluwa then huddled her hands into the pouch of her grey sweatshirt.

Luluwa smiled at the study-abroad student while trying to push the drawings into her tote bag. Followed by Mary, she walked toward the library exit, hoping Amna hadn't heard a word.

Luluwa had endured such pleading and cajoling when Noor tried to insist that they pursue fashion together. That pressure would surely resurface if her cousin realized that her interest in engineering was purely a desire for financial independence. No one knew about her stash of other drawings, failed versions of a concept that wouldn't quite materialize—either the wrong color or pattern, or some elusive element missing, something she couldn't figure out. The stack of sketches she worked on during nights when the insomnia returned piled on the table next to Luluwa's bed. She kept the bridal sketches, gowns with etched paisley on brocade, in a notebook buried in the closet.

"It's an *abaya* inspired by a sari," she said.

Mary's eyes widened, indicating a stream of questions was sure to follow. "Based on your sister-in-law?"

"My cousin-in-law," Luluwa corrected.

Just keep your mouth shut. The American girl was polite, punctual and kind. But Luluwa couldn't take any more of her searching questions today. *Why does everyone let their maids carry their bags in the malls? Why do the maids get out of cars and take people's portfolios at university? Why don't students use backpacks?*

Luluwa's phone buzzed in her hand. She flipped it to answer, treating

Mary to the photo on her home screen—herself with Sangita at her henna night, palms up, flashing the red swirling patterns and smiles at the camera.

"She's beautiful," Mary said. "Even in every day."

Luluwa was not in the mood to talk about the family's biggest scandal, and definitely not to a more or less stranger. She swept the phone up in one hand and hoisted her bag higher on her shoulder. "See you tomorrow," she said before Mary could say more.

Luluwa pulled her *abaya* closed over her leggings and white tank top and raced toward the building's south exit, an ornately studded metal door in the local vernacular style. Hurrying, she caught the edge of her *abaya* under her Converse. In her eagerness to put the building behind her, she stumbled and almost catapulted into the guard station before catching her balance. Behind her she heard a titter—girls coming back from their stroll to Starbucks in the Student Center. Luluwa righted herself, ignoring the urge to turn around and look at them.

"Careful, ma'am," called the security guard, an older woman with a square haircut and shoulders that gave her the stocky appearance of a small man.

"I'm okay." Luluwa smiled at guard's dubious look. She burst through the burnished bronze door, skipped down the three marble steps outside the building, and paused on the curb to let a maroon Mercedes pass before it crushed her toes. Across the street in a black Land Cruiser idling on the side, Sangita was adjusting her *shayla*.

Luluwa sprinted toward her, dodging a Nissan Patrol that braked at the last minute.

"Hello," Sangita said as Luluwa clambered into the vehicle, tossing her bag into the back seat.

"Drive," Luluwa replied. "As fast as you can, away from here."

"Yes, madam. I cracked the driving test because your wish is my command." Sangita made a clucking sound. She turned the SUV around in the parking lot, passing several occupied vehicles waiting with drivers asleep and maids in uniform staring out the windows. "That bad?"

Luluwa shook her head instead of replying. She played with the dials on the radio, moving from one station to the other. The British DJ on the national network was the best of the worst, though the '80s song he introduced had them both wincing. The car's high-pitched beep as it picked up speed past the guard station made Sangita snap her fingers. "Seatbelt."

Luluwa pulled it on, the metallic click drawing Sangita's gaze from the road.

"*That* bad?"

So bad you forgot how your sister died? The unspoken words hung between them. Luluwa took several deep breaths, not wanting to think about Fatima, not now, not in the presence of Abdulla's new wife. This still felt disloyal somehow, the fact she enjoyed Sangita's company, like a betrayal. The unhappy memories would only taint a day that she was hoping would turn around now that the yellow university building was receding in the rear view mirror.

"How are *you* feeling?" she asked brightly instead, hoping to distract them both.

"Fine," Sangita said. "I guess. I mean, I keep thinking maybe they're wrong. Maybe I am the problem. I'm still not pregnant."

Luluwa flipped down the mirror to avoid replying. The American's penchant for bluntness still took her by surprise. No other cousin-in-law could so explicitly identify the cause of family angst.

A car sliced through the roundabout and skidded in front of them. Sangita stomped on the brakes, leaning on the horn. "Watch where you're going! Asshole," she muttered, then gave Luluwa a sidelong glance. "Sorry." She flexed her fingers against the leather of the steering wheel. At the next stoplight her fingernails dug back into the curved top.

The houses whizzed by. "You shouldn't drive," Luluwa said. They turned right then sped onto the entrance ramp of the highway. "It upsets you too much."

Sangita honked again as another SUV kept her from getting over into the middle lane. "And you'd rather be picked up by Naren or wait for Noor every day?" she muttered, her eyes on the rearview mirror, watching a vehicle riding so close they couldn't see its front license plate.

"I could drive myself," Luluwa said. "Then no one would have to pick me up."

"The thought of you on these roads ..." Sangita shook her head, then checked the side mirror before switching lanes. The Land Cruiser behind her, which had begun flashing its lights for her to go faster, sped on past. "Plus this gives me something to do. A reason to get dressed."

"It can't be as bad as all that," Luluwa said. "What about volunteering?"

"To do what? Organize million-dollar dinners? Looks like we're stuck with each other."

"That's not what I meant." Dusty palm trees bobbed in the median as three lanes of traffic inched forward toward the roundabout.

"Finish this degree," Sangita said, "and then we'll see."

Luluwa scrunched down in her seat with a groan. The family didn't have many original lines any more, and the few they had seemed to be permeating even the newest member. Maybe they'd all heard them so much they'd come to believe them. Luluwa chewed on the edge of her finger. She found it hard to believe graduation would bring anything other than mounting pressure to find an eligible bachelor and settle down—the same fate as all her cousins and friends.

Sangita exited the highway and crawled forward in the line of cars to make a left. "Don't be so glum," she said. "You'll remember these as the best days of your life."

"Things are bleaker than they appear," Luluwa said.

Sangita laughed. The adobe-colored houses and boundary walls blurred together as they picked up speed. Scaffolding stood like a skeleton around an unfinished mall at the side of the road. Of course another mall project, ongoing, sat on the opposite side of the street; sand tinged the glass top of the atrium.

"We don't have to go back yet," Luluwa said. "How about some *karak?*"

Sangita shrugged. Neither of them enjoyed living on the family compound under mild surveillance by the rest of the family. Luluwa gave her directions to the Tea Time, a staple in her high school years when she and Noor often picked up an order before heading home. They beat the post-work rush hour and parked in front.

"Wait, the guy is coming." Luluwa lowered her window. A man in uniform with a mustache came to take their order. Luluwa threw in a few items for her younger cousins, who were always starving.

"Brings a new meaning to curbside service," Sangita mused. "No wonder people are so big here. Don't have to do anything."

"Don't say that again too loud," Luluwa said.

Sangita chewed on her lip. "You know what I mean."

"I do."

They contemplated the other cars filling up the parking lot; one driver with much less patience than Sangita beat out a staccato rhythm on his horn until a waiter came out to take his order. After a few minutes their own steaming tea arrived.

"Chapatti with cheese?" Sangita took a bite. "My mother wouldn't believe this. Guess you can't go wrong with cheese."

Luluwa laughed and dipped her plain flatbread into the tea. "It can't hurt."

The phone rang through the SUV's speakers. "That's our cue," Sangita said before telling Abdulla they were on their way. "He's as nervous as you are about me driving." She reversed, taking them back into the traffic.

"That's family," Luluwa said. The years Sangita had spent in London on her own, pursuing a master's degree was the dream of many local girls. Concerns about family reputation prevented most of them from seeing it come true. Her cousin Hind had found a loophole—getting engaged meant she was more or less settled while in graduate school. But in the end it'd backfired, since that was when she lost her fiancé.

Within a few minutes, the SUV nosed past the wrought iron gate and into the family compound where the four houses loomed over the courtyard like sentinels. Theirs was the first car back in the fold.

"Women in Saudi Arabia have been arrested for driving," Luluwa complained. "But it's legal for me to drive here, and still no one will let me."

Sangita stopped the car next to Luluwa's childhood home and slid the key out of the ignition. She turned to look at Luluwa with a steady gaze. Sangita was becoming one of the few people, even in the family, to actually see Luluwa or bother listening while she spoke. Sangita's brown eyes were focused, her brow furrowed in sympathy.

"If I lived in America, I wouldn't need anyone's permission."

"We don't live in America," Sangita said quietly.

Luluwa fidgeted for her bag in the back seat. She fiddled with the strap, her bracelets, anything to avoid that tone in Sangita's voice, the one that said, "Don't remind me of all that I gave up to be here." Luluwa took in the marble arches of the entryway to her grandfather's house, the gold calligraphy above the door, the hot pink hibiscus shrubs—all physical reminders of where they were—all the while hoping that the tears that had sprung quickly to Sangita's eyes were dissipating.

"Have you heard from Hind?" Luluwa asked, hoping for a diversion. She'd intended to lift the mood, but the drooping corners of Sangita's mouth suggested her question had not had that effect. Although Hind and Sangita were on speaking terms, the two former best friends couldn't reconcile Sangita's marrying Hind's fiancé. "I'm sure she loves India," Luluwa rushed on. "Anywhere has to be better than here."

"I'll see you later," Sangita said in a low voice. She slid from the driver's seat and out the door and tried to scurry away, but her lack of familiarity with the voluminous folds of her *abaya* caused her to stop several times to avoid tripping.

The wind had picked up during their drive home, carrying with it the smell of charcoal. Someone was probably burning trash a few houses away, despite the municipality's campaign to get people to dispose of trash in other ways. Luluwa sniffed, but there were no accompanying odors of rubber or refuse, only the crispness of winter finally approaching after having skipped the desert's non-existent autumn. Despite the cooler temperatures of recent days, she wiped a line of sweat from her forehead. She pulled her *abaya* closer, juggling bag, laptop and mobile phone in her other hand. Petals from the bougainvillea skittered across her path, and the wind whipped the *shayla* from her head, casting the headscarf on the ground behind her like a mischievous child.

Luluwa bit her lip, though no one would hear her if she swore. Years of training made her mindful that if any of her cousins saw her outside without her *shayla* and told one of the adults, they would surely rethink their support of her going to the American university. She wedged her phone and laptop into the mouth of her bag and bent to get her *shayla*. Not with her knees, as her mother would have liked, but from her back, sticking her butt out in a way that would have her Aunt Maryam shaking her head. *No one was looking anyway, so what did it matter if she carried herself like a man?* She was inside the cream walls of the family compound, the perimeter that ran around the houses of the three brothers and their father. She straightened, letting the sheer black fabric dangle in her hand.

The fountain Sangita had had installed in the entryway to what had been Luluwa's childhood home tinkled in welcome.

Luluwa heard the meows of kittens. Yet another group of the tiny beasts were nestled in the patio chair. She didn't shoo them away. They were so scrawny she could have held one in the palm of her hand. When she approached, the mother cat appeared from behind a leg of the wrought iron table, green eyes watching her without blinking. Luluwa shivered as the wind whipped her uncovered hair around her. Engrossed in the cat, she didn't notice the man standing to the left of the path until she was nearly upon him. His arms shot out to stop her stumbling into him.

"Oh!"

He stared at her, muscles taut along his arms and the plane of his stomach. The sharp ends of his collarbone protruded under an angled chin.

She stepped back. A gardener would have made way for her, but he didn't move.

Despite the fierce wind, his cut-off trousers, in tatters below the knees, barely stirred. He radiated heat and the tang of barbecue.

The wind whipped her bag off her shoulder, strewing her sketching supplies everywhere. She bent to pick them up. A few pencils rolled under the tires of her cousin's car. Abdulla was home.

"Get out of this wind!" he ordered, shouldering the strap of Luluwa's bag and lifting it from the pavement.

She looked up and saw her cousin's bemused expression. He had one hand clamped on his *ghutra* to keep it from flying away and the other on her arm, tugging her into what had been her father's house. Luluwa looked back over her shoulder, but the gardener was gone.

"Inside," Abdulla said. He pulled the corner of his *ghutra* over his nose and across his mouth so that only his eyes were visible, like boys did in the desert. "The sand is going to start flying soon. The air along the Corniche was orange."

"Did you just see anyone?" Luluwa asked, holding her breath. Abdulla was unpredictable these days. If he knew a guy roamed the compound, the women might not be let out of the house for days until the man was found.

"There's no one here." Abdulla let go of her arm to open the door. "Come on."

The rising wind swept away the whoosh of her pent-up breath. Luluwa was curious, though. She wanted to search for the man, see what he was doing on the family property, and tell him that whatever his plan—begging or asking for work—he was likely to end up in jail if he dared to enter again. Abdulla pulled her forward, like another element of nature, as the wind whipped their garments around them. She glanced around one more time, across the vehicles and the courtyard, for a sight of the bare-chested man, but he was nowhere to be seen.

Not normally one to be superstitious, she nevertheless said a quick prayer as Abdulla closed the door behind them. They had had enough misfortune in the family with the death of Fatima and her baby—the child the family found out about only after the accident. No one needed any more bad luck.

Chapter Seventeen

Abdulla ignored his phone as it buzzed on the tabletop while he tasted yet another sample of a gourmet take on *machboos*.

"This I've made with lamb instead of chicken and also added cranberries to soften the metallic taste of meat." The chef's lilting accent plucked at Abdulla's heartstrings, and he made an effort not to groan audibly.

"It tastes fine," he said under his breath to James, "but this is not an authentic traditional dish."

James smiled, nodding, and ushered the chef out by the elbow, full of platitudes and promises to be in touch.

Today was supposed to be devoted to tasting bits and pieces from various chefs. Abdulla tossed his fork down. Yet another person favored fusion over tradition. Maybe they were right. After all, what did he know about what was going to be the next big food craze? He still hadn't got over how similar samosas and sambusas were.

"You keep frowning at everyone even before you've had the first bite, while they're still just describing the dish. Word is going to get around." James came back into the small room adjacent to the kitchen that would eventually be the bathroom. Right now the four bare walls and concrete floor betrayed how far behind the project was on the redesign. "That guy was from the Food Network."

"Final round pick for Chopped is hardly anyone to be worried about," Abdulla muttered.

James leaned his forearms on the table. "People talk," he said. "We're using up all our cards."

"Why are the chefs all men, anyway?" Abdulla said. He pushed back from the table. "Maybe we need a woman's touch to get traditional home cooking."

James flopped into a chair opposite him. "Feminist now, are we?"

The buzzing phone interrupted their increasingly terse banter. A tenseness Abdulla was beginning to recognize as resentment had replaced the playful tone of the early days. He'd seen it all too many times during circular discussions at the ministry. "Hello," he snapped.

"Abdulla," a man's voice said.

"Yes, who is this?" He glanced at the number. A landline. He recognized nothing else about it.

"This is Ali." Abdulla paused as he recalled his friend, the police officer. Surely he wasn't calling to shoot the breeze in the middle of the workday? "Yes, how are you?" He feigned interest.

"You need to come down to the Maamoura police station." Bin Youssef never had minced words.

Abdulla's blood ran cold. His aunt had received a call like this after the accident when Fatima died. "Who is it? What's wrong?" Abdulla held up a finger to James, turning away for some privacy.

"Everyone's fine. We'll talk when you get here."

He hung up and told James to schedule a new round of chefs, female this time, for later in the week. The glaring irony of speeding to the police station struck Abdulla as he zipped under flashing yellow lights and wove his way into the outside lane around a white sedan that was slowing down. On this rare occasion, ignoring everything they had learned from Fatima's accident, he texted Sangita and Luluwa as he drove to make sure they were safe. They were not the ones he should've been worrying about.

"*As-salaam alaikum,*" an officer said, his braces gleaming as he greeted Abdulla at the station.

"*Alaikum as-salaam.*" Abdulla took a deep breath. "I'm here to see Captain Ali." The young policeman sat straighter and pointed to the bank of elevators to the left. "Top floor."

Abdulla rode the elevator, adjusting his *ghutra* and *agal* in the mirror. They'd fallen askew in his rush to find out what his friend wanted. The doors opened onto an entire floor of gleaming polished tiles. Banks of computer screens lined both walls. Only a few officers sat scattered in front of them.

"Abdulla." Bin Youssef came forward and shook his hand.

"What—"

His friend led him to the nearest computer. He pressed a few buttons on the keyboard, which made the screen whirr to life. Abdulla hunched over, peering at grainy images of a parking lot. A black SUV sat in the corner.

"What is this——" he began again, but stopped when a group of gangly boys filled the bottom right of the screen. He recognized one by the high-top black sneakers. The boys tried all the doors of the SUV and found them open. The camera lost them for a second as they disappeared inside. "Tell me they didn't steal someone's car." Abdulla clenched his jaw, waiting for the vehicle to jerk into motion.

"No." Bin Youssef patted his shoulder.

The boys emerged again and circled to the back bumper. Each held a different object. One showed off a pair of sunglasses, then tossed them back into the interior. Another showed off a lighter. Again tossed back. The third produced a bottle of cologne that sent the others coughing. And the last, the one with the high-top sneakers under his *thobe,* Abdulla's younger brother Saad, grinned as he produced an iPad. The camera then lost them as the boys whooped and ran off screen together.

Bin Youssef tapped a few more keys and the screen went blank.

"You're doing surveillance?" Abdulla looked up, unsure of what else to say to his friend.

"We were watching this lot for something else." He held up a hand. "I can't say what. You shouldn't be in this room. But the minute I saw your neighborhood ..." His voice trailed off. "You want to call him, or should I let the guys deal with it? Call your dad?"

Yuba can't find out about this. Theft was a serious crime, not something Arab fathers took lightly. Even if it was only young boys out for a lark. *Next thing you know, Saad and Khalid will be shipped off to boarding school.* Abdulla adjusted his *ghutra,* folding it one way and then the other. "I'll deal with this," he said. "Though I might bring the boys back here."

Bin Youssef shrugged. "As you wish. I'm on assignment, so you won't see me. The guy wants his property back, that's all. Expat. He's downstairs. Want to talk to him?"

"Not yet," Abdulla said grimly. He shook hands with Bin Youssef again. Whatever his friend was involved in now, he was thankful it had brought them together.

His drive home was much more measured. He played over and over in his mind what he would say to the boys when he found them. If he yelled, the moms would overhear, and that could go either way. Wadha would protect Khalid. She always did, since he was the baby in their household, and the only boy. His own mother—her temper was mercurial, depending on who had done what to her that day. That could work for or against him and Saad.

Abdulla burst into the foyer, keys jangling. "Where's Saad?" he asked a startled Anita.

"At your uncle's … your house."

Abdulla turned on his heel for the house.

"Your wife is teaching him chess," she called after him.

Abdulla burst through the door. Saad sat at the table with Sangita. "You get over here this minute," he said to his brother, his temper flaring with the heat.

"Hello to you too, dear," Sangita said. She looked up at him, head to one side, as he glowered at them from the doorway.

Saad moved a piece. "Check." He clapped his hands.

"Hey, that's really good." Sangita paused, taking in the board.

"Now," Abdulla growled.

Saad stood. "Okay, okay, take it easy."

"I'll take it easy when you stop doing illegal things." Shaking his head at Sangita's questioning look, he shut the door behind them, then grabbed Saad by the shoulder and steered him towards the car. When they were about to get in, he stopped short. "Go and get it."

Saad raised his arms, his mouth opening in question.

"The iPad you stole," Abdulla snapped. "As if we couldn't buy you one!"

Saad went white as a sheet. "I didn't steal—"

"The police have you on camera." Abdulla folded his arms. "Go ahead. Try and get out of this one. But we're going to the station first."

"It's at Faisal's house."

Abdulla pinched the bridge of his nose. "In Wakra?"

Saad nodded, his eyes on his brother's shoes.

"Get in." He slid into the car and slammed the door on the driver's side. "Oh, and get your cousin out here, too," he shouted. "We're all going for a drive."

An hour to Wakra, the next town, and an hour back, then who knew how long at the police station? There was another day of work gone.

Chapter Eighteen

She tossed and turned that night, fuming because she'd had to take the Bose meeting alone. How could he leave her to deal with that man? After he'd asked for her help, calling it "family business!" She pummeled the pillow to soften it and cradled it around her head. He was no one to her. Just someone she knew. A relative of a relative by marriage. So he didn't technically owe her anything. But hadn't there been that spark, begun accidentally those many months ago? Hadn't he been glad of the excuse that brought them back together?

Hind sat up, turning on the bedside lamp. She pulled Ravi's folder toward her, flipped to the consultant profile and started punching numbers into her phone.

Seething, she didn't wait for Ravi to say hello. "If you're neck deep in this why go through the pretense of asking for my help?"

"Hind?" The muffled voice brought her up short. "I'm not sure what you're talking about. What time is it?"

Belatedly, she flashed a glance at the clock, which was showing just after 1 a.m. "Are you asleep?"

Ravi cleared his throat. "I was."

"Sorry." *I'm not the one who should be apologizing.*

Sheets rustled in her ear. Was he alone? "None of my business," she muttered.

"What's that?"

"You left me to meet with that man," Hind sputtered, the awkwardness of the meeting coming back to her. "I had no idea what he was saying. Charts, and tables, and graphs. Seismic movement and ocean currents. And apparently my grandfather's already been invited. I was waiting for you."

"I'm sorry." Ravi's voice was warm without any of the animosity from earlier that afternoon. "I was on the other side of town, trying to figure out who Bose's funder is."

"You couldn't call?"

"My battery died." A pause. "I didn't know my help meant so much to you."

She bit her lip, taking a few breaths to steady her voice. "You're the one who knows what's going on."

"I'm not leaving you out on purpose." He sounded fully awake now, his voice taut.

"Aren't you playing both sides behind my back? Why do you care if someone else knows? They gave you the bid, right?"

"Hind, there's more on that boat than skeletons and history," Ravi said.

"Okay. But I mean, this is not the *Titanic*, right?" She laughed. "There's no old lady with a diamond to throw back in."

"No. But the pearl that sank with the boat was worth three times that fake diamond in *Titanic*. Anyone who knows the maritime history of the region knows there's a chance of finding it."

"And that's why the government would spend so much money dredging up a decaying old wooden boat?" Hind said.

"Your grandfather is the legal owner of that pearl," Ravi said, "but whoever finds it can lay claim to it. He could spend the rest of his life in court trying to get it back. If we find it at all." He went through the history of the boat and the pearl again, explaining the complicated legal framework if they did manage to raise the boat, then promised to send over more material for her to look at.

When the call ended, Hind was speechless. She stared at her phone. All those years, all those stories, and she had dismissed her grandfather as an old man with delusions of a heroic past. They could be true. She slid down into the bed, trying to set aside her growing excitement at being reunited with Ravi. They brought the best out in each other when they had a project. She still had photos of the village school they worked on during that first trip.

Her dreams filled with smiling, dark-eyed children writing on blackboards with chalk made of pearl dust. They wrote a word half in Arabic and half in English, then died.

Chapter Nineteen

Luluwa padded to the kitchen in her house slippers. Friday was the maid's day off, and she was grateful for the privacy. No mother to jar her out of bed, demanding she get dressed to go to family lunch. No, Hessa had bigger fish to fry. Luluwa, on the rare occasions when the women gathered, had heard her aunts and their friends whispering that her mother was trying to catch the eye of an older man looking for a second, younger wife who might bear him one or two more children. The whispers fell silent whenever she drew near.

"Oh." She stopped short at the sight of her grandfather clutching a glass of water at the kitchen table. "*Salaam alaikum, Yeddi.* Feeling okay?"

He sighed. A shiver racked his frame. Jassim perched on the edge of his chair; his once massive frame appeared shrunken in the overhead kitchen light.

"Yes, my child." He rubbed a hand over his face.

"Let's go somewhere more comfortable." Luluwa picked up two cups and a teapot, and made for the living room. Jassim remained seated behind her. "I'm fine here."

Luluwa returned the items to the table, unsure whether fatigue or a craving for comfort kept her grandfather in the kitchen. A slew of letters and leaflets in English spread across the table. "I'll tidy this up," she said. "No need for all this junk. They stick it on the car windscreens, you know. Menus, whatever."

Jassim put out his hand, stilling her for a second time. "Those are for me."

Luluwa sat down. Her fingers felt the bumps of the raised seals on the top envelope. "You read them?" Most people of her grandfather's generation spoke halting English at best. Few made the effort to read it—especially in their own country.

"Check," Jassim said, with a twinkle in his eye. "From what I can see, they're hosting an exhibition about pearl diving." He rested his hand on his leg, eyes focused on her and really seeing her, not looking past her as he did so often now, as though listening to someone somewhere else.

"In the Cultural Village? That's wonderful!" She scanned the letter that explained the nature of the exhibition, a celebration of maritime friendship between Qatar and India.

A cough prevented him from answering, racking the old man's shoulders and causing Luluwa to shudder at the sound of the phlegm.

"I thought you were better," she said, rising. "I'll go get someone." She set the papers down.

His leathery hand on her wrist stopped her. He gasped for a moment before subsiding into normal breathing. "I'm old. What ails me is nothing that anyone can do anything about." He knocked on the table top.

Luluwa picked the papers up and read them again. "*Yeddi,* this says the exhibition will be in India."

Jassim nodded; his chin dipped to his chest and rested there.

"India," Luluwa repeated. *Al-Hind.* The name hung in the air between them. She knew her cousin's name was an Arabic word for a herd of camels. Many names had significance in Arabic. Like her own, the word used for a pearl. But the fact that Hind was also the name of a country, the country of her grandfather's youth, was not lost on Luluwa. "That's far."

"Three hours by plane." The gleam in his eye grew brighter, lighting his face; the wrinkles dissolved into the creases of his smiles. "In my day, it used to take weeks, a month if the waves were unkind."

"You're not thinking of going."

"When you get to this age, *en sha'allah,*" Jassim said, "time plays backwards and forwards in your mind. The things you leave undone, they haunt you."

"My past won't be the same," Luluwa murmured. *Unlikely to be troubled by a secret marriage or a love child.*

"They want to reconstruct the trade route, tell those old stories." Jassim's lips lifted in a smile, as if he could see his audience.

Luluwa kept reading. The papers were signed by the Indian minister of culture. "They found a *baghlah,*" she murmured, flipping past the letter of invitation. "Submerged for decades, they found her while looking for the flight from Malaysia."

"*Al Muhanna.*" Jassim gripped the table.

"Doesn't say." Luluwa sank back against the kitchen chair, a thousand unvoiced questions racing through her mind.

A voice in the doorway barely broke the spell. "*Yuba*," Uncle Mohammed rumbled to his father. "We want to see you for lunch."

Jassim ignored his son, draining his glass of water.

"Lulu, you come too." Her uncle nodded in her direction.

"I have to study, *Aami*," Luluwa demurred. Lunch with the family was such a raucous affair.

"I'm telling the girl stories, important ones," Jassim said. "I'll be in later."

Uncle Mohammed took a seat at the kitchen table and pushed up the sleeves of his shirt.

"What about lunch?" Luluwa asked.

"Well, if these stories are so important, then I guess I should hear them too," Mohammed said with a wink. "No one gets him to talk like you do." He folded his large hands over the back of the chair next to him and eyed his father.

Jassim cleared his throat. "This is not a joke, you know."

Luluwa tucked the papers under her elbow in case her uncle looked any more closely at the table.

"I know," he said. "Tell me too." Mohammed's voice softened conspiratorially. "Not like I want to be at lunch either," he said in a stage whisper. "Saad and Khalid are arguing over who gets to play what on the Xbox, since it's the weekend."

"1972," Jassim began, his voice gravelly with emotion. "Thirty men set sail for India, hoping for a rich pearl harvest. Only one would survive."

"Lunch time, and the three of you are in the kitchen!" Aunt Maryam stood in the doorway, hands fisted on her hips.

Mohammed jumped up like a guilty schoolboy. "I came to get them."

"You come to eat this minute," Maryam retorted, pointing a bony finger at her husband. "There will be order in this house; I don't care what year it is."

Jassim pushed up from the table with a sigh. "Yes, yes. I'm never as important as I am on a Friday." The wink and flash of teeth reminded Luluwa that her grandfather had been a debonair young man before growing into the stately figure she saw every day.

"I thought that ship was lost forever," he said in a whisper. "Like an Arab *Titanic*."

"You too, Lulu, come on."

"They found even the *Titanic, Yeddi*," she whispered back. Luluwa fell into step behind her uncle and aunt. Jassim rubbed his hands together. "Technology, you young people are always saying, can do anything."

"I can't believe India is interested in an old boat." Luluwa snuck a peek at the papers under her arm. "Seems we need a good news story," she said, eyebrows twitching, "with one of the biggest sending countries for migrant workers here. And—" She cut herself off, unsure how to phrase the next part.

"Tell me about university." Jassim smoothed his fingers into the crevice made by her elbow. "You're happy there. You don't miss your old school? Your friends?"

Luluwa's thoughts swam as she tried to construct a happy narrative about university, one without the backstabbing Mustafa, and all the while her mind churned with the possibility of her ailing grandfather traveling to India. They walked through the courtyard toward the dining room adjacent to the *majlis*, the only space large enough to hold them all.

"Tell me the truth," he said, pinching her cheek as if she were still a child. "I'm an old man. There isn't much I haven't seen."

"University has been …" Luluwa wrinkled her nose at him, searching for a cover story.

"Is it a boy?"

"*Yeddi!*"

His laugh ended in a wheeze. She gripped his elbow until it passed.

"I told you; there's a lot I've seen. All this business …" He waved his hand at the arched features of the building ahead of them. "We didn't need all of this when I was your age. We lived on the land or the sea. And we made our way. Life on a ship was simple. You kept each other alive for another day, for the chance to find a pearl that everyone could live off for the rest of the year."

Where her other arm braced him, she felt the vertebrae through the fabric of his shirt. "Did you ever fight on those boats?"

Jassim chuckled. "There were rivalries, sure. Not on our boat. Usually our competition was between captains."

"I bet it's hard to cheat at pearl diving," Luluwa muttered.

"I told you my story," he said. "Of love, secrets kept too long and then lost. Tell me yours. Is it a boy from a minor family?" He gave her a playful nudge with his elbow. "Someone your aunts would turn their noses up at for being from a smaller tribe? We weathered one such scandal. We'll be fine."

She stopped short of entering the dining room. "There's a strange man following me," Luluwa blurted out. Unbidden, the image of the dark eyes staring straight into her, unblinking, rose before her. She shook her head. There was no reason why she should be thinking of that man now.

"What do you mean?" Jassim trained his eyes on her, all trace of amusement gone. "In the car? Did he follow you home?"

She felt tension building in his spine, drawing him straighter. Luluwa bit her tongue, and the metallic sting of blood made her stop talking. She regretted the moment of honesty. No one else in the family would've been able to coax it out of her, but she had a very soft spot for her grandfather.

"You tell me his plate number, and we'll send it to the police. These boys, they don't have any manners."

"Here's where everyone is!" Sangita walked up to them, her long hair wound into a bun at the nape of her neck. The angular planes of her face still came as a shock to Luluwa, who was used to the rounded features of their family.

"Are you coming for lunch?"

"I already ate," Luluwa said. Her grandfather pinched her arm. They couldn't speak of anything bad around a woman trying to get pregnant; it could attract the evil eye. Luluwa shivered. She'd erased Khalid and Saad's chalk markings in the living room, but she'd need to keep Sangita out of there. She would give the boys a talking-to—playing Ouija in a house desperate for a baby!

"How are you feeling?" Jassim asked, surprising both women.

"*Hamdullah.*" Sangita's hands fluttered at her side.

Such a simple word. Sangita knew many more, could have held an entire conversation in Arabic, but knowing the right phrase at the right time was what counted, and each time she got it right, it made her a little more of an insider.

"Bu Mohammed," Maryam called.

"I'll let you young people enjoy the day," Jassim said, and he shuffled into the *majlis*, his slippers dragging on the concrete paving stones.

Sangita smiled at the elderly man as he made his way across the courtyard, then turned to Luluwa. "Let's order our own thing," she said. "I don't feel up to them."

"Abdulla will be upset if we don't show."

Sangita waved her hands in the air. "He's working."

Luluwa frowned. "He should be here with you."

Sangita pinched her cheek as Jassim had done a few minutes ago. "But I have you to keep me company."

Luluwa swatted her hand away. "I mean it. He said he'd learned from … about being a workaholic …" A shadow crossed Sangita's face, and for the second time that day Luluwa could've bitten her tongue in half. *From the last time.* The words she'd almost said hovered between them in the silence. The car accident that killed Fatima, Luluwa's sister, pregnant with Abdulla's baby. *While he was at work.*

"I feel like Bukhari." Sangita led Luluwa by the arm into the adjacent house and reached for her bag on the entryway table to rummage for her phone. "Do you fancy some *dahl makhni?*"

Luluwa groaned, taking the conversational bait. "How many times do I have to I tell you, that's not the Indian food we eat," she said. "Aren't you paying attention at these family meals?"

"Ma'am." Sally appeared in the doorway. "What you want me make?"

"We're ordering," Sangita said, slumping against the sofa. "Let's order the *naan.* At least they can get the bread right."

Sally stepped back into the hallway, disappearing without a sound into the shadows beyond the circle of light from the overhead lamps. Luluwa shivered and rubbed her arms as the phone rang on loudspeaker. Sangita rattled off a list of dishes, adding a few extra items in case Khalid and Saad decided they were hungry after the meal at the main house.

Luluwa unbound her hair.

"Be right back," Sangita said. "Ovulation test."

Luluwa ran her fingers through her hair, frowning. It seemed her well-educated cousin-in-law still couldn't quite believe she was a stranger in a strange land waiting to get pregnant.

A movement at the periphery of her vision startled her. "Not funny, Khalid," Luluwa snapped. No response. Luluwa pushed up from the settee and stomped over to the window, hands on hips, ready to give the boys a piece of her mind. But instead of the chubby outlines of her cousin, she saw the firm muscles of the man she'd spotted twice already in the driveway.

Her heart beat faster, the sound thudding in her ears; her skin prickled as if she were standing near a fireplace with heat rising into her face. She gasped and took a step back from the redness emanating from his eyes. His skin glowed, as if it were dull copper, lit from the inside.

"Whew," Sangita said, re-entering the room. "Tomorrow could be the day."

Luluwa whirled, her heart in her throat. "Out; let's get out of here now."

"There's food coming," Sangita said. "I won't make you eat lentils if you don't want to."

"Forget the food," Luluwa retorted. She turned, ready to point out the stranger, to share with someone else her growing fear that they were being stalked. But again, he was gone. "A man was here." Luluwa swallowed. The sound of her heartbeat receded, undistinguishable from the other involuntary sounds of her body. "Right there."

Sangita opened the door to scan the courtyard. "There's no one there now." She came to stand next to Luluwa. "Probably one of the drivers. I can't get used to how many people actually live in this little walled community of ours." Sangita enfolded her in a sideways hug. "You need more sleep." She gave Luluwa's braid a tug. "And maybe some food. When's the last time you ate?"

Luluwa allowed herself to be led out of the room like a child. To resist would have bigger consequences—a talk with Abdulla, maybe one of the uncles, more visits to the Western-trained therapist, who would give Luluwa adult coloring books and encourage her to find something she liked doing for fun, for the sheer pleasure of it. Sangita prattled on about the differences between north and south Indian food. Luluwa glanced back over her shoulder and could have sworn she saw two red pinpricks glowing in the window, even in broad daylight.

Chapter Twenty

Steam rose from the bowl of seasoned rice in the middle of the table. Luluwa reached for it.

"You're in here?" Abdulla rapped against the door frame. "Everyone else is having dinner."

Luluwa dropped her fork, which clattered against the glass table top. She reached for it, but the utensil skidded off the edge. Abdulla caught it before it hit the ground, clinking it against her water glass as he returned it to her plate. Luluwa started.

"There's so much food *Ummi* is packing up portions to give to the neighbors," he said.

"Lulu got caught up in a problem set," Sangita said. "And we didn't want to go in late."

Abdulla's gaze narrowed on her like a falcon's.

"Sorry," Sangita mouthed from across the table.

Luluwa stepped on her cousin-in-law's foot under the table.

"School going okay?" Abdulla raised an eyebrow at her as she scooped up the lentils with half a piece of *naan*.

"University is fine," she muttered. A movement caught out of the corner of her eye sent a chill down her arms. Luluwa slipped from her seat and drew the curtain across the door to the back garden.

"Don't they have clubs or something, a few fun things to do as well? Like high school?"

He doesn't know anything, she reminded herself. *I need more information about that man or I'll be on lockdown until they figure it out.* "I maybe one of the youngest, but I'm not a kid." She sat down again, reaching for butter chicken to distract herself, and then passed it on to Abdulla in the hope that it would do the same for him. In the process, the edge of her long-sleeved satin blouse dipped into the dish of *dahl*.

"There's a guy," Sangita supplied.

Luluwa kicked her in the shin this time.

"Ouch." She waved a hand in front of her mouth to indicate the curry was hot.

Abdulla looked from one to the other. "Skipping your last year of high school was not a good idea."

"Not that kind of guy problem." Sangita rolled her eyes. "One of the other kids in class is cheating on exams."

"I'll deal with it," Luluwa leapt in. She'd shared the details of the incident with Sangita while her indignation at Mustafa's smug attitude was fresh. Luluwa forked a heap of rice into her mouth, chewing slowly to avoid having to add any further detail. She wiped at the dark brown sauce on her sleeve with a napkin.

"Let the teacher find out on his own," Abdulla said. "You don't want it to be your word against this guy—what's his name?"

"Mustafa," Luluwa muttered.

"That's intellectual fraud," Sangita protested. "She has every right to be upset. It's against the honor policy."

"We have twenty cupcake shops in town," Abdulla said drily. "Do you think originality is one of our national strengths?"

Luluwa kept eating. She couldn't shake off the feeling of those eyes burning into hers or the sound of her blood rushing in her ears. The Mustafa episode was the furthest thing from her mind. Her hand trembled as she spooned more rice, spilling a few grains onto her plate.

"Why not regale us with news of the battles you're fighting, oh mighty warrior?" The tightness of Sangita's mouth belied the joke.

Luluwa's cousin-in-law was becoming increasingly frustrated at being made to wait in the compound for everyone to come home, day after day. Luluwa heard their voices over the television in the living room late at night when they thought she'd gone to bed. Sangita would burst into tears because, unlike herself, all her American friends had lives, and none of them could visit.

Abdulla cleared his throat. His leg moved under the table to press against Sangita's.

Luluwa's twinge of relief that the spotlight was no longer on her turned to remorse when Sangita's lower lip trembled.

"Well," Abdulla said, pouring himself some water. "The noise around the World Cup plans is heating up."

Sangita pushed a piece of chicken around her plate like a mulish child.

"Everyone is concerned about the migrant workers. How many will die building the stadiums?" He showed Sangita the headline on his phone. She barely raised her eyes. "I thought you would be pleased at the scrutiny," he said, putting the phone down. "People are talking about this now for the first time in years."

Sangita snorted. "It will take decades before any real change can help these people."

"I saw guys dangling from ropes," Luluwa said, grateful for the change of subject. "On at least the fortieth floor or higher in West Bay. They were tied onto the roof."

"That's the least of their problems," Sangita retorted. "Those guys may not like the work, but at least they have jobs. The poor bastards who have no IDs and no way home are much worse off."

"Sangita," Abdulla said sharply.

"*Yeddo* says they need some good news about the Asians," Luluwa piped up. "So they're doing an exhibition about pearl diving and the trade routes with India."

"Oh," Abdulla said.

"It's going to be in India. The embassy is organizing it. Hind's involved, I think."

"Sounds like a good idea," he said, helping himself to a spoonful of rice.

"*Yeddo* wants to go."

"Hmph."

"They're going to dredge up his boat," Luluwa said. "I think he wants to revisit his old haunts, see the graves of his wife and child."

Abdulla sipped at his water. A grimace crossed his face like a shadow.

"What? Like we don't all know about his other family?" Luluwa said, sitting up straight. "The one before he had us?"

"Knowing is not the same as discussing it at the dinner table," Abdulla said.

"Well, who else I can talk about it with if not you two?"

The air hummed with unspoken words, more than made up for in glances across the table. For a diversion Luluwa spooned more *dahl* onto her plate.

"I'm not sure if you're trying to bring us closer together or further apart with these topics of yours." Abdulla placed his hands flat on the table and rubbed away invisible smudges on the glass surface.

"I didn't know there were taboos," Luluwa said. "We are the House of Taboo."

Abdulla made a strangling noise as he swallowed a mouthful of curry.

"If *Yeddo* goes to India, I'm going too."

Abdulla choked on his food. "India!"

"He's daydreaming," Sangita said. "When it comes time, he'll stay home."

"No, he has so many memories tied up with that boat," Luluwa said. "He says losing the boat triggered all the other things that went wrong so he couldn't live the rest of his life the way he wanted. It was why he left his pregnant wife for too long—he had to come back with enough pearls to pay the cost of the voyage. And that's when she got sick. His whole life was payment for what his father wanted, not him. I didn't know these kinds of things happened to men," she ended in a murmur.

"I'll check with *Yeddo* to see how his health is," Abdulla said.

"Don't stop him telling me his stories," Luluwa said anxiously. Her throat constricted at the thought of losing her main ally.

"He's an old man," Abdulla said. "He needs to get his rest, not fill an impressionable young girl's head with regrets from the past."

"Open your eyes," Sangita put in. "Can't you see she's a young woman?"

Abdulla held up a finger. "Teenager."

"Meaning what? I won't be adult enough to talk about this stuff until I'm twenty? Uff, this is like living with my dad."

"About that," Abdulla said. "Your father called."

"No." Luluwa lowered her voice. She tore into another piece of *naan*. "No."

Sangita rapped her knuckles on the table. "Not okay," she said. "They can bully one of us, but both? No."

"Okay, I'll go." Abdulla raised his hands. "I'm outnumbered. I'll move out, and you two can invite me over for dinner. I surrender to the feminists."

Like water on a fire, his joke soon doused their irritation. Luluwa looked from one to the other, and they all burst into laughter. "I get to have the bigger bathroom," she said. "*Yeddo's* house needs new plumbing."

"I'll go," Sangita said, playfully swatting the air with a serving spoon. "No one likes me here anyway."

Their chuckles died.

"I like you." Abdulla leaned over to squeeze her hand.

"And you're all I've got," Luluwa added. "So there we are."

Sangita took a sip of water. "Back to Lulu. She's not getting enough sleep. She's so nervous about this guy at school, this cheater, she thinks there are strange men in the compound."

The silence was absolute.

Luluwa didn't bother breathing for a full minute.

Abdulla's gaze turned to her. "There's no one here besides us and the drivers."

"I'm not seeing anyone," she said.

"I can tell you're lying," he snapped.

"You wouldn't understand," Luluwa began.

Abdulla's palm hit the top of the table, sending all the cutlery rattling. "That's not the point, and you know it," he said. "There are consequences. Things are different, because ..."

"Because I'm a girl!" Luluwa spat. Tears filled her eyes. "I can't drive because I'm a girl. I can't study abroad because I'm a girl. God alone knows why He made me this way if he didn't want to make my life miserable."

"Luluwa," Sangita reached across the table, elbowing aside the white ceramic dishes. "It's not that bad. Look at all the freedom you have."

Luluwa's hollow laugh reverberated through the kitchen. "My cheating father and my vengeful mother don't care what happens to me. There we are again, the useless girl—who cares what she does, as long as she keeps her *abaya* closed."

Sangita's mouth gaped. "You're studying well beyond your years, and you come and go as you please," she said. "What's more, you live most of the time with us, not your parents or your grandfather."

"Don't joke with me," Luluwa said. "This isn't freedom. Look what they've done to you, faster than it takes most people to get pregnant. You're as bad as any of them."

"Enough," Abdulla thundered, provoked to anger by the shocked expression on Sangita's face. "To your room."

"What I do, I do for us," Sangita said. "You wouldn't understand. You have only yourself to think of."

"Easy for you to judge me." Luluwa jumped up from her seat. "You were making eyes at an engaged man." She blinked, and a tear coursed down her cheek. The room spun slightly; she couldn't think what had come over her to say such awful things.

"Out," Abdulla repeated, leaning across her line of vision. "Now. We'll discuss this man later."

Sally came in and started picking up the plates as quietly as possible.

Luluwa spun around and left the kitchen. She stormed through the living room, out the front door, and thundered up the steps into Jassim's house. Her grandfather's door was shut tight, though the blue flicker of the television from the kitchen said the maid was still awake. Luluwa headed straight to her room. Unable to stop herself, in the grip of emotions she hadn't known she had, she flung the door closed behind her. The wood gave a satisfying smack and shuddered into the frame. She threw herself on the bed as she'd done a hundred times before, waiting for Noor to launch into a story about the latest gossip. But this time she was alone. The memory of time shared with her cousin and best friend brought on the tears in earnest. Ever since Abdulla's wedding, Noor had grown more and more distant, even though they lived only a few meters apart in the compound, the roofs of their houses almost touching.

As Luluwa sobbed, her eyes alighted on a photo of her sister. She'd never felt alone when Fatima was alive; she always had someone to listen to her and give her counsel, someone patient, kind, loving, maternal, everything their mother was not. Her shoulders shook with fatigue from crying. "Come back, Fatoom," she said, her voice breaking. "Come back."

"She can't," a man's deep voice answered. "She can't."

Luluwa raised her face and met the eyes of the man she'd seen in the courtyard. He was sitting on the bed beside her. She sat up in a rush, scrambling away from him, and fell off the side of the bed in her haste. *This is a dream, a dream, a dream,* she thought, clutching the edge of the bedspread. *Wake up!*

A head of curly black hair appeared over the edge of the bed after her. The eyes—the irises not red, but amber—peered over at her.

"How did you get in here?" she whispered.

"The same way as you." He smiled, revealing blindingly white teeth. "Though I walked through the wall and not the door."

She followed his gaze to the closed door. "If anyone finds out you're here—"

"Do you mean the man in the kitchen who was shouting at you?" The stranger's eyes turned dark, smoldering.

She could smell something burning, like chicken left too long in the oven. "Abdulla will be furious." She sat up, hoping this was the moment that the dream and the strange man would dissipate. Luluwa willed herself to wake up in a pile of sweaty sheets, as if from a nightmare.

"Have no fear. Leave him to me," the man said.

"You're out of your mind." She stood and pulled him up with her from the edge of the bed, but the instant she touched his skin, she gasped. The heat emanating from his arm scorched the inside of her palm as though she'd grabbed a pan from the oven without a cloth. She fell back against the wall, cradling her right hand.

"I'm sorry." He hovered over her.

The sensation of heat drew closer, and she averted her face. The warmth caused a flush to spread across her cheeks.

"I'm doing it again," he muttered. "I'm sorry. You cannot yet come as close to me as that. I have to learn to control it."

"How?" she asked, noticing for the first time that his feet weren't touching the ground. "How are you doing that?"

He gave her a small smile. "I am not like you."

"If Abdulla calls the police, they'll find out an Indian was in my room," she said. "All hell will break loose. They'll deport you."

He laughed. The sound wasn't exactly musical, but she couldn't say she'd ever heard anything quite like it.

"They'll jail you," she corrected herself. "And then, when you've suffered some more, they'll send you home."

"If they try to remove me before I want to go …" The skin around his eyes crinkled. He looked older than she'd guessed at first glance. "As you've said, all hell will break loose."

Another rush of heat trickled up her arms, causing all the fine hairs to stand to attention. The back of her neck grew sweaty. She felt drowsy, which didn't make any sense, because wasn't she already dreaming?

He hovered over her again, lips close to her neck.

"Are you a vampire?" she whispered in alarm.

He laughed, a warm sound again, yet eerie, drawing her further outside herself until it felt as if she were hearing her own voice from somewhere on the ceiling.

"Nothing as modern or foreign as that," he said.

Or did I hear him only think it? Luluwa had a hard time figuring out where his thoughts ended and hers began.

"I am what your people call a *jinni*," he said. "The boys playing with the board made the job of finding this place much easier."

At that word, one that would send most girls rushing to the corner of the room with their hands covering their ears, shivers ran across Luluwa's body. Everyone whispered stories of the *jinn,* beings made of fire or water living in a parallel world, forbidden to make contact with humans yet causing them mischief and mayhem—or worse. Luluwa always dismissed such tales as stories for children when other girls told them. A *jinni* summoned by

Ouija—no one would believe a word of it.

"What's your name?" she asked, entranced by the rings of fire that appeared in the pupils of his eyes.

"You cannot speak it in any of your human tongues," he said—or more like sighed, a whisper caressing her mind. "But it sounds something like Khaldoon."

She shuddered, her body overwhelmed by the heat radiating from him. Sweat beaded across her forehead. "You came to curse us?"

His laugh echoed in her head, reverberating in her ears, making it difficult to remember where she was, what year it was, her very name.

"No," Khaldoon said, his breath flowing over her skin like silk. "I came to save your grandfather."

The heat coiled around her like a snake, weighing down her eyelids. Luluwa's knees gave way. She fell toward him, her palms stinging on contact with the burning skin of his chest. Yet she couldn't draw away, even though the heat increased, the burning feeling like a thousand stinging nettles. "Oh, please, go away if you are making him sick."

"It is not I who make him ill," Khaldoon said, "but I know who is."

Luluwa pushed at him, gasping in pain as she made contact with his fiery flesh.

"Take care." He pulled away her hands, each of his fingertips branding her wrists with a perfect oval singe mark. "Don't come too close to me."

"Or you'll burn me?" She felt herself melting like a wax doll, losing sensation in her arms and legs. The corners of the room rounded. The periodic table poster on the wall—a joke present from —blurred, the letters and numbers running together. Khaldoon's face loomed before her, his eyes framed by long lashes.

"No," he said, brooding over her, his eyes glowing like flames. "If we do not take care, it is possible I will possess you. And that will only add to our problems."

The furnace-like heat from his skin enveloped her, searing her eyes, toasting her own skin like a bonfire on the farm in winter. Luluwa surrendered to the insistence of sleep. In her dreams she tumbled through a series of ever-deepening waves as the sun shone brightly on the surface of the sea hundreds of yards above her.

Chapter Twenty-One

Luluwa went through the next day expecting Khaldoon to show up at any moment, like a spectator, or hovering as her reflection in the bathroom mirror. However, unlike the horror movies of her childhood, he showed no sign of pursuing her to her demise. He showed no sign of anything at all.

Noor came within inches of the bumper of the vehicle in front of them.

Luluwa clutched the inside of the car door.

"You okay?"

"Fine," she squeaked, not wanting to take Noor's attention away from the road. Today in the blistering desert daylight, she couldn't summon the words to describe what had happened yesterday. What she *thought* had happened yesterday. *There was a* jinni *in my room.* Even in her own mind the words sounded ludicrous.

"I'll get a booth next time," Noor said. "At the next big *abaya* exhibition."

Luluwa made encouraging noises, letting Noor prattle on through the morning traffic toward the education complex housing six American branch universities. On any other day she would've asked subtle questions about how to register, how much a booth was, what sort of margin Noor was planning on. Today all she could think about were the embers she'd seen floating in the *jinni's* eyes. And when she thought of them, a shudder like a breath of cold air shivered down her back.

"Anyway, what's going on in the world of the math genius?"

"Exam results today," Luluwa said.

"Oh, that's great."

Noor slowed before one of the many speed bumps on campus. "*Yuba* says one more ticket and that's it, back to riding with the driver. But the speed limit here is 40—we might as well walk."

Luluwa made an appropriate sound of dismay, at both the inconvenience of the speed bump and the idea of walking fully cloaked in black in forty-degree heat. She wasn't sure which was more distressing.

"Uff, this place is so packed." Noor pulled up behind a row of cars discharging their passengers next to the steps leading up to the plaza where two universities sat like chess pieces on a blanket of green grass. "All right, out you get, my dear. See you later, genius. Find that equation to make us rich."

"Thanks," Luluwa murmured. "Enjoy sewing class." This was their standing joke.

Noor sped off without a backward glance. Luluwa clutched the strap of her tote bag and made her way past the water features, her flats soundless on the sandstone, and through the twenty-foot entryway into the university. She found a seat near the front of the auditorium, once again beating Dr. Roberts into place by only a few seconds. He ambled in, deposited some papers in a neat stack on the desk, and started scrawling across the whiteboard in his precise handwriting—left-handed, Luluwa noticed. *If he'd grown up in the Arab world, someone would've cured him of that dirty habit.*

Dr. Roberts leaned against the board, his arms crossed. "Only one student in class got this problem right."

Luluwa flushed. Was he going to tell everyone who it was? She hoped not. She couldn't bear their scrutiny today. She would've sat in the back if she'd known. Or skipped class altogether.

"One student who did the homework, I take it, in preparation for this test. Congratulations, Abdulaziz!"

A pulse of shock took her breath away.

The class applauded; a few of the boys hooted in recognition. Abdulaziz came forward to collect his exam paper, along with a high five from Dr. Roberts.

The rest of the exams were handed back, supposedly in no particular order, but the students quickly worked out that they were in order of marks from highest to lowest. Luluwa received hers in the middle. The number eighty floated on the page in red. *Eighty.* She couldn't remember a time when she hadn't got ninety at least, or even ninety five. The day's lecture washed over her like discordant notes at a concert, then the hall emptied as students trudged out. The boys called to each other to wait, and Abdulaziz paused for one more congratulatory clap on the back from Dr. Roberts. Luluwa remained in her seat after the others had gone.

"Can I help you, Luluwa?" Dr. Roberts asked.

"Professor, I …" Her throat closed. She thought of Noor and her *abaya* dreams, and of her mother waiting for her father to send money every month.

"This is a big step for you," Dr. Roberts said. "It's difficult to go from being number one in high school to join the big fish in a much bigger pond." He erased the problems scrawled across the board. "Do you have a question in particular?"

"I got no points for the problem about the ski jumper?"

Dr. Roberts came to sit next to her in the front row.

She showed him number three, the one that had a large zero next to it. "A ski jumper takes off at an incline parallel to a mountain. The drop is sixty feet. He's ten feet above the mountain's top at the drop, and the lip at the bottom is level with the mountain's horizon. What is the friction?"

They scanned the page together, looking at the neat diagram measuring the height, the drop, the force.

"No, you got that part right," he said. "Friction is point zero five. But the problem asked you to include the details and assumptions."

"Other people got that right?" Luluwa leaned in as he turned the page toward her.

"One," Dr. Roberts smiled ruefully. "And we know this time it wasn't you."

"That's not why I'm upset." She looked at the smaller font, right below the space where she'd put her answer. She'd left the entire details and assumptions part blank, thereby losing most of the points for the section. "You neglect air resistance, factor for gravity, and start from non-movement pre-jump."

Dr. Roberts nodded. "Yes, well done. It's good that you know that now."

Luluwa glared at him. "Professor, I knew it then. I just didn't see that part of the question."

Dr. Roberts looked down at his hands. "Luluwa, much of university life is being able to follow directions. There is nothing to be embarrassed about with a B."

"But professor, Abdulaziz …"

His dark eyes trained on her again, a wrinkle in his nose indicating concentration, but also something else, not mirth, like when he smiled, but possibly … disgust? Disappointment?

"He was cheating. I saw him," she rushed on as the wrinkle curled his upper lip. "He wouldn't be paying attention to nuances like that."

"Luluwa," Dr. Roberts leaned away from her, "cheating is a very serious accusation. You cannot level it at people because you're upset with your own performance."

"*Wallah,*" Luluwa burst out, despite her best intentions. "*Wallah,* I swear to God, I saw—someone else—with the answers written on his arm."

Dr. Roberts gave a long sigh. He stood, gathering his things. "Please think about this long and hard. And if you want to pursue it, come to my office before Thursday. Otherwise we will pretend this never happened." Dr. Roberts turned at the double doors. "I was the one who advised them to take you early," he said, his eyes jumping around the room behind her. "You were done with high school math. They were worried about your adjustment."

The metal doors clanged behind him. Luluwa clutched her exam paper. Her breaths became shallower despite her efforts to deepen them.

"Can I help?" a voice whispered in her ear.

She turned and felt the heat from Khaldoon, rather than saw him. "I thought you didn't exist," she muttered, even though they were the only people in the room.

"The problem is greater than that," Khaldoon said solemnly.

"I know, I know, possession."

"Oh, it is far graver." His voice was inside her head, caressing her mind again. "We have to save your grandfather's life from the one trapped in the pearl."

"The Pearl? You mean the apartments?"

"No. I'm speaking of the one trapped on the boat they're planning to raise."

Her exam fluttered to the ground.

"Allow me, please."

"I can take care of it myself," she retorted, slapping her hand against the desk next to hers. A stab of heat caused her to double over.

"Gently, gently," he said. "Warn me of your movements when I'm close to you."

She took a quivering breath, and then another.

"Very well, I'll leave that to you," the *jinni* conceded.

She nodded, her shoulders relaxing.

"Then I'm the one who needs your help," Khaldoon went on. "We need to go to India. And the sooner we depart the better."

Chapter Twenty-Two

The pilot's voice droned through the business class cabin. Luluwa adjusted the blanket over Jassim's legs. His head lolled to one side, eyelids flickering when his forehead bumped the window shade.

"He's fine," Abdulla said from across the aisle. "You shouldn't even be here. You're better off at your desk, studying."

"I'm going to rest now." Luluwa gave him a small smile. "I told my advisor there was a family emergency." They pressed back into their seats as the plane accelerated into takeoff.

"You said this would be better than a boat." Khaldoon was shaking in the space beneath her seat, compressing himself like a child. His large eyes, now an almost human brown, peered around the cabin. "Are you sure this ship won't fall out of the sky?"

"This is the safest airline in the world," she said. "And yes, you have a higher chance of getting hit by a car than being in an air crash. Come out of there." She laughed. Who would have believed a centuries-old being made of fire could be afraid of flying? She wondered if all *jinnis* were like humans in that way.

Khaldoon shook his head, burrowing further back. "Certainly not."

"Are you okay?" Sangita leaned across Abdulla, her forehead bunching in concern.

"Give me some space," Luluwa murmured. She kept forgetting that although no one could see Khaldoon, they could hear her talking to herself and feel his heat if they got close.

"She has a fever," Sangita said to Abdulla under her breath.

"Now you're pregnant and a maternal expert." Luluwa felt a stab of guilt at Sangita's look of surprise. But Abdulla seemed to agree; he patted Sangita's arm until she sat back out of view.

"Ouch," Luluwa said.

"I'm sorry." Khaldoon moved back into the corner, making himself even smaller so Luluwa could stretch her legs.

Having a *jinni* as a companion was much more complicated than anyone would've thought. Luluwa wondered if anyone had thought to update the folktales they told children, to take into account the modern inconvenience of nosy relatives.

The large television screen facing her flared into life with advertising for the in-flight entertainment, only to be interrupted by the safety instructions. Luluwa giggled. This was a safety briefing unlike any other she'd seen before. Instead of featuring smiling flight attendants, the video showed football players in the airline logo striding out onto a pitch with a row of airline seats. Screaming female fans and the players' smug waves in response gave Luluwa pause. What would older people like her grandfather think of such a video campaign? A sideways glance revealed that he'd fallen asleep, chin dragging toward his chest.

The footballers went through the motions of putting on their seatbelts and oxygen masks. "There's an idea: get a celebrity ambassador for your company," Luluwa said. She tapped her screen to catch Abdulla's attention. "You know, product placement?"

The Fasten Seatbelt sign switched off with a ding. Sangita, along with two other women in the cabin, immediately shed her *abaya* and *shayla*. Luluwa followed suit with her *abaya*, tucking it into her carry-on bag, but she kept her scarf on. A dozen people got up and pushed their way down the aisle to the toilets. A flight attendant in a grey skirt and patterned blouse came forward to draw the curtain between the two cabins.

Luluwa's words were lost on Abdulla; he was helping Sangita to hoist herself out of her seat. She caught the back of the chair in front, righting herself with a laugh as the bottom of her belly bumped the embedded television screen. She stepped to the toilet near the cockpit. Abdulla followed and lingered outside the door. *Never mind.* Luluwa settled back in her seat and slipped on the noise-canceling earphones. The plane climbed to its cruising altitude.

Jassim coughed.

Luluwa passed him a bottle of water, but he waved her away. She pulled out her math notebook, trying to focus on the problem set in front of her. The numbers swam before her eyes. She wiped away a film of sweat above her lip. Across the aisle Abdulla, back in his seat, sat his laptop on his tray table and opened a few .pdfs, then looked over the top of the laptop at the movie Sangita was watching.

"Have you had a chance to look at the dinner menu?" The petite flight attendant crouched in front of Luluwa. "Ouch, that's hot." She rubbed her shin, eyeing the wheel of Luluwa's carry-on with suspicion.

"Yes, it's hot in here." Luluwa leaned around her grandfather, who'd nodded back into sleep, and lowered his screen shade. "I don't want any dinner, thank you."

The flight attendant raised her eyebrows and swiveled round to Abdulla. Sangita murmured to him as they placed their order. "You should eat something," he rumbled at Luluwa. "We won't arrive until early morning."

Luluwa made non-committal noises and shook her head when the flight attendant came back to her. "And the gentleman?"

She ordered for Jassim without looking at the menu. "Arabic mezze."

"Certainly." The flight attendant continued on her culinary mission to the seats behind them.

"Maybe some ice cream?" Luluwa asked.

The flight attendant brightened. "Yes, madam. Would you like it at the same time as everyone is having dinner or would you like to wait?"

"Sure," Luluwa said. Somewhere behind them a baby wailed.

"I know how he feels," Khaldoon muttered.

"Hush," Luluwa said. "Go to sleep."

"I am not a human creature like you," he grumbled. "I don't need sleep."

The plane hit an air pocket, and Khaldoon let out a moan. "You're fine," Luluwa tutted.

She pulled out the sheaf of papers Hind had emailed her and tucked them under her elbow so Abdulla would see the math notebook first. *The Lao Tzu Pearl is mostly rumor,* the article read, *hatched as part of a plot to increase the pearl's value. It has also been called the Pearl of Allah because of the shape of the pearl's head, which resembles a turban.* No Muslim would call it that, Luluwa knew instantly, because of the basic tenet of Islam forbidding idol worship of any kind, especially objects in human form.

Valued at sums ranging from thirty-eight million USD to ninety million USD, the Bombay pearl has been confirmed by gemologists as having formed inside a clam. She underlined this sentence, listing her questions in the margin. What type of pearl had *Yeddo* found? Was it also real or a hoax? When could they ask him about what he'd found all those years ago? On the next page she stared at the grainy photo of a man on a boat surrounded by smiling faces.

Though scanning had compromised the quality of the image, Luluwa would recognize the slope of that nose anywhere, because it was exactly the same as her father's. *Twelve pounds? Fifteen?* She tried to estimate the weight of the sphere this younger version of her grandfather was holding above his head. If it were true—if, as Hind said, they could find the pearl—then there was no telling what would happen. Both countries might try to claim it. The government could commandeer the pearl to put it on display.

Her grandfather groaned in his sleep.

Luluwa shoved the papers back into her bag. Abdulla had been easy enough to convince that coming to India was a good idea. Sangita wanted to see her family before the baby was born, and there would only be a few more months during which she could safely travel. Already her cousin-in-law's cheeks bloomed with excitement at being out from all the watchful eyes that monitored her every move in Doha.

"School going well?" Abdulla asked Luluwa when the flight attendant returned with a linen napkin and tablecloth.

She pulled out Luluwa's tray.

"Fine." She'd been ignoring emails about registering for next semester.

"A selection," the flight attendant said with a smile. She presented a ceramic bowl with three different scoops of ice cream.

"Thank you," Luluwa murmured.

The woman turned to assist Abdulla, taking mini salt and pepper shakers as well as hot sauce from the tray.

"Oh!" She gazed in dismay at Luluwa's tray: a multicolored puddle swirled where the ice cream had been moments before.

"That's okay. It's like a smoothie." Luluwa lifted the warm bowl to her lips.

Khaldoon groaned as the overhead sign dinged on again. This was going to a bumpy ride.

Despite the steward's directives over the intercom that passengers should remain seated until the *Fasten Seatbelt* sign was switched off, a man stood up and clicked an overhead bin open. Luluwa's grandfather stirred and peered out the window like a young boy, his nose millimeters from the glass. A few rows back two women wearing gold necklaces and earrings rocked the still-crying baby. Their bangles clanged together as they passed the child back and forth.

"Bombay," Jassim breathed.

"They call it Mumbai now, *Yeddi,*" Luluwa said with a wink.

A carpet of white cloud screened the ocean from view. She tried to relax her grip on the armrests. Flying never came easy; she did it so infrequently.

Khaldoon's face appeared in the next window, hovering in glee outside the plane. "I could crash this air-ship, you know." His eyes narrowed until a flame danced in the pupils.

"Oh, God, no." Luluwa's heart dropped.

"But that would pollute all this beautiful air." He threw his arms out and gulped big breaths. "Humans stink, you know." He floated away.

"What's that?" Jassim turned back to her, the dreamy gaze gone. His eyes narrowed, focusing on her features.

"I'm fine." Luluwa hoped Khaldoon would be too busy enjoying the ether to pay them any more mind during the rest of the flight. "Really." She patted her grandfather's hand so that his scrutiny returned to the window rather than her face.

* * *

Luluwa dozed on and off, and woke with a jerk when the plane landed on the asphalt like a ton of bricks.

"Where did he learn to land like that?" Abdulla grumbled.

Luluwa gave a short laugh and unclenched her hands on the armrests. The cabin crew pleaded again with passengers to remain seated, but this time they paid no heed at all. They surged forward through the cabin, ignoring the flimsy curtain. Men with oil-slicked hair and shirts in all shades, girls in shiny shoes, and women with powdered cheeks. The eagerness on their faces struck Luluwa. What would their own group find at their destination?

Swatches of green flanked the asphalt runways like ribbons made of grass. When both cabins were nearly empty, except for other elderly passengers, a short, burly man with muscular arms came onto the plane pulling a folded wheelchair backwards. Abdulla helped their grandfather into the chair, then they left the airplane and made their way down the jet bridge. Luluwa walked behind her grandfather, and Sangita brought up the rear.

"Did you know about this?" Abdulla hissed. He suddenly stopped short, and they all piled up behind him.

"What?" Luluwa and Sangita peered around him.

Their cousin Hind stood in the boarding area along with a man whose features were familiar in a way Luluwa couldn't quite pinpoint. *A boyfriend!* A thrill went through Luluwa, more than excitement to get off the plane.

Her cousin's rebellious tendencies clearly hadn't faded in this new setting. Hind and the not-quite-familiar stranger stood at a slight distance from each other, almost as if they didn't want to be seen together. *Probably a staffer from the embassy.* She must have skimmed one too many romcoms during the flight.

"No," Sangita said. "Not me. I didn't know." She twisted her wedding and engagement rings together.

"*Yeddi.*" Hind came forward, kissing their grandfather on the head in the traditional gesture of respect.

"Tell me the truth," Abdulla said, his lips barely moving.

"Nothing. We had no idea," Luluwa and Sangita assured him.

"Ah, my girl." Jassim held onto Hind's wrist while she kissed him repeatedly in a show of affection. "This country is treating you well."

"What is he doing here?" Abdulla asked, eyeing the man.

"*Hamdullah as-salaama,*" Hind continued, crossing to greet Luluwa and Sangita with a series of air kisses close to their left cheeks. Two women in matching saris, airport custodians, walked past, their eyes flashing with interest at the reunion scene. Overhead, the airport intercom droned details of the next departing flight.

Khaldoon seemed entranced by this spectacle. "Is that your cousin?" He crossed his arms, regarding Hind and then Sangita. "Two beautiful women. And Abdulla had his choice of them."

"You're burning up," Hind said, peering at Luluwa's face.

"I'm fine." She brushed away Hind's concern along with the beads of sweat at the edge of her forehead. "Not now," she whispered to Khaldoon. He walked away with a shrug to take in Hind's companion.

"Hi, I'm Ravi," Sangita's brother said. He made to extend his hand, first toward Luluwa and then to Jassim, but dropped it before either could respond.

"Bombay," Jassim murmured again. Luluwa took over from the airport employee wheeling him toward the baggage claim. "So modern. We didn't have all this then."

"I swear to God," Abdulla gritted out.

"No one knew," Hind said, straightening up and turning to Abdulla.

Understanding dawned on Luluwa when she saw Sangita in the stranger's embrace. Their features were so similar they could've been twins. *The infamous brother who'd broken up her cousin's engagement. Or was it the sister who'd torn Hind and Abdulla apart?*

"You have to listen to him," Hind said. "Just hear what he has to say."

Abdulla opened his mouth to object.

"Not here." Sangita put out her hands, one on Abdulla's arm and the other on her brother's. "Let's go."

Abdulla's jaw clenched, but the wheels of Jassim's wheelchair were turning again. They made their way through the airport as another PA announcement urged travelers to Dhaka to proceed directly to their gate to avoid missing their flight.

"The driver will get the bags," Hind said, sweeping them through the baggage claim area.

At the sight of Hind and her group, a skinny man with black-rimmed glasses sprang forward from the wall where he'd been leaning. He scurried forward and took the baggage tags Abdulla handed over.

Jassim emerged from the air-conditioned terminal building and took a deep gulp of air, moist and heavy like a cloud. The street lights still glowed in the last few hours of night. "Bombay," he said once again.

Luluwa saw tears glittering in his eyes. He got up stiffly when an airport agent took away the wheelchair but stood tall, almost even with Abdulla, and for a moment Luluwa could visualize the young man of the bedtime stories he'd filled their ears with when they were children. He stepped forward, Abdulla's hand hovering at his elbow, and they shuffled at his pace across the receiving area where other passengers were being greeted with garlands, and businessmen in rumpled suits spotted their names on pieces of paper held up by waiting drivers.

"Land," Khaldoon echoed at Luluwa's side, looking to right and left. "But something has changed. Something is different."

They followed Hind and Ravi across the parking lot, marching past a waiting sea of humanity, mostly male, leaning against the curved metal barriers and taking in their every step as if they were on stage.

"Taxi, madam? Taxi?"

In English and Arabic, the offer went out repeatedly like the chatter of pigeons. Their guides remained impervious. Dozens of drivers in an array of sedans waited in the parking lot. Other passengers were being embraced by relatives or haggling over prices.

"These cars are new," Jassim said, a note of surprise in his voice.

"Things do change," Ravi said. "There's some big money in this city."

Hind held open the rear passenger door of a black Mercedes for Jassim, indicating to Luluwa and the others to get into an identical car waiting in front. Jassim ducked into the vehicle's interior; Hind climbed in behind him.

"He's like a bad penny," Abdulla muttered, diving into the front seat of the other Mercedes. "Did you know they were back on speaking terms?"

Sangita burst into tears. "No one," she said with a gulp, "tells me anything."

Luluwa scrambled for a tissue.

Khaldoon bounced in the back seat between them. "This is going to be an interesting week."

Thankfully most of them couldn't hear him stating the obvious.

Chapter Twenty-Three

Abdulla's voice rumbled on the other side of the connecting door of their suite. Luluwa collapsed onto the bed face first, the tension draining from her body. She'd been holding her breath ever since they'd arrived in the baggage claim. First with worry about *Yeddo,* and now because of the tension between Sangita and her cousin Hind.

What are you going to say to the traitor? Her phone pinged with Noor's alarmed text.

Our cousin-in-law, she typed back. For Noor this would be all about Hind. Knowledge that her sister's former best friend, along with her ex-fiancé, were paying a social call could have her on the next flight out. From what Luluwa had seen that morning, Hind was doing just fine. She'd blended in with all the other women at the airport.

Luluwa had never noticed how similar Arab and Indian features were: same glossy black hair and caramel skin. Without the blue jumpsuits that marked the Asian laborers in Doha, the men here resembled the heroes of the Bollywood posters plastered on concrete walls across the city. She deleted her reply. She had to focus—not exchange a flurry of dramatic texts.

A knock at the room's main door brought her to her feet. Her grandfather stood in the doorway, wheezing slightly.

"*Yeddi.*" She grasped his arm.

"I can do short distances." He waved her away and took a seat beside the desk. His veined hands pressed on the glass-topped surface.

"Couldn't sleep?" She hovered, not sure what to do next. Should she get Abdulla? She bit her lip, regretting the pressure they'd allowed the old man to put himself under to make the journey.

"I haven't been honest with you," Jassim muttered, clasping and unclasping his hands.

Luluwa leaned in to make out his words, which were coming out in the dialect of the Gulf.

"*Yeddi.*" Luluwa drew closer, pulling the ottoman over to the desk. She sat a head lower than her grandfather. "Cancer?" The word escaped before she could put it away as she'd done the many other times she'd thought it.

"No, no," Khaldoon whispered in her ear. "This is about the living, not about dying."

"I didn't come," Jassim said resolutely, "to help with this exhibition. I came to see her."

Luluwa sank her chin onto steepled hands. "Your first wife."

"Aziza." Jassim's eyes watered. "Will you go with me?"

"Yes," Khaldoon said. "Say yes."

Jassim sniffed the air. "Can you smell something burning?"

Luluwa smoothed her hair and found the tips on the right side of her scalp hot to the touch. "Probably someone smoking somewhere on this floor," she murmured. Khaldoon hastily slipped off the ottoman. "Yes, of course we'll go, but where?"

"To her grave," Jassim said with a shudder. He stood up. "The car is waiting."

"Waiting? Now?" Luluwa rose with him. Her grandfather's limbs creaked like those of a marionette at the end of its strings.

"You said you'd come," Jassim said.

Luluwa threw on her scarf and pulled on some ballet slippers. "I am, I am," she said. "But Abdulla—"

"They'll stop me if you tell them," Jassim said. "We have to go now, while they're sleeping, or not at all."

"Okay, okay." She slung her messenger bag over her head and across her shoulder, stuffing the hotel key into the side pocket. "What do you know about this?" she whispered under her breath to Khaldoon, who floated alongside her, trailing behind her grandfather as he made his way determinedly down the hall toward the elevator.

"It is all a big surprise," Khaldoon said with a mysterious smile.

Luluwa stopped short. "This is not a joke," she said crossly.

Up ahead Jassim stumbled, grabbing the wall to steady himself.

Luluwa shot the *jinni* a withering look, though he continued to grin from ear to ear. She hurried forward to take Jassim's elbow.

* * *

Luluwa settled against the leather upholstery of the hotel car and studied the architecture of downtown Mumbai. Wide tree-lined avenues and the brick façades of buildings reminded her of summers spent in central London.

"How do you know where she's buried?" Luluwa asked.

Her grandfather gulped from the bottle of water thoughtfully placed in the armrest between them. "There are seventy-one Muslim burial grounds in Mumbai." He capped his water and gazed out his window.

"We're going to visit them all?" A few hours while Abdulla and Sangita were sleeping was one thing; days of searching graveyards would not be so easily explained.

Jassim chuckled. "It's not so bad as all that," he said, patting her hand. "I have been reading about this. Most people are buried in the graveyard closest to their neighborhood."

"Reading about this," Luluwa repeated. Her grandfather was turning out to be a well of mysteries. Yet she was supposed to be the teenager.

"On the Internet thing. You know, that Google, it's very useful."

"Right." Luluwa leaned back against the seat. Yes, he was like a teenager. The city raced by them in the emerging light of day; the sky went from inky black to a ribbon of blue as the stars surrendered to the dawn.

"Here, sir," the driver said. They idled on the side of the road across from acres of grass stretching in every direction. A yellow police line separated them from the cement markers of the graves. Two men held a sign that read *Hunger Strike* in English with Hindi characters below. "Please do not get out."

The men stiffened and hoisted the sign at the sight of the white hotel Audi.

"Problem," the driver said. The locks of the car doors clicked. "They fighting, the Sunnis and others, about who bury here."

Luluwa drew closer to Jassim and peered out the window at the men, who stared back without blinking.

"I am here," Jassim said. He took a shuddering breath. "I didn't come this far to turn away."

He unlocked his door and climbed out, even as Luluwa grasped at his shirt sleeve.

"You stay, madam," the driver said. He gave Luluwa a nervous glance and cast about the front seat for something to give him authority. He stepped out of the car and hurried after Jassim, who'd made his way across the road.

Luluwa lowered the window, trying to hear what they said. To her relief, the men on the other side of the road lowered their banner as Jassim approached, his loose black slacks and white shirt underlining his frailness and age.

"She is not here," Khaldoon said, bouncing on the seat next to her.

Luluwa loosened her scarf, the tense feeling inside her starting to subside. One of the men offered Jassim his plastic stool. He took it, sinking down, and accepted an offer of tea from a smudged glass.

"1971," Jassim said as the men huddled together in front of him, squatting on their haunches, arms folded.

"Abad?" This sparked some excitement between the men. They switched from their broken Arabic to Hindi.

Aziza Abad, Luluwa repeated in her mind. The woman who might've been their grandmother. *What a different life that would've been.*

The men gesticulated up the hill as the driver scribbled their instructions onto a piece of paper. He asked questions as quickly as they provided answers, while Jassim stood and headed to the car.

He and the driver got back into the car, Luluwa scooting over to the other side. "I'm glad you're safe—"

"Her family is here," Jassim said. He pressed the bottle to his lips. "The house is not far."

"*Yeddi,*" Luluwa said, as the car lurched into reverse, "we're going back to the hotel."

He shook his head.

Khaldoon clapped his hands. "Oh, oh; you have no idea who is waiting for you."

"She's not alive," Luluwa snapped.

"No." Jassim pressed her hand. "She's gone. They wouldn't let me walk down to the grave, because they're protesting the use of the land. Some sect hasn't been allowed to bury here for some years."

The car's tires screeched as it made a U-turn in front of a pair of scooters, which squeaked their high-pitched horns. Others cars dotted the roadway as the somnolent residents of the city woke up to a new day.

"We're going to the hotel," Luluwa repeated, even as the car took a sharp turn, throwing her against the window.

"There," Jassim breathed.

They arrived in front of a three-story house, the stone façade sporting curved balconies that overlooked the street.

"They've done well," Jassim said. "So well."

Luluwa, irked by the look of awe on her grandfather's face, took in the towering mansion, the one traditional structure against a backdrop of high-rises. "They would be lucky to see how you did," she said with vicarious pride.

"They didn't want to give their daughter to a fisherman," he mumbled, as he craned out the window like a child at a theme park.

"You were a merchant." She wanted to yank him inside, remind him of the zoo he built several neighborhoods away, bringing in a baby elephant, one of the first in the country.

"Now," Khaldoon said, lurking outside the window. "Now."

She turned to tell him to stop it, to ask him to help end this madness. Luluwa could no longer tell whether it was the *jinni* or the rising heat of the day that caused her to sweat. Her phone buzzed as the wrought iron gates of the property swung open before them. Abdulla flooded her phone with messages, increasingly dire in their warnings. *Yeddo is very weak. Do you know which hospital to take him to if something happens?*

A tall man in black mesh shorts and a white t-shirt emerged from the house. He leaned forward, hands flat against the brick wall surrounding the house, stretching his calf muscles.

"Bhai," the driver called to the runner. "Is this the Abad house?"

The runner glanced up and down the road and trotted over to them. He leaned into the window. "Private property," he said with a British inflection.

"No harm," Jassim said. "Visiting an old friend."

The man looked in the back seat, his face softening at the sight of Jassim. His gaze skirted over Luluwa.

"You knew my grandfather?"

"Grandfather," Jassim echoed. "No." His brow wrinkled in confusion. "Maybe. Are you a new family living here?"

"We've lived here my whole life," the man said.

"But this house, all this, is new." Jassim's eyes clouded; his head bobbed back and forth like a bird as he looked past the younger man into the street.

The stranger took a step back, giving the car another once-over. "Where did you say you were from?"

"My grandfather knew someone who lived near here once," Luluwa blurted into the silence. "A woman named Aziza."

Jassim started at the sound of her name.

"Aziza?" The man took another step back from the car. Dust from the street clung to his white sneakers. "That's not possible."

"Thank you," Luluwa said. She swallowed past a lump of disappointment. "Let's go a little further down," she said to the driver, winding up the window. "Around the corner, maybe. We'll find it." The wall around the big house took up the rest of the block, so they would have to search the neighborhood. She took Jassim's wrist in her hand, circling it with her fingers. His pulse beat slowly under her thumb.

A thud against the window brought the car up short. "Wait, wait." The runner bent over at the side of their vehicle. "No one who knew her is still alive."

Luluwa lowered the window. Sweat gleamed on his brow.

"You know where Aziza lived?"

He stretched up, hands on hips, catching his breath from the effort of chasing them. "She was my grandmother."

Grandmother. The word hung in the air. Jassim gripped Luluwa's hand, squeezing the bones together.

The man pulled the sweatband off his forehead. His Adam's apple constricted as he cleared his throat and coughed. "Sorry. No one has spoken her name in years. How did you say you knew her?"

"An old friend," Luluwa said. "Why don't you get in?"

"I'll meet you at the house."

"Well, I—"

"Yes, yes, yes!" Khaldoon breathed in her ear, so close that the heat he radiated made her sweat.

Jassim nodded in agreement.

"Okay."

The vehicle swung around, this time trailing the man in shorts as he jogged back to the wrought iron gate. He pressed a button and waited for the car to enter before following it inside. Shards of glass poked up from the cement top of the perimeter wall, a deterrent to thieves. Though if you could scale the ten or so feet to get up there, you would likely persist over the glass. Luluwa helped her grandfather from the car, and Jassim leaned on her arm as they followed the man up a set of rose marble steps. The second-floor balconies at the front of the house curved out on either side of the entrance like arched eyebrows.

"Show them to the sitting room, please."

A woman in a blue and white sari bowed in their direction. Cool air enveloped them as they entered a rectangular room filled with light, the interior benefit of all those windows and balconies. Silk rugs absorbed their steps as they made their way to a wooden sofa, raised off the floor on carved legs.

"Well," Luluwa said, perching on the edge of a beige cushion. Tin-roofed tumbledown shanty—clay hut—the road to Aziza had taken them in a completely different direction from their speculations. With the maid gone, Luluwa took in every detail to recount later to Sangita. The framed silver dagger on the wall belonged in a museum.

"Where is everybody today? My tea is late." A silver-haired man grumbled through the hallway. "Hello? Hello? Anyone? Oh. Yes?"

Luluwa coughed to hide a laugh at the man's startled expression. She saw echoes of the runner's long nose and high forehead, grooved by the years with wrinkles. She pulled at the edges of her tunic. Explaining their mission to someone even older than her grandfather would be much harder than simple name-dropping. Jassim began, in halting English, but the man remained in the doorway.

"You're from where? What do you want?"

"Papa, I met them on the road." The runner re-emerged in dark slacks, a white polo shirt and brown leather sandals. He ran his hands through a shock of black hair, causing it to stand on end.

"Oh. And invited them to tea. Is that why I can't get any?"

He laughed. "No, come in, come in. They say they know about Aziza."

The older man stiffened. "Who?"

"Ah, Papa, come on." The younger man took the tray from the maid, who appeared at his elbow.

"That name has not been spoken for many, many years in this house," Khaldoon warned. His hot breath in Luluwa's ear sent a trickle of perspiration down the inside of her tunic.

"Stop doing that," Luluwa said. "You're making me sweat."

"We do not speak that name in this house."

"And why not?" Jassim asked. His voice rose to match the volume of the other man's. Papa was likely old enough to be their host's Great-grandpapa.

The maid scurried forward to pull out a table from beside the sofa. She took the tray back from the younger man, placed it in front of the visitors, and poured milky tea into gold-rimmed cups with saucers.

"You have been a guest in this house, and now you may leave." The old man's voice shook.

"Papa, no one is leaving." The great-grandson came back into the center, pulling a teak chair behind him.

"This is my house!"

"It isn't," he said calmly, tilting the sugar bowl toward Luluwa. "I bought the land from the government, and these people are my guests. They're going to tell me about Aziza. You can stay to hear it or take your tea in your room."

She held her breath at the sharp words, delivered in an even tone, almost matter-of-fact.

"Such insolence," Papa snorted. He turned and shuffled away.

"He's not well. The years are weighing on him."

"As they do on us all," Jassim murmured.

"Now, tell me everything you know." His hands clasped and unclasped between his knees.

"You are?"

"Oh, right." Another run through those unruly locks, kicking them up again in every direction. "Laith." His fingers touched the middle of his chest. "My name's Laith Abad, and I grew up here. That's my great-grandfather. My parents died ten years ago. My father had an interest in sailing. I sold the company and made us into software moguls. Modern India and all that." He flashed Luluwa a smile. "I'm an only child. I live here alone. Except for Papa, of course." He laughed. "Sorry, we don't get many visitors."

"You're an orphan?" Luluwa blurted out. She gazed at him in wonder, and with a little pity. In Arab families it was rare for a child to be down to one relative.

Laith cleared his throat. "I'm a bit old to be Oliver Twist, but yes, yes, I am."

Jassim took a sip of tea. "I knew your grandmother," he said in a low voice. "But not your father or mother."

Laith gulped. "I can show you some photos if you like." He wiped his hands on his slacks and made to stand.

"What was your father's name?"

Luluwa sipped her own tea to hide her embarrassment at *Yeddo's* bluntness. At this rate, Laith would throw them out himself.

"Jassim," Laith said, settling back into his chair.

Her grandfather took a shuddering breath.

Tea burned down her throat, making her cough. "That's not a common Indian name," Luluwa said.

"No. Papa doesn't like to talk about this, but my father wasn't full Indian," Laith said in a stage whisper. He leaned forward, his hands gripping the arms of his chair. "He was a love child who never knew his father."

"Oh, God help me," Jassim croaked. He slumped against the back of the sofa.

"Is he okay?"

"This is a lot to take in," Luluwa said. She pulled out a plastic handheld fan from her purse; the motor jumped to life with a whirr. "Your grandmother— did she die in childbirth?"

"Aziza? No." He looked from Luluwa to Jassim and back. The older man gasped for air. "She raised my father, telling him stories about a merchant who had sailed away and would one day come back. Papa said she could keep the baby as long as she never spoke of little Jassim's father. I think it was one of the neighborhood Casanovas," Laith said with a conspiratorial wink. "Before we had all this", he waved a hand around the house, "the family was very modest. My grandmother was a great beauty, and Papa wanted what he saw as the best for her, the daughter of a merchant who was a rising star. A good marriage for her could have established us among the upper echelons of society."

He rolled his eyes, taking a biscuit from the plate on the tray. "But she fell in love with someone. They shut her up in the house for nine months and said she'd eloped abroad with a foreigner. Then she returned one day with a baby, and they said her derelict husband had left her. She lived the rest of her life as a shamed woman, bringing up my father. Never breathed a word to anyone. It was all a lie."

"Yes," Jassim said unevenly. "Her husband would have never left her."

"You knew him?"

"I am him," Jassim said softly. "Argh." He clutched his chest again. A trail of saliva slid from the corner of his mouth, running toward his chin.

"*Yeddi*." Luluwa dropped the fan.

"Oh, oh, oh." Jassim's body shook with a forceful tremor.

"Call an ambulance," Luluwa said. She pushed aside the table, sending dishes clattering. Tea sloshed over the sleeve of her tunic.

"Did he say he knew my grandmother?"

"This is the first Jassim," Luluwa said. "When he came back for her and the baby, they told him she was dead."

Laith's face went as pale as Jassim's.

"And he'll be dead too, if you don't get an ambulance."

Laith ran to the hallway and shouted for a doctor.

Luluwa pulled up her grandfather's feet, putting him into a reclining position like in the videos Abdulla had shown her. "What good is—?"

A balding man rushed into the room, his startled gaze taking in the situation in a triangle of confusion. "Papa, sir?"

"No," Laith said, taking the man by the elbow. "This is our guest. I—"

Jassim convulsed again.

"Call the nurse," the balding man said, pulling a stethoscope from his pocket.

"Your doctor lives with you? You're practically Saudi," Luluwa said.

Laith managed a strangled laugh. "Papa is all I have left in the world. I won't take any chances. Dr. Vivek lives in the house behind ours. His whole family is there, and the kids—"

"Quiet," thundered the doctor. "Everyone out of here." He barked instructions to the nurse, who hovered at his elbow.

"I have to call my cousin," Luluwa said. "He's going to kill me." She dug in her purse for her phone.

"No one is going to die today," Laith said, pacing the hallway. "Not when I just found you."

Chapter Twenty-Four

Footsteps up and down the hall maintained a steadier beat than the beeps from the machine hooked up to Jassim. Luluwa clutched a wad of tissues in one hand and prayer beads in the other as she recited cycles of *duaas* in prayer for her grandfather. She slumped in her chair, diagonal to the bed, watching for any sign of wakefulness. All the desires and decisions leading up to this moment raced through her mind. While she sat at his bedside the years of listening to her grandfather reminiscing about being out on the sea flooded back. His hopes for this trip. His wish to see his ship again, and some trace of his lost love, this one last time. And these white walls in a crowded hospital were their reward. The number of tubes hooked up to his shrunken form and his overall pallor made it difficult to distinguish Jassim himself among the sheets.

The door creaked open, jolting her from the dark bend of her ruminations. "The doctor is sure he's stable," Laith said, closing it behind him.

She nodded. No words squeezed past the lump in her throat. "I did this to him," she whispered. "This whole trip was irresponsible."

"You brought us together." Laith leaned over and gripped the arm of the chair. "How would I have ever known—ouch!" he exclaimed as he knelt down beside her. "This floor is really hot. They'll have to look at the wiring in here."

"Leave him alone," Luluwa muttered to Khaldoon, whose eyes were boring into Laith.

"Sorry, I know this is hard." Laith stood, his cheeks flushing. "I only meant to help."

The door swung open, the metal handle whacking the wall. Abdulla burst in and strode to Jassim's side. He swiftly surveyed the room, his gaze locking on Luluwa. "Is he—?"

"Alive," Luluwa managed to get out. After that one word, the floodgates opened. Tears coursed down her face and into the corner of her mouth in what Noor would surely call an ugly cry.

"Allah help us." Abdulla gripped the opposite edge of the bed, unsure, as she'd been, whether or not he could come closer.

"This was what he wanted," Luluwa whispered. No one spoke for several minutes. Laith stood in the corner, his eyes trained on the machines.

Sangita came in, closing the door with a purposeful click. At the sight of the woman Luluwa now regarded as her cousin-in-law, she flung herself into her arms.

"It's all okay. You're okay now."

"I told you this was a bad idea."

Sangita shushed both Abdulla and Luluwa.

Jassim coughed from the bed. The four of them jumped to his side.

"*Yeddi.*" Abdulla took their grandfather's veined hand, but the old man drifted back into sleep. "I have to call everyone," he said in the ensuing silence, broken only by the beep of the monitor.

"He's getting the best cardiac care in the city, I assure you," Laith said.

"Good to know," Sangita said, keeping hold of Luluwa's hand. "Are you our doctor?"

The door opened again, and this time Hind stood on the threshold, her eyes darting from the bed to the faces gathered around the supine figure. "This trip was a bad idea."

"Hind?" Jassim's voice didn't stir the covers.

She rushed forward at a rustle from the bed. They made way for her, Abdulla stepping aside to let her take his place by Jassim's shoulder.

"*Yeddi,* I'm so sorry. We never should have let you come."

Another coughing fit seized him. Laith hoisted the much smaller man higher up on the pillows. They waited for Jassim to catch his breath.

"India agrees with you," he croaked.

Luluwa let her own breath out in a rush. Yeddo was still with them. Weak, yes, but clearly alert.

"I suppose it does," Hind said with a laugh. She clutched his hand tighter.

Voices rose outside the door. "I'll just stick my head in and come back out again."

"I'm very sorry, sir, but you can't go in there. Two people maximum."

The door opened again to reveal Ravi towering over a nurse in a blue and white uniform.

"Look, Sister, these people are new here, and they won't understand how everything works."

"As I mentioned, the visitation policy—"

"Ravi!" squeaked Sangita in delight.

Luluwa smiled, despite the tension radiating from Abdulla as the siblings embraced.

"Wow, you sure you shouldn't get a bed for yourself?" Ravi chuckled, putting his hand on Sangita's belly.

"Still many months away." Sangita smacked at his hand.

"Too many people in here," the nurse said, her voice rising. "The patient needs his rest."

"The doctor says it's fine," Abdulla said, waving his hand toward Laith. "Tell her."

"Well, I'm not—"

"He's not a doctor," the nurse objected. "His company just—"

"I'll make sure they don't tire the patient out." Laith ushered the protesting nurse back out the door.

"What is this? Like a price gouge or something?" Ravi said, when Laith re-entered the room.

"Um, no," Laith said, clasping and unclasping his hands.

"What was the bit about the company then?" Abdulla glared at Laith from the corner.

"Well, yes, it's true that my company provides software to this hospital, and so, right, in a sense—"

"So that's why you brought us here. Not because we were close by, or because it's the best hospital, but because you make money here." Luluwa spun around to face Laith.

"No, as I told you, this is the best hospital for cardiac cases, partly because all their software is up to date for medical files and the machines. Wow, there are a lot of people in this room. Are you all descendants?" Laith fingered the collar of his shirt.

"There'll be one less once you leave," Hind snapped. "Out."

"No," Luluwa said.

"Not a word from you, Miss Memory Lane," Abdulla said. "Let them deal with this," Sangita said.

"He stays," Jassim wheezed from the bed.

"*Yeddi,* you're tired," Abdulla cajoled. He smoothed hair over the crown of Jassim's head. "Let us take care of these things."

"He has as much right as any of you." They leaned in to hear him, his voice thin and high like a sleepy child's. "He is family."

All four of them turned to look at Laith, who shifted from one foot to the other.

"People make random connections like this when they get older," Abdulla said in a subdued voice. "Their minds start to go. Did you hear him make any offers or extract any promises?" he asked Luluwa. "Was he asked to sign anything?"

"Nothing like that," she said. "We went to find Aziza's house, and we found," she gestured to the man standing next to her, "Laith."

"Who's Aziza?" Ravi, Hind and Sangita asked at the same time.

"Jinx," Luluwa said. "One, two, three, four, five. I'm the only one who gets to talk." No one laughed.

"Aziza was *Yeddo's* first wife," Abdulla said, understanding dawning on his face.

"And we're all cousins," Laith said with a small smile. "Right, Granddad?"

Jassim's snore put a hold on the slew of waiting questions.

Chapter Twenty-Five

They trooped down to the cafeteria to give Jassim a chance to rest, instructing the nurse to call them immediately if his condition changed. She assented with a complicated series of head bobs, happy to see the back of them.

Luluwa strained to catch snippets of the terse discussion Abdulla had with Sangita and Hind at the table in the corner.

"That must be a difficult conversation," Khaldoon whispered in her ear.

"Shush." Luluwa sipped at a bottle of water.

Ravi scrolled through his email on his phone, not looking up at the tense triangle of gazes. Laith alternated between fielding phone calls and greeting staff members who recognized him.

"There's no proof these claims are true. This could all be an elaborate plot," Abdulla said in an agitated tone.

"For what?" Sangita asked, winding a napkin between her fingers. "From what Lulu said, he's not after money. He's a successful businessman."

"If what he says is true," Abdulla countered, "then he's the oldest grandchild."

"Ah." Hind sat back.

"Ah?"

"Ah, someone is taking your pride of place."

Abdulla squinted at her. "Is that what you think of me? That's not what this is about."

"Why don't they answer it?" Khaldoon said.

"Answer what?" Luluwa muttered.

Screeching musical tones interrupted the calm of the cafeteria. A few nurses shot them disapproving looks, gesturing to a sign on the wall with a barred mobile phone inside a red circle.

"One second. It's the ambassador." Hind left the table, drifting toward where Luluwa sat with Ravi and Laith. Luluwa intercepted a glance between her cousin and her cousin-in-law's brother.

"They seem attracted to each other," Khaldoon said.

"Uff, give me a moment of silence, please."

"Sorry, I only wanted your thoughts on dinner arrangements," Laith stuttered. "Didn't mean to disturb."

"Not you," Luluwa said. Khaldoon gave an irritating chuckle. "I meant— never mind."

"We have more problems," Hind said, putting the phone into her bag.

"More long-lost relatives?" Abdulla said, propping his chin on his hands in mock interest.

"They have the boat." She adjusted her headscarf, smoothing the hair over the crown of her head.

"Again, I'm lost," Abdulla said, spreading his arms. "What else haven't you told me?"

"We didn't come to India only for fun," said Luluwa.

"The dhow exhibit, right?"

"Centered on *Yeddo's* dhow," Hind said.

"*Yeddo's* dhow? That's impossible. The boat is over forty years old, and at the bottom of the Indian Ocean." Abdulla pressed his hands flat against the table. "A wooden boat sitting in water for forty years would be a heap of rotten splinters."

"A wooden boat at the bottom of the ocean preserved in silt, however, is recoverable," Ravi offered.

"And that's why you're here, because you're a boat expert?" Abdulla shot back.

"Your cousin does not cope well with change," Khaldoon noted.

"Enough," Luluwa said to the *jinni*. She made her way to the table of people who, until now, she'd thought of as her elders. Their floundering conversation was evidence they needed her help. "I should have told you, *Yeddo* wanted to come here to settle his past. He wanted to remember his days with Aziza, and also be there for the restoration of his boat."

"Speaking of which, the cage has been brought up," Hind said. "I'm going to the dock to see it transported to the workshop."

"When is the last time anything like this ever happened?" Abdulla asked Sangita. She rubbed the crook of his arm.

"2003," Ravi called over his shoulder. "They found a boat in Yorkshire.

From the Dark Ages. That one, though, they reconstructed piece by piece. Wasn't as well preserved."

"How do you think the boat came to be buried in silt?" Khaldoon muttered. "Doesn't happen by accident."

"No one cares about that boat as much as *Yeddo*," Abdulla said. "Who would spend all that money to dredge up an old relic?"

Trust her cousin to get straight to the heart of the matter. "There are rumors," Luluwa said, "of a pearl of great price."

"She's right." Hind produced a sheaf of papers from her handbag, giving Luluwa a grateful look. "You know how we grew up learning about the different categories? Remember, *dana* being the best, the most perfect? Well, turns out there were others as well."

Abdulla and Sangita leaned on their elbows flipping through the pages together.

Luluwa went back to her seat at what she now viewed as the kids' table, where Laith had his phone pressed to his hunched shoulder. Did people still make phone calls for things like food? Seeing Ravi and Laith on their phones as well pricked Luluwa's conscience to check on the world she'd left behind, the one of tests and university classes. She pulled hers out of her purse. None of the missed calls or social media notifications that most other millennials would find. Just one email, marked *Urgent*, from Dr. Roberts.

Dear Luluwa: Please come to my office as soon as possible to discuss your issues with the course.

She grunted in mild satisfaction. What had Abdulaziz done this time? Scored one-hundred percent, the unthinkable in physics class? She made several attempts at typing a reply, each of them starting with variations on: *Dr. Roberts, I'm away in India on a lifesaving mission. Your course*—Raised voices at the other table captured her attention.

Abdulla pressed his fingers against his eyes and groaned. "So that's what he wants. The long-lost cousin. He's magically found us because of this pearl."

"I didn't find them; they found me," Laith said in a low voice.

"No one wants that pearl to be found," Khaldoon hissed.

"Valued in the millions," Luluwa confirmed. "And *Yeddo* has first claim on it."

"If that pearl comes up," Khaldoon said menacingly, "none of you will be long for this world. The spirit I have trapped in it will probably take half the city to hell with her. Benita has been down there for a long time."

"There are two of you?" Luluwa's eyes opened wide.

"Of course, my dear," Khaldoon said. For the first time in many days he materialized before her. "You don't think I came just to look at your pretty face, do you? I came to save your grandfather's life. And help him protect the pearl of great price."

Chapter Twenty-Six

Like limping camels, their cars moved through the congested streets of Mumbai, Ravi and Hind leading the way in his car, followed by the others in the hotel Audi.

Luluwa fidgeted in the back seat as Abdulla flipped through the file of papers she'd prepared about the boat.

"A natural pearl of immense value …" he read aloud.

So much for her cousin skimming ahead.

"You thought no one else needed to know?"

Sangita gave her hand a squeeze.

"I was given assurances we wouldn't find the boat," Luluwa said archly.

"I didn't want you to find it," Khaldoon sighed. "I am not the only spirit tied to the boat."

"You still haven't explained that," Luluwa hissed. "There are more of you?"

"You knew I came to protect your grandfather."

"No, I didn't! You should have told me."

"Stop whispering back there," Abdulla said. He twisted abruptly in his seat, causing the driver to flinch.

"Are you feeling okay?" Sangita asked. "This whole business with your grandfather must have been stressful."

"I'm fine," Luluwa ground out. "Besides," she added, looking at Abdulla's reflection in the car window, "we don't know if it's even on there."

"How many people know about this pearl? How many of the funders want to get their hands on it? If it is found, who can lay a claim to it? And if it's awarded to us, will they let us take it out of the country?" Abdulla enumerated the concerns listed in the margin of Luluwa's document.

How can we contain the spirit trapped inside it? Luluwa added silently.

"So many people are at the dock today," Sangita remarked. The cars crawled to a halt in the gridlock before the Mumbai port.

"Sir, you are walking from here," the driver said. He squeezed their vehicle into a space between a dumpster and a vegetable vendor.

"Where to, exactly?" Abdulla asked. Men with their pant legs rolled up streamed past them like a school of fish.

"You show your permit card there." The driver's bony finger pointed to a throng of people pushing and shoving at a gate a few hundred meters away.

"Wait here," Abdulla said. "We don't have permits."

Up ahead, Ravi climbed out of his vehicle and headed toward them with purposeful strides. He came around to the passenger side, knocking on Abdulla's window. "I've got cards. And there's a separate entrance arranged by the embassy."

"Thanks, Bai," Abdulla said.

A bubble of hope surfaced, and Luluwa smiled at the first words exchanged between the brothers-in-law.

"You mean 'Bhai'," Ravi said. "'Bai' means maid." He walked a few paces from the car.

"Honest mistake," Abdulla muttered gruffly.

"We need his help," Luluwa whispered. The cacophony of sound filled her ears: the tooting of boats coming in or going out of port, the idle chatter of the passers-by, the hawkers calling people to come and look at their wares. They all got out and waited for Hind to catch up.

"I'm coming too," Sangita said. She grabbed the handle above the door to hoist herself out of the car.

"No, don't, the heat alone ..." Abdulla began.

"My Hindi is terrible, but it's better than yours."

"We could manage with Arabic," Luluwa reminded her as the two men looked everywhere but at the loose folds of Sangita's tunic.

Women sat on the sidewalks peddling yellowish green mangoes spread out on plastic bags. Potential customers clustered around them, haggling over the price.

"Come on, then," Hind said. "We'll be crushed by this tide of humanity if we don't get going." They elbowed their way through the crowd, keeping Sangita protected in the middle like a child rather than a mother-to-be.

"This way." Hind waved a red handkerchief at them. Light bounced off her ornately embellished sunglasses.

The humidity enveloped them as they inched closer to the water. Dampness and a powerful smell of worms and fish and soggy wood permeated their skin. Sangita doubled over, dry-heaving into the sleeve of her *kurta*. "I'm fine, I'm fine." She waved off Abdulla and Ravi's anxious protests.

"Fish," Khaldoon moaned. His normally fiery red cheeks and lips shimmered a mixture of pale orange and yellow. "Water."

"I have to worry about you, too? You're supposed to be supernatural," Luluwa said.

"Created of fire." He brushed against her as the guard checked their permits.

"Careful," she reminded him. The contact didn't scorch her as it had the other times he got too close. This was just a temporary flash of heat, like nicking your forehead with a curling iron.

"No smoking on the dredge site," the guard said, sniffing the air.

"Understood," Luluwa smiled politely. *You try traveling with a fire jinni.*

"Your Excellency! You're here!" A short man, so thin his head bobbed like a bubble, came forward to clasp Hind's hands. "I would have come to meet you, but they didn't call me." His fingers reached for hers.

"I'm actually the first secretary," she corrected him, sidestepping the proffered hand of welcome.

Abdulla stepped forward instead to accept the man's eager handshake.

"Your Excellency." He grasped both of Abdulla's hands in his, making a sandwich of their palms.

"The ambassador sent us ahead to check the site," Abdulla said. Their hands continued to pump up and down. "You are?"

"Professor Sridhar Ganapathy," Ravi said. "He's seconded to us from the university to advise and oversee the lifting."

"Please, please, call me Sri." He released Abdulla and raised his hands to dismiss the suggestion of formality. "It is my true honor. This is a most exciting discovery. Think what we'll learn from analyzing the wood and the microorganisms and—"

"Where is the boat?" Ravi broke in.

"Yes, yes, of course. Right this way." Sri gave a laugh, light and bubbly, like a boy who'd just won a game. "Step carefully. Everything is a little wet. Proximity to water." The professor lifted his pant legs to reveal neon yellow sneakers with orange laces. "If you'd let me know you were coming, I would have arranged footwear for you."

"Those are bright," Sangita said with a smile. "You won't get lost on site."

"He's the best marine archeologist we have," Ravi said under his breath as Sri bobbed his way ahead of them, winding in and out of laborers in brown uniforms and fishermen tying up their nets. "Oxford-trained, worked on the recovery of over three hundred vessels."

"Didn't know the English were so keen on ships," Sangita said. She stepped around a bucket of bait, holding her sleeve to her nose.

"This way, this way. Stay together now." Sri called them aboard a metal ramp like a group of errant schoolchildren. Behind him towered two metal shipping containers, one stacked on top of the other, their backs toward the dock. In the left side of the lower one someone had sawn a door, already rusting orange at the edges. Sri waved a laminated pass at another set of guards, this time with machine guns looped over their shoulders. "With me, they're with me. Diplomats."

The guards looked them over. "IDs?" the darker one asked, his voice like gravel.

"We didn't bring any," Luluwa said. "Everything is in the car."

"I am the site supervisor." Sri stood straighter. "I say they're okay, they are okay."

The guards looked at each other. The darker one spoke into a walkie-talkie on his shoulder. From the smart fit of their shirts, these were not like the men who checked IDs at the university buildings in Qatar. "No ID, no entry," he said, stepping across the entrance.

"Listen, we didn't come all the way out here …" Abdulla began.

"I'm the manager," Ravi said. He pulled out his wallet and flicked through a dozen plastic cards before brandishing an orange one. "See?"

The guard took it and passed it over to his partner, who gazed at the front, flipped it over, smoothed his mustache, and spoke briefly into the unit on his shoulder. "Sorry, sir, you know policy. Restricted area."

"Sure," Ravi said smoothly, sliding the ID back into his wallet. "We appreciate your diligence."

They moved forward, past the metal barricade.

"Here she is," Sri said reverently. "Here." They rounded the corner to the screech of buzz saws and pounding of hammers, which instantly drowned out his hushed tones.

Blinking in the fluorescent lighting, they entered a utilitarian space formed out of two identical empty shipping containers welded together, end to end, to form one long tube, one door on land, the other opening onto the sea. Beyond the edge, beside a lowered platform, ocean water lapping the sides, was a rectangular metal cage the size of a small airplane.

"Come, come." Sri picked his way through an army of men wearing plastic visors and orange coveralls, who were scrubbing the interior of the container in preparation for the precious cargo that would soon be moved in.

Their group stood at the edge of the platform gazing down into the metal cage.

"Orders to wait for you," Sri said, looking at Ravi, "before opening."

"Proceed," Ravi said.

Sri called a few words down to a man in a hard hat. "Put these on," he said to the party at large, passing a set of headphones round to each of them. They slipped them on; Luluwa had to hold hers on the crown of her head so they didn't slip off her ears. Hind's and Sangita's looked equally out of place. The floor beneath them jolted as a motor kicked into operation. They surged forward to grab the rail of the descending platform.

"*Bismillah*," Luluwa said.

"*Bismillah il-rahman il-rahim*," Khaldoon echoed.

She made out the faint outline of where his hair had been. "You're fading."

He gave a twist of a smile with half of his lip.

The platform came to a shuddering stop before the cage, which now towered two stories above them. Inside, like a child's plaything, a wooden boat lay on its side.

"Open!" Sri called to some other men in orange jumpsuits and hard hats, who waited attentively at a control panel at the side of the dock. "Stand back."

The metal jaws over the boat creaked apart.

"I'll be the first one on board," Sri called out cheerfully.

"You'll destroy it the second you set foot on it," Abdulla protested.

They faced the hull of the boat. It curved sideways like a pregnant woman's belly.

"Not to worry," Sri tutted. His eyebrows drew together. "We'll use this robot camera. Only the best." He gestured for them to follow him to a video screen on the far wall. They crowded behind the Plexiglas barricade which served as a splashguard against the ocean spray and the drips from the boat and her metal container.

"She is here," Khaldoon said. "Benita is still inside the pearl. Make these people leave this place at once."

"How?" Luluwa retorted. "No one is going to listen to me. Besides, did you see how big the ship is? The pearl could be anywhere on there. This could take days. We need another plan."

"Very well," said Khaldoon. "If you will not act, then I will."

"Wait," Luluwa called, but he was already gone.

"Yes, you wish to say something?" Five pairs of eyes turned toward her, Sri's blinking rapidly as he waited for an answer.

"Is there a restroom?" Luluwa asked lamely.

"Up top only, I'm afraid," Sri said, turning back and continuing toward the screen. "Can you escort her?" he asked one of the orange-clad men.

"I'll wait," she said.

They turned their eyes back to the excited professor hurrying ahead of them. Abdulla squinted at her.

Luluwa gave her cousin a weak smile.

Chapter Twenty-Seven

Sri positioned the group in front of a jumbo control panel dominated by images of the murky water below. They strained their eyes to see what he promised was there—Jassim's long-lost dhow. Humidity rose from the water like a wave and cloaked them in moisture.

Yeddo should be here, thought Luluwa, a sharp pang stabbing her heart.

"No, no, no, no," Khaldoon breathed in her ear.

"The whole thing is there." Luluwa blinked to make sure she hadn't conjured a vision of *Al Muhanna* after years spent listening to her grandfather.

"Uff, this smell! It's even worse now that I'm out," Khaldoon muttered. "Like a million pounds of meat left out to rot."

Until that moment, she hadn't noticed the stench. Luluwa raised her sleeve to mask the odor of the docks. "Where have you been?" she whispered.

"I can't get any closer to the water," he admitted. "Whatever can be done has to be done from up here." The *jinni's* face was downcast as he contemplated the machinery. He strode over to the panel, raising his hands in front of him like a magician about to cast a spell.

"No!" Luluwa wanted a photo of the ship, if it was the last thing her grandfather saw in his hospital room. Then they could lower it once more, smashing it to pieces for all she cared, along with Benita and her threats. She grabbed onto Khaldoon, forgetting for a second that he wasn't human.

"Let the man work," Abdulla snapped.

Luluwa couldn't reply because her insides were on fire. She tried to make her mouth move. All that came out was a squeak.

So this is what it feels like. To have a beating human heart. Khaldoon's voice boomed in her mind. As if through a screen, Luluwa saw her relatives crowd closer to her.

"You two should rest," Abdulla said. "All of this has been too much."

"We're not children," Sangita said. "The boat will be fine. They've looked into this," she said to Luluwa in a lowered voice that, despite her declaration to Abdulla, did sound like it was addressing an infant.

Sri began slowly to lower the claw-like metal jaw in search of the boat. His mouth pursed in concentration, he maneuvered the joystick incrementally to the right, like a child operating an arcade game.

Smashing it to pieces, Khaldoon echoed. *I like the way you think.*

Get out of my body! This is mine! Moving her limbs took unusual effort, as if she were underwater. She grabbed onto her cousin to steady herself. Khaldoon's presence left her as easily as it had entered. "I'm fine," she insisted, though trying to reassure Abdulla with chattering teeth was hardly going to be effective. Luckily for her, a flurry of movement in the water below pulled all of their attention.

"I see it!" Sangita rubbed her belly with one hand, tracing the outline of the boat with the other.

"There she is." Sri wiped his palms on his slacks. "Now to the right ..."

Gears whirred along as the seeking arm shuddered to one side. "Now."

With a force that shook the platform, the cage pulled up through the depths of churning water, obscuring the dhow from view for a few moments until it broke the surface. Luluwa let out her breath in a rush; the dhow dangled a few yards in front of her. Teetering in the sky, the crane arm shuddered like a double-jointed elbow before making a one-hundred-and-eighty degree turn and swinging the dhow toward the dock with a metallic whirr. With the dhow hooked to the crane, it gave the appearance of sailing along on the water's edge. Luluwa's fingers slipped on the phone as she recorded the floating boat for her grandfather. "Never do that again," she said under her breath to Khaldoon.

"You ran into me." He put his hands over his ears. "Can't you hear that infernal din? She is in the seventh heaven, broadcasting her presence to any other *jinn* nearby." He folded into a sitting position at the edge of the platform. "I told you we couldn't get too close."

"Yes," Sri said under his breath, as if he were the only one on the platform, alone with his toys. The screen flickered and went dark, before brightening again with an up-close view of the wooden planks of a ship. "Now we'll get Fish One going. Dropped him down earlier in the week. He's on loan to us."

"From the British Museum?" Sangita asked. "Do they do many excavations like this?"

Luluwa and Abdulla exchanged glances. Anything could get the most bookish among them off on a tangent.

With the dhow now fully out of the water, Sri manipulated the joystick more forcefully, like a teenager playing a video game. A shock of hair fell into his eyes. "What? Heavens, no; they wouldn't have this kind of money. There you go, Fishy. There, there." The camera wobbled as the robot vehicle, the size of a remote control car, jerked its way down the galley of the ship. Sri manipulated the controls to weave the robot in and out of tarnished utensils scattered along the floor. "Debris, excellent," Sri muttered, his eyes fixed on the screen. The rest of them might as well have disappeared.

"This isn't going to be ready for the exhibition," Ravi said, speaking for the first time since they came down from the upper level of the dock. "At this rate they may have to build a replica."

"Restoration," Sri repeated, not taking his eyes off the screen. "We won't restore all of it. Only the part—" He gasped as the roving robot fell through a hole in the deck. The screen filled with a blur of grey, black and brown as the camera on the front of the rover tumbled through the open space. After transmitting a rapid series of blurry shots, it blinked off. "Call the engineers," Sri shouted to a group of workmen lurking behind them watching the screen. "We'll need the arm to get him out and start again."

He ran his fingers through his hair, then started chewing on his fingernails and muttering to himself. "Of course, there's a back-up for situations like these. But on the first day. The first day!" He stretched and squeezed his hands open and shut into fists. "Hours. It will take hours to get the other machine." The breeze rustled his hair, adding to his wide-eyed mad scientist look.

"Uff, is that the fish market?" Sangita buried her nose in her wrist.

"We must be downwind," Abdulla said.

A spray of water splashed up against the platform as the wind picked up.

"Terrible, terrible. Get the tarps," Sri called to the workmen.

"Let's leave them to it," Ravi said. "We can ask for updates." The loss of the robot had sent Sri into a frenzy of energy, but deflated the rest of them. "Come on." No one protested, not even Abdulla, who might have done so just to be contrary.

"We are not needed here," Khaldoon agreed. "I sent that diabolical contraption to the bottom of the bay." His voice was ragged, weary.

"You did that?" Luluwa whispered.

"Anything man-made, I can destroy by heat. Even in water. It is actually a good conductor. I ... fried the circuits?" He coughed. "The device came close to the pearl. Too close. We will have to find a way to sink the whole boat again." He struggled to rise.

"Are you insane?" she said. She stretched out a hand to help, but he waved her off. "Right, no contact. What's wrong with you?" Luluwa had never seen the *jinni* short of breath. She wasn't aware that supernatural beings could get tired.

"Proximity to water, momentary possession, suppressing Benita." He ticked off the exertions of the day. "You would be tired too."

"Lulu, come on," Hind called. They stood in a group further back on the platform, waiting for her.

"Coming." Luluwa scurried forward. "I'm not going to be a part of that," she whispered to Khaldoon. "New plan."

"You're the whole reason we're here," Abdulla reminded her.

"I mean, yes, I want to be here, but I ..." She cast around in frustration for a plausible reason for her outburst. These public chats with Khaldoon had to stop. Luluwa tilted her head further away as the face of a tall man in a black suit peered down at them from the dockside.

"We're all tired," Sangita said.

"And with all these decades-old bacteria and who knows what, I don't think you should be down here anyway," Ravi said.

"I don't need another mother, I have one," Sangita retorted. She waved off her brother and husband's worried glances.

The platform shuddered to a stop. Without waiting for them to exit, the man in the suit shouldered his way on. Abdulla shot him a look as he moved between Hind and Sangita into the center of the space. The women maneuvered around him to step back onto the dock. A second after they exited, the platform lowered again to sea level, the man its only occupant.

"That is most unfortunate," Khaldoon whispered.

"Who is that guy?" Luluwa asked.

Hind snorted. "Someone with bad manners."

"Someone with access." Ravi stared after him.

"I'm hungry," Sangita said.

Ravi's attention snapped back to his sister.

"We'll talk tomorrow," Hind said. "You can all come to my office, and we'll figure out what is going on."

They loaded into their respective cars, each lost in their own thoughts.

Chapter Twenty-Eight

With Jassim's condition now stable, the rest of them split up, each looking forward to a change of clothes and a hot meal. Ravi and Abdulla agreed to meet again in the morning to discuss options for the boat. No one mentioned the pearl. Hind left in Ravi's car, avoiding her former best friend. Luluwa itched to talk to Sangita about the trip and the proximity of her brother and friend, but back at the hotel Abdulla and Sangita retired to their room, and the suite door closed on Luluwa's questions. Everyone was with someone.

"Everyone but me," she said, flopping back onto the bed. The familiar pain of her teenage years, alone, without her sister, clutched her heart.

"You have me." Khaldoon shimmered through the floor-to-ceiling hotel window. His glowing outline floated on the top of a building under construction.

"You're not a person, though, are you?" Luluwa retorted. She turned over to avoid his steady gaze.

"I am real, however." He appeared at the side of the bed in the same cast-off black trousers he'd worn when she'd first seen him.

"Why can't you wear some proper clothes?" she asked, scooting herself upright, her back against the headboard.

"They burn up," he said. "It requires much effort even to keep these on." She looked away.

"And that is only possible because these are what I drowned in."

She drew up her legs, resting her chin on them. "What's it like to die?"

"Ah." His breath came out in a warm whoosh, like opening an oven. "Those dark days are behind you now." Khaldoon sat on the edge of the bed. "You no longer have such thoughts."

A knock at the door kept her from asking how he knew that. Abdulla was the only one who'd witnessed her suicidal days, and no one in their Muslim society would ever talk about such things. Abdulla didn't judge her for having those feelings, because he'd felt much the same way in the months following Fatima's death. Luluwa opened the door cautiously, mindful of how on family summer holidays the boys would play tricks on her, saying it was one of her uncles, or—the other favorite—room service.

She jerked the door open. Of course, the boys were hundreds of miles away, but still likely up to no good.

Laith tripped as he entered the room. "Sorry, am I disturbing you?"

She put out her arms to stop him from falling. "Laith!"

"You were talking to someone?" He brushed himself off, looking around the room. "Sorry, I didn't mean to interrupt."

"Stop apologizing," she snapped, irritated yet again with Khaldoon. "What are you doing here?" she continued more calmly, moving on to the logical question in order to keep Laith from asking more of his own.

"I wanted to see if everyone was comfortable. I didn't have your number. Our grandfather's condition improved, and he checked himself out of the hospital."

"That's impossible," Luluwa said. His use of "our" rang hollow in her ears, coming from the mouth of this stranger. Lights flickered on in the streets below them as darkness fell across the city like a blanket. "Did you take him home?"

"No, that's why I'm here," he said slowly, as if speaking to a child. "I came to make sure you have everything he needs."

"He's not here," Luluwa replied at the same measured pace. They eyed each other.

"Benita has called him," Khaldoon said, raising his arm behind Laith's back. Bizarrely, his hand seemed to be missing. "We must go now."

"The boat," she said, closing her eyes. She pinched the bridge of her nose. "How could we be so stupid?"

"He couldn't have gone to the dock," Laith insisted. "Who would've taken him? No taxi driver should've picked him up in his condition, paying customer or not."

"Now, now, now," Khaldoon said. The shoulder socket where his right arm should've been appeared to be a gaping hole.

"Let's go." Luluwa grabbed her purse and threw on a pair of sandals.

"Should we tell—?"

"Hind is at her place, Ravi with her. Sangita needs her rest, and Abdulla will panic." Luluwa improvised, realizing there was no way to explain what she knew. "Let's get there and assess the situation. Then we can call for back-up."

"My car is downstairs." Laith raced down the hallway behind her, the carpet absorbing their thundering footsteps. "Why would he take this risk? He's so frail."

"He doesn't think he has much time left," Luluwa said.

"He is quite right," Khaldoon moaned. His left hand had now disappeared as well. "And he is not the only one for whom time is running out."

Laith weaved through the crowded parking lot to a black Mercedes convertible. The engine sprang to life with a growl. He put his hand on the back of Luluwa's seat as he reversed, bringing his profile within inches of her face.

In all the excitement she'd failed to notice the aquiline slope of his nose, so like their grandfather's, or the even whiteness of his teeth against his olive skin.

Laith maneuvered the vehicle into the narrow exit from the parking lot with ease. "To the dock?" he asked, interrupting her contemplation of him.

"The dock." She nodded.

Laith's phone buzzed on the dashboard. He glanced towards it.

"He must not get any closer to the boat," Khaldoon muttered from the back seat. "And I do not think you should sit so close to this gentleman."

"Not now," Luluwa said. *So I'm not the only one impressed by Laith's confident grip on the steering wheel.*

"It's probably Papa anyway," Laith said, "wanting to know where I am. He thinks I'm going to run away with one of you and never come back to India."

The realization that she was sitting next to a newly discovered cousin tingled through Luluwa's veins. "Do you want to leave?"

His eyes darted across to her. "A whole family I've never seen? Never known? At least for a visit, yes."

A first cousin, even if he was only a quarter Qatari.

"Pay attention to the task before us," Khaldoon warned.

In a car with a real cousin, and her jinni. She hoped that would be enough to face whatever the spirit Benita might throw at them.

Chapter Twenty-Nine

A blueish glow from lights across the harbor backlit the dock at night, as if someone had left a giant television on. Luluwa directed Laith to the area of the port where the containers loomed over the edge of the water.

"He doesn't have a pass," Luluwa said. "The security is very strict. He's probably sitting in a chair by the gate, waiting for someone to pick him up."

Jassim wasn't at the guard point, however. Two bored security guards, different from the ones who had eventually waved them through earlier that day, looked scrawny enough for Luluwa to outweigh them by at least fifteen pounds.

"Passes?"

"Have you seen an older man come through here?" Luluwa asked. "Did you let anyone through?"

The guard looked her up and down, eyeing her Converses and jeans. "We ask the questions."

"Answer her," Laith said. "We're looking for our grandfather."

The other guard crossed his arms over his chest. "Matter of security, sir. Company rules."

"Here." Laith shoved a wad of bills into each of the men's hands. "Tell us what you know."

Luluwa protested, expecting them to toss the money aside.

"An older man came through here with Mr. Jefferson. They went down about ten minutes ago."

"Let us pass," Laith said.

The guards looked at each other.

"Let us pass, and there will be more where that came from."

"If Mr. Jefferson finds out—"

"We only want to take the old man back to hospital," Laith said. "He's not well."

The older one gave a flick of his hand to indicate that they should board the platform. Luluwa's stomach clenched as they lowered toward the ocean.

"We'll find him," Laith said, patting her hand.

An electric current shot up her arm.

"Concentrate," Khaldoon reminded her. "I can smell Benita."

"Stop it," she said, shaking the feeling back into her hand.

"That wasn't me," Khaldoon said.

She squinted at him. In the humid night, the *jinni's* shimmering form appeared to have only one remaining leg.

They shuddered to a stop as the platform connected to the dock below. An army of scientists no longer crowded at the monitor, which stood blank against the inky night sky. No sign of the enthusiastic Professor Sri.

"There." Laith tugged her toward the yawning metal jaws of the cage. "How did they do that?" he asked in awe at the sight of the boat upright in a steel frame.

"*Yeddi!*" Luluwa called. A spotlight lit up their grandfather's frail frame. Next to him, his outline obscured in a black suit, stood the mysterious man—presumably Jefferson—who had passed them on the platform earlier that afternoon.

Jassim shuffling forward, the other man holding on to his elbow.

"No, no, no," Khaldoon groaned, and a shudder wracked his frame.

"Who's that?" Laith asked.

"You can see him?" Luluwa turned to Laith as Khaldoon buckled. They grabbed him, one on each shoulder as his other leg disappeared.

"What the hell?" Laith said.

"Over there." Luluwa cocked her head toward the wall of monitors. They hauled the upper half of the *jinni's* body across the platform.

"Keep the old man off the boat," Khaldoon wheezed. "Benita is calling to him. He will find her, and we will all be lost."

"Stay here with him," Luluwa said. She spun around, eating up the distance between herself and the man in black. "*Yeddi!*" This time Jassim turned, but his eyes looked past her.

"Lulu?"

"I'm here." She grasped his arm, jerking him away from the man in the suit. "Leave my grandfather alone."

"He asked me to bring him here."

"There she is," Jassim whispered.

They teetered at the end of the metal structure, which up close resembled a steel cage of intricate wires enclosing the ship.

"You're sure I can walk aboard?" Jassim whispered.

"*Yeddi,* no."

"Sign this, and you can explore to your heart's content." A pen glimmered silver, like a sword, against the black lapel of Jefferson's suit.

"Don't touch him," Luluwa warned.

Her grandfather held the paper up against the metal frame and signed, the pen tearing through, then he proceeded down the ramp toward the boat.

"What are you going to do?" Jefferson growled. He shoved her roughly aside, knocking her to the ground. She tasted blood in her mouth.

Laith skidded to a stop in front of them, panting to catch his breath. "You'll pay for that," he shouted at the man in black.

Khaldoon hissed in agreement. Without legs, he scooted forward on his stomach, undulating like a worm. "There," Khaldoon grunted.

"There what?" Luluwa said.

"Push that." He tilted his head toward a huge silver knob on the panel of levers that maneuvered the container surrounding the ship. "Now!"

Luluwa kicked at the knob. Her foot just grazed it. She kicked again; this time the ball of her foot connected with the lever.

"Khaldoon?" Silence enveloped her. Jefferson and Jassim disappeared below.

"Khaldoon," Luluwa whispered.

A deep rumbling vibrated beneath her. The ship rattled inside the metal encasement. As the vibrations increased, the entire shell slithered to the ground. Luluwa scooted backward as fast as she could, her tunic catching on a nail. Mud flew in all directions as the ship groaned above her.

"Luluwa!" Laith ripped the edge of her tunic free. They crab-walked as far back as they could on the platform.

"*Yeddi,*" Luluwa whispered.

The metal structure groaned again, like a living beast, shuddering as it sank into the ocean. Incredibly, the boat remained upright. A luminous white figure stepped onto the swaying dock, picking his way through the debris.

"He's alive," Laith said, squeezing her arm.

"Not for long if we don't stop him." Luluwa darted forward, running straight for the edge of the platform they'd vacated only a few minutes ago.

Laith clambered behind her, over and under the steel structure.

"*Yeddi,*" Luluwa called. Water lapped at her sneakers, coming up to her ankles within a few seconds. Her grandfather's white trousers were soaked to the knee. "Come back!" The wind tossed back her voice, like a playful child.

Laith ran ahead of her. The ship groaned when he stepped onto the steel girder.

"Don't let him touch the pearl," Luluwa said.

"Leave them be," Jefferson shouted, grasping at the edge of the platform.

"Leave us alone." Luluwa stomped on his fingers.

Jefferson gave a yelp, released his grip on the platform, and fell back into the water. The waves swallowed him in their watery embrace.

Chapter Thirty

Salty spray hit Luluwa on the cheek, causing her to sputter. She covered her mouth as, below, Laith and Jassim inched along the steel structure under-girding the dhow. Within minutes they were drenched, water running off their hair and clothes in rivulets. The earth rumbled. Vibrations sent the dhow tottering back and forth like a toy in the bathtub. Waves lapped higher and higher. Strips of wood fell off *Al Muhanna* as the trembling in the water increased. Without the protective covering of mud, the dhow could not withstand the elements, much less supernatural forces.

Jassim picked his way through his old boat as nimbly as a spider on a web, his jaw set in determination. Laith crawled behind at half the pace, bent over until he was almost on all fours, using his hands to grip as the ship twisted beneath them. Despite being in excellent shape, he wasn't as agile as the man three times his age.

Once a seafarer, always a voyager, Luluwa thought, her heartbeat thrumming in her ears. Jassim made his way along the lowest part of the boat, adjusting his balance as it tilted to the left. Maintaining his pace, he reached the middle of the ship first.

Jassim's lips moved rapidly. He raised trembling palms to the sky. Luluwa closed her eyes and said a quick prayer with him. To lose the same vessel twice—how would he be able to bear it? The ship creaked, bobbing in the water. Jassim lifted his foot and pushed it against the railing in front of him. A thunderous crack reverberated all the way to the platform, rattling Luluwa's teeth. Jassim raised his foot again, breaking the aged wood. He moved further down, and kept breaking up the edges of the ship to help her sink.

"She's here," Khaldoon said, his head floating at Luluwa's shoulder.

A blue bubble rose above the ship, round and magical like the ones they played with in the garden as children. Only this one was a harbinger of evil.

"Khaldoon," Luluwa cried, tears mingling with the salt water running down her face. "Do something!"

"Take me there," he said.

She pulled at the sleeves of her blouse, making sure there was a barrier, however thin, between them, then cradled the *jinni's* head in her arms. All that remained of him. After weeks of experiencing his presence as being as hot as a burning flame, his tepid warmth now felt more like a cup of half-drunk tea. She scooted on her knees toward the edge of the platform. A gust of wind blew them both back. Luluwa put out a hand to steady herself, clutching Khaldoon to her stomach.

"Closer," he said. "Throw me in."

"You'll die," she said.

"Now," he insisted. "Or all is lost for everyone you know." He pressed his lips against her arm.

"And you?" A clap of thunder swallowed her question. She yelped as Khaldoon's kiss turned into a bite. Freed from her embrace, he fell onto the platform and rolled toward the edge.

"Jassim," boomed a voice that resounded across the sky.

Luluwa froze in place as a vast figure rose above them, blocking out the moon and any sight of stars, rendering everything pitch dark. A cavernous mouth grinned, revealing teeth like stalactites.

"You thought you would trap me in that pearl," the towering phantom cackled as waves crashed against the boat. "Watch as I free myself forever." Her hands curved into sharp talons, sending bolts of lightning searing across the sky.

"Benita! Leave them alone!" Luluwa shrieked. She stamped her foot.

The imperious *jinni* shifted her gaze to the platform, squinting.

Luluwa gulped. She had to give Laith and Khaldoon enough time to sink the ship. Or die trying, if that was what was going to happen anyway.

"You dare to speak my name, girl." Benita surged forward, her face twisted in a scowl.

Luluwa ran for the other side of the platform. Water poured onto the rocking structure as it tilted toward the sea.

At last Laith reached Jassim. He enfolded the older man in his arms from behind, like an adult holding a child to watch fireworks. They braced themselves against the steel support beam as another wave rocked the entire length of the ship, obscuring them from Luluwa's view.

"Get back to where you belong!" Khaldoon shrieked, launching himself into the half-submerged ship. He plopped onto the deck, rolled into the corner, sparking as drops of water hit him, and then he burst into flames, igniting everything he touched. Tongues of fire sputtered in the corner, going from bright red to a dull orange and then to yellow.

Benita laughed, a booming sound that hurt their eardrums. "So much for your hero. Damned pest, keeping me down there for decades."

Luluwa held her breath until the tops of Jassim and Laith's heads became visible above the waves again. Her relief was short-lived, though, because her cousin and grandfather were dangling, panting, like a human offering, balancing against a metal spire. Her mind raced through the possible options, a pathetically short list of non-solutions. Could she try to get a rope to them, and haul one up after the other? You didn't need to be a first-class engineering student to calculate the odds of saving them like that. *Better to die together.* The old whispers from her sister's death bubbled to the surface, like the shards of *Al Muhanna*. She couldn't watch another person she loved die. She wouldn't be able to survive this.

Benita swooped toward Jassim and Laith. Waves buffeted the two men. "Humans, you are flotsam, scum," she crowed. "Let's see how you like being in the water for decades. Don't worry, the fish will pick your bones clean. What the—"

A curl of smoke rose behind her like a tail, snaking around her neck before enveloping them all in a dark cloud. Up on the platform Luluwa coughed, the air burning her lungs.

Below, the stern of the ship exploded in a ball of fire.

Benita roared as the fire raced the length of the wooden hull.

"Run," Luluwa screamed, though there was no way Laith could hear her above the roar of the burning ship. Flames licked upwards, skipping onto the edge of the platform. A blast of heat singed Luluwa as flames gobbled up the machinery along the wall and grew in strength. She took a deep breath and jumped off the edge, pulling her arms tightly around her legs as she had done in the pool at home in summertime.

Laith wrapped Jassim against him in a rescue dive position and jumped after her. They hurtled into the ocean, the waves swallowing them whole. The sound of sirens filled the air along with Luluwa's cries.

Chapter Thirty-One

She woke to the sound of steady beeping, persistent like an alarm. "I'm coming," she said groggily, pushing aside the covers. *What day is it? Do I have homework?* Luluwa stumbled against a metal pole and blinked in the harsh light. There was no dresser, no purple duvet cover, nothing familiar. A large bandage covered the right side of her face.

I'm in jail, she thought, falling against the bed. That beep again.

"Lulu, rest." Sangita loomed over her, a deep groove of worry forming on her forehead.

Luluwa opened her eyes wide and found an IV with a steady drip hooked up to her right arm. "Ohh," she said, fading back against the pillow. The last few hours raced through her mind like a rip tide: Khaldoon incinerating himself, Laith and Jassim facing off against Benita. What fools they'd been. Tears streamed from the corners of her eyes. *"Yeddo."*

"Yes," Jassim said.

"Oh God." Her nose ran. Sangita wiped at her face with a tissue.

He clutched her hand, his fingers squeezing her knuckles.

Luluwa looked up to see her grandfather standing, as if it were the most normal thing in the world, and smiling down at her. "But … you jumped. I jumped. Laith …" She struggled again to sit up, her head swimming. Both Sangita and Jassim pressed her back onto the pillows, ignoring a string of protests. "How is this possible?"

"Laith is a good swimmer," Jassim said. "Come." Her grandfather beckoned to a figure in the periphery of her vision.

"He's being kind." Her newfound cousin limped forward into focus, his arm in a sling. "The current brought us back to the platform," Laith said, with what she now recognized to be characteristic humility. "All we had to do was stay afloat. You did me a favor and hit your head, so it was easy to hang on to you. The old man though …"

The two men elbowed each other in mock outrage.

"We're all happy and alive, and what—" Luluwa's head spun. "You're all on the ceiling," she said.

"I'll get the doctor." Sangita hurried to the door. "Keep her awake."

Luluwa's eyes fluttered closed.

"Running off in the middle of the night," Abdulla said, squeezing her toe.

"After *Yeddo*," she protested, sitting up awkwardly. "He couldn't go on his own."

"That's the spirit," Abdulla said. "Stay alert. Stay angry."

Everyone laughed.

Her eyes skipped around the faces. "Benita is gone," she said, holding her breath.

"Yes," Jassim said. He sat on the edge of the bed, the twinkle gone from his eyes. "She will plague us no more."

"The fire …" Luluwa trailed off. She pawed at a strand of hair with her bandaged left hand and tried to flex her fingers. Under the thick white dressing, only four of them moved. Nausea rolled through her. "My pinky …"

"You'll carry the memory of this forever, I'm sorry to say," Jassim said.

"We burned that dock down," Luluwa said, to herself as much as to the others.

Hind came in with the doctor, who cleared his throat sternly at the number of people in the room. "Please, everyone. She needs her rest."

"Don't anybody leave," Luluwa said, her voice cracking. She might never want them out of her sight again.

The doctor studied her vital signs on the monitor. "Are we still standing on the ceiling?"

"Yes," Luluwa admitted, swallowing.

"Close your eyes, then. I'll give you something to help you relax." The doctor paged a nurse from the bedside table.

"Hind and Ravi are coming up with something to tell the authorities," Sangita whispered in her ear.

They were all getting more used to hearing those two names together.

Luluwa peeked through the screen of her eyelashes, scanning the room again. She turned to the window. One more person should be there celebrating with them.

"Seriously, with this much loss of blood I don't advise much effort," the doctor said.

Luluwa frowned at the room at large.

"Come on, let's let her rest," Abdulla said.

They each squeezed her shoulder, and relief swirled around the room as they left one by one. Jassim was the last to approach her.

"You should be in this bed, not me," Luluwa croaked.

The nurse came in and flicked the IV bag.

"I'm no longer sick," Jassim said. "As long as Benita was after me, I couldn't get better, but now I'm fine."

Luluwa's good hand worried at the bandage where her missing small finger would've been.

"Hands straight, please," the nurse said in a sing-song voice.

"He isn't here," Jassim said, brushing a kiss against her forehead.

"*Yeddi?*" Luluwa complied with the nurse's instructions as the doctor passed her a cup of water and a set of pills.

"He's gone forever." Jassim's eyes took her in. "Khaldoon."

She coughed at the sound of the name, some of the water going down her windpipe. The doctor and nurse frowned, but Jassim waved them away.

"You knew about him?"

"He warned me this day would come," Jassim said. "All those years ago. There would be a pearl of great price, above all worth, and he and I would protect her together."

The words took several minutes to sink in. "Her?" Luluwa blinked. "Me?"

"You," Jassim said, squeezing her elbow. The wrinkles that used to hang around Jassim's face, deep grooves that aged him beyond his years, were gone.

"There was no pearl?"

"The actual pearl was the prison that held Benita. Any effort to raise it would've released her and sent her looking for a new home."

"In me?" Luluwa said, realization dawning on her.

Jassim nodded. "In another pearl. And the pearl is safe." He smoothed the hair back from her forehead.

"All of this, the trip, the boat, everything, was about me?"

"You." Jassim pressed another kiss to her forehead.

"And Khaldoon?"

Jassim let out a deep breath. "He owed me a debt. Let him go. He wouldn't have found peace roaming the earth in love with a human."

Tears scorched the back of Luluwa's throat. "I could see him," she said.

Jassim stroked her cheek. "*Jinn* and humans are not meant to meet," he said. "Don't waste time grieving for what could never be when there's plenty we've been given right here."

Laith stuck his head around the door. "The car is here."

"Coming," Jassim said.

Luluwa gave her newest cousin a wan smile.

Laith returned it with none of his earlier shyness. "I'll see you later," he said.

She nodded, letting her eyes slide closed. *We did it.* Emotions swirled through her like the current that had smashed the dhow to smithereens. *We found the boat; we lost the boat. We had the pearl; we lost the pearl.* Images of ember-red eyes in a dark face glowed in her mind.

And the pearl is safe. The words lulled her into a deep sleep.

Glossary of Arabic terms

Aami – term of address for one's paternal uncle.

Aamti – term of address for one's paternal aunt.

Abaya – a black robe worn by women in the Arabian Gulf.

Agal – a black coiled circle of wool or cloth, used to keep a man's *ghutra* (worn over the head) from slipping.

Ajnabiya – a foreign woman.

Allah yerhamho/yerhamha – "God have mercy on him/her." Said in reference to a deceased person.

As-salaam alaikum – "Peace be upon you." The response is, "(Wa) alaikum as-salaam," meaning "(And) upon you be peace."

Baghlah – a type of dhow or traditional wooden ship of the Arabian Gulf.

Duaa – a prayer of supplication.

En sha'allah – "God willing."

Fajr – dawn, or dawn prayer, one of the five daily Muslim prayers.

Fatayer – small pastries, usually stuffed with meat, cheese or spinach.

Ghutra – a soft square cotton cloth folded diagonally into a triangular headdress, worn by men in the Arabian Gulf along with a circular black cord (*agal*) to hold the *ghutra* in place.

Hamar – an insult, roughly meaning donkey-driver, peasant.

Hamdullah – "Praise God."

Hamdullah as-salaama – "Praise God, (you've arrived) safely."

Khaleeji – adjective describing something of, or pertaining to, the Arabian Gulf

Kosha – lavishly, even theatrically, dressed stage set for the bridal couch where bride and groom sit and receive well-wishers.

Ma'a salaama – "Goodbye." Literally, "(Go) safely."

Machboos – a rich, spicy rice dish.

Majlis – salon, in both senses of sitting room and social gathering.

Ma sha'allah – a phrase used to ward off the evil eye. The literal meaning is "what God willed", thus attributing a blessing or positive attribute to God's will and not one's own deserving.

Shayla – a head covering worn by women in the Arabian Gulf.

Sheikh – term used in the Arabian Gulf for Muslim clergy or men of high status.

Shukran – "Thank you." "Na'am/la, shukran" means, "Yes/no, thank you."

Souq – market or bazaar.

Tabaaba – apprentice pearl diver.

Thobe – a full-length white starched robe with long sleeves worn by men in the Arabian Gulf.

Ubooy – name for one's father in the Gulf dialect.

Ummi – name for one's mother in the Gulf dialect.

(Wa enti,) tabeen? – "(And you,) would you like (some)?"

Wallah – "By God." An expression of surprise or affirmation.

Yeddo – word for grandfather in the Gulf dialect.

Yeddi – term of address for one's grandfather in the Gulf dialect.

Yella – informal expression meaning, "Come on, hurry up, let's go."

Yema – another name for one's mother in the Gulf dialect.

Yuba – another name for one's father in the Gulf dialect.

Zein – Okay, good, fine.

Family Tree

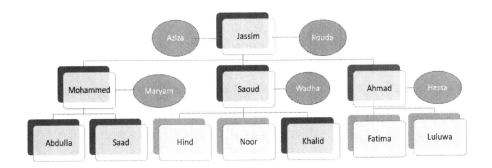

You're reading a writer who loves literary fiction. If you enjoy reading about people in overseas settings, consider signing up for my newsletter. In addition to updates, you'll also receive a free copy of the award-winning Love Comes Later about an unusual love triangle. I got the idea for the story from living in Doha, Qatar, a small country on the tip of the Arabian Peninsula.

http://mohadoha.com/newsletter/

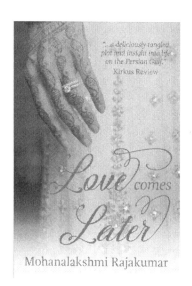

Mohanalakshmi Rajakumar is a South Asian American who has lived in Qatar since 2005. Moving to the Arabian Desert was fortuitous in many ways since this is where she met her husband, had two sons, and became a writer. She has since published eight e-books, including a momoir for first time mothers, *Mommy But Still Me;* a guide for aspiring writers, *So You Want to Sell a Million Copies;* a short story collection, *Coloured and Other Stories;* and a novel about women's friendships, *Saving Peace.*

Her coming of age novel, *An Unlikely Goddess*, won the SheWrites New Novelist competition in 2011.

Her recent books have focused on various aspects of life in Qatar. *From Dunes to Dior,* named as a Best Indie book in 2013, is a collection of essays related to her experiences as a female South Asian American living in the Arabian Gulf. *Love Comes Later* was the winner of the Best Indie Book Award for Romance in 2013 and is a literary romance set in Qatar and London. *The Dohmestics* is an inside look into compound life, the day-to-day dynamics between housemaids and their employers.

After she joined the e-book revolution, Mohana dreams in plotlines. Learn more about her work on her website at www.mohadoha.com or follow her latest on Twitter: @moha_doha.

If you enjoyed this book and have a few minutes to leave a review, you'll help more readers find stories like these.

You can also receive a FREE copy of Mohana's short story collection, *Coloured and Other Stories*, by signing up for her email newsletter: http://www.mohadoha.com/newsletter/.

Mohanalakshmi Rajakumar
www.mohadoha.com
@moha_doha
www.facebook.com/themohadoha

Before you start reading, check out the book trailer for any of Mohana's titles!
www.youtube.com/themohadoha

The Migrant Report, Book One, Crimes in Arabia series

The penalty for stealing is losing your hand. No wonder Ali can leave his wallet overnight in his office. Yet crime hovers on the fringes of society, under the veneer of utopia.

Police captain Ali's hopes of joining the elite government forces are dashed when his childhood deformity is discovered. His demotion brings him face to face with the corruption of labor agencies and also Maryam, an aspiring journalism student, who is unlike any local girl he has ever met.

Ali and his unlikely sidekick must work together to find the reason so many laborers are dying. Against the glittery backdrop of the oil rich Arabian Gulf, Ali pursues a corrupt agency that will stop at nothing to keep their profits rising. As the body count rises, so does the pressure to settle the source. Can Ali settle the score before the agency strikes again?

The Opposite of Hate

"....this is a book which lingered in my imagination long after I finished it, and offered an invaluable insight into Lao culture and its recent history."
--Kate Cudahy

During the 1960s and 70s, more bombs were dropped on a landlocked part of Southeast Asia than in any other war - and it wasn't Vietnam. The turbulent history of the Land of a Thousand Elephants, the Kingdom of Laos, is the backdrop for this family saga, told as a historical novel. THE OPPOSITE OF HATE opens a window onto a forgotten corner of Southeast Asia and brings little known history to life through vivid characters and settings which explore the cultural heritage of Lao history.

This is a tale of intermingled violence, love and ambition. Seng and Neela embody the historic cultural struggle of thousands who fled the threats of communism only to face the challenges of democracy.

The Dohmestics

"On the surface, it appears to be about six women whose lives intertwine, three are privileged women and three are their servants. But, there is so much more to this book."

--Aya Walksfar

Edna, Amira, and Noof are neighbors but that doesn't mean they know what happens behind closed doors or that they have anything in common with their hired help.

Maria, Maya, and Lillie live in the same compound as their employers but that's where the similarities begin and end.

There's never a dull moment for anyone in this desert emirate.

The unending gossip and unrelenting competition may be business as usual for expatriate communities but the unspoken secrets threaten to destroy life as everyone knows it.

Love Comes Later

**Winner of the Best Indie Book Award 2013, Romance
Short listed for the New Talent Award, Festival of Romance
2012**

"*Love Comes Later* is about love, choices, culture, bigotry, family, tradition, religion, honesty, forgiveness and friendship, to name just a few. The story allows a Westerner to actually see and feel what it is like to be a Muslim, with strong family ties, living in Qatar."

--*Diana Manos*

Hind is granted a temporary reprieve from her impending marriage to Abdulla, her cousin. Little does anyone suspect that the presence of Sangita, her Indian roommate, may shake a carefully constructed future. Torn between loyalties to Hind and a growing attraction to Abdulla, Sangita must choose between friendship and love.

From Dunes to Dior

**Winner of Indie Book of the Day September 2013
Witty, Intriguing and full of stories and curiosities worth
reading.**

"Which country in the Middle East is safe and hip and quirky? How does an ex-pat survive in a world completely unlike anything they know? Mo is one of those rare joyful writers who will walk with you through these answers."

--*Shariyousky*

Called everything from the world's richest to fattest nation, Qatar has been on the breakneck path towards change for several decades. The capital city Doha, is where our family of three has lived since 2005.

Mommy But Still Me

Enjoyable, honest, very real and funny

"… a funny and entertaining journal that takes you inside the upcoming changes of a working women who is about to embark in one of the most important journeys of her life: becoming a mum!"

--Alejandra

Imagine a man volunteering to trade in his game nights for heart burn and back ache. Good thing there are women around to ensure the survival of the species. This hilarious look at the journey from high heels to high blood pressure, as a jet setter turns into a bed wetter, is what your doctor won't tell you and your own mother may have forgotten in the years since she was blessed by your arrival.

So, You Want to Sell a Million Copies?

Helpful, informative guide every author needs!

"This book is such a helpful guide and is chockfull of tips, exercises, humor, and practical advice for any writer, whether you are just starting out or finding yourself consumed with the minutiae of daily living and looking for a way to get your ideas down into some form of structure."

--Rachel Thompson

If you've had a story idea in your head for a day, year, (or longer) that it doesn't seem to be writing itself, you may want to take a closer look at this book. Designed as a concise guide for aspiring writers, you'll find here the key principles of how to get started, keep going, and finish a manuscript, all told by a fellow accidental writer who took the long way developing a writer's formula.

Coloured and Other Stories

5.0 out of 5 stars **Brilliant short stories**

"The stories in Coloured are instantly absorbing- which is a triumph with short stories where the writer only has a limited number of pages to win you over."

--Phoebe

What's it like being the ant in the ice cream? The characters in this short story collection will show you. Experience life as they know it as transplants from across the world into American suburbia.

An Unlikely Goddess

Winner of the SheWrites New Novelist Award 2011
4.5 out of 5 stars
"When a title fits the book in every way with everything within the tale, its like the sprinkles on top of a cake"

--Cabin Goddess

Sita is the firstborn, but since she is a female child, her birth makes life difficult for her mother who is expected to produce a son. From the start, Sita finds herself in a culture hostile to her, but her irrepressible personality won't be subdued. Born in India, she immigrates as a toddler to the U.S. with her parents after the birth of her much anticipated younger brother. Sita shifts between the vastly different worlds of her WASP dominated school and her father's insular traditional home. Her journey takes us beneath tales of successful middle class Indians who immigrated to the U.S. in the 1980s. The gap between positive stereotypes of South Asian immigrants and the reality of Sita's family, who are struggling to stay above the poverty line is a relatively new theme for Indian literature in English.

Sita's struggles to be American and yet herself, take us deeper into understanding the dilemmas of first generation children, and how religion and culture define women.

Saving Peace

4 out of 5 stars

"I do not know whether to laugh, cry or throw my Kindle because of how this book ended."

--Suzie Welker

You go to college to meet your bridesmaids," or so the saying goes in North Carolina, on the campus of the all female Peace College. But what happens when the friends you thought you were making for life, betray you? The same ones you'd be in the retirement home with aren't speaking not ten years later? The ups and downs of women's friendships are tested in SAVING PEACE. Thirty years intervene in the friendships begun at the all female Peace College.

Sib, the local news anchor with dreams of going national. Mary Beth, the capable, restless mother of three. Kim, the college president who admits male students.
SAVING PEACE is the story of promises made and broken, love found then lost, and redemption sought for the past. Three women. Two choices. One campus.

What if there's nothing worth saving?

Please enjoy this complimentary preview of the award-winning novel *Love Comes Later*.

Prologue

Abdulla's mind wasn't on Fatima, nor on his uncles or cousins. Not even when he drove through the wrought iron entry gate, oblivious to the sprawl of family cars parked haphazardly in the shared courtyard, did he give them a thought. Despite the holy season, his mind was still hard at work. Mentally he clicked through a final checklist for tomorrow's meetings. *I can squeeze in a few more hours if Fatima is nauseous and sleeps in tomorrow*, he thought, rubbing his chin. Instead of the stubble he had anticipated, his whiskers were turning soft. A trim was yet another thing he didn't have time for these days, though longer beards were out of fashion according to his younger brother Saad, who had been trying to grow one for years. Beard length. Just another change to keep up with.

Change was all around him, Abdulla thought. The cousins getting older, he himself soon to become a father. Abdulla felt the rise of his country's profile most immediately in the ballooning volume of requests by foreign governments for new trade agreements. By the day, it seemed, Qatar's international status was growing, which meant more discussions, more meetings.

He slid the car into a gap in the growing shadow between his father's and grandfather's houses. It would have to serve as a parking space. The Range Rover door clicked shut behind him as he walked briskly toward his father's house, BlackBerry in hand, scrolling through his messages. Only then did the sound of wailing reach him, women in pain or grief, emanating

from his Uncle Ahmed's house across the courtyard. He jerked the hands-free device out of his ear and quickened his pace, jogging not toward the *majlis* where the rest of the men were gathering, but into the main living area of Uncle Ahmed's, straight toward those unearthly sounds.

The sight of Aunt Wadha stopped him short. Disheveled, her *shayla* slipping as she howled, she was smacking herself on the forehead. Then came his mother, reaching her arms out to him with a tender, pitying look he hadn't seen since his pet rabbits from the *souq* died. But it was Hessa, his other aunt – Fatima's mother, his own mother-in-law – who sent him into a panic. Ashen-faced, her lips bleeding, she was clutching the evil eye necklace he had bought Fatima on their honeymoon. At the sight of it, the delicate gold cord in Hessa's hands instead of around his wife's neck, Abdulla felt his knees buckle and the BlackBerry slip from his hand.

"What has happened?" he said. He looked from one stricken face to another.

Numbly, he saw his female cousins were there. At the sight of him, the older ones, glamorous Noor and bookish Hind, both now adult women in their own right, whom he hadn't seen in years, jerked their *shaylas* from their shoulders to cover their hair and went into the adjoining room. In his haste, he hadn't said "*Darb!*" to let them know he was entering the room.

"Abdulla, Abdulla..." his mother began, but she was thrust aside by Aunt Hessa. "Fatima," Hessa screamed, staring wildly at him. "Fatima!"

Rather than fall onto the floor in front of the women, Abdulla slumped heavily into the nearest overstuffed armchair. *Fatima...*

They left behind gangly nine-year-old Luluwa, Fatima's sister, who resisted when they tried to take her with them. His father, gray-faced and tired, entered. Abdulla slouched and waited, the growing dread like something chewing at his insides. His father began to talk, but on hearing "accident" and "the intersection at Al Waab" he remembered the Hukoomi traffic service SMS. Then he heard "Ahmed," and a shiver of horror ran up his back. The driver had been Ahmed, his uncle and father-in-law.

Later that night in the morgue, in the minutes or hours (he couldn't keep track) while he waited to receive her body, Abdulla flicked his Zippo lighter open and struck it alight. Holding it just so, he burned a small patch on his wrist just below his watchstrap. Even this couldn't contain his rage at the truck driver who came through without a scratch, at his uncle, or at himself.

The morgue was antiseptic, mercilessly public. The police advised against seeing her, insisting that he wouldn't be able to erase the memory of a face marked with innumerable shards of glass.

Surrounded by family and hospital staff, he couldn't hold her, talk to her, or stroke her slightly rounding stomach, the burial site of their unborn child. Any goodbyes he had hoped to say would have to be suppressed.

He would mourn the baby in secret. He hadn't wanted to tell relatives about the pregnancy too soon in case of a miscarriage. Now it could never happen: the need to visibly accept God's will in front of them would prevent him from crying it out—this woe upon woe that was too much to bear.

Fatima's body was washed and wrapped, and the prayers said before burial. His little wife with the round face and knowing eyes he'd grown up next to in the family compound, and the baby he would never see crawl, sleep or walk, were hidden from him now for all eternity. The secret she was carrying was wrapped with her in a gauzy white *kaffan,* her grave cloth, when he was finally allowed to see them. The child would have been named after Abdulla's grandfather if a boy, his grandmother if a girl, whose gender would now remain a mystery.

At the burial site, as was customary, he fell in line behind his father and uncles. Ahmed, the father, carried his daughter's slight form.

They placed her on her right side.

Men came to lay the concrete slabs that sealed the grave, so her frame would not rise up as it decomposed in the earth. Abdulla regretted not having been able to stroke the softness of her chin or the imperceptibly rounding curve of her belly. *I am burying my wife and our unborn child,* he thought, the taste of blood filling his mouth from the force with which he bit his cheek to stem the tears. Their secret would have to be lost within her lifeless womb. News of a *double* tragedy would spread with the sand under doors and into the ears of their larger circle of acquaintances. Someone would call someone to read the Qur'an over him. Someone would search out someone else for a bottle of *Zamzam* water from Mecca.

None of it would stop the acid from gnawing through his heart.

In swirls of conjecture and pity, his newly-assigned role as the widowed and grieving almost-father, would replace his role as the eldest grandchild in a fertile and happy extended family. His birth order had focused their marital intents on him. Caught between duty and tradition, he did the only thing he could do. He tried to forget that he had been too busy to drive Fatima that day, the day he lost a wife and a child because of his own selfishness. He had thought they had years ahead, decades, when they would have time to spend together. A chubby infant growing into a child who went to school, for whose school holidays they would have to wait to travel abroad, and eventually another child, maybe several more. Now none of this would ever be.

He should have died with them. But he kept on breathing—as if he had a right to air.

They returned from the funeral to gather at the home of the grieving parents for the ʿazaa, the receiving of condolences. Abdulla rode in the back seat of the Land Cruiser, his father at the wheel, his cousins and brothers messaging friends on various applications. For him there was no sharing of grief. This was his burden to bear alone.

He was the last to climb out of the car, but the first to see Luluwa hunched on the marble steps of Uncle Ahmed's entryway. The lines around her mouth, pulling it downward, aging her face, drew his attention; the stooped shoulders spoke of a burden heavier than grief for her sister. His mother saw it at the same time and hurried over to the girl, concerned.

"Yalla, what is it?" she said, pulling her up.

Luluwa shook her head.

"Go inside, habibti," said Abdulla's mother, but Luluwa shook free and drew back, panic in her wide eyes. Abdulla's mother turned her face back to the men. Then they heard the shouting.

"When? When did this all start?" Hessa's voice screamed, raw and startling, from inside the open door. "Leave this house."

The family halted in their tracks, exchanging uncertain glances.

Ahmed emerged, looking shaken but defiant, a weekender bag in one hand. Abdulla's father, the eldest of the brothers, stepped forward and took him by the arm.

"Everyone is upset," he whispered harshly. He was trying to lead him back inside, as his wife had done a moment ago with Luluwa, when Hessa burst forward into view, her face aflame with indignation.

"Tell them," she spat at her husband. "Tell them now, so when you don't come back here everyone will know why."

The words made no sense to Abdulla. His first thought was to speak up and still the voices. He had already forgiven Ahmed in his mind. The accident hadn't been his fault. "There's no reason to throw him out," he called out, half-climbing the steps. "It was my fault, not his. I should have been driving them."

Hessa turned towards him and laughed in a way that made the hairs on the back of his neck stand on end. "Who needs to throw him out when he's leaving?" she said. "Leaving his daughter to a house with no man to look after her. She might as well have died with her sister."

"Yuba, no," Luluwa cried, moving toward her father, but her mother grabbed a fistful of her abaya and spun the girl around by the shoulders.

Abdulla's mind whirred to compute what they were witnessing. A sudden white-hot rage stiffened his spine. His gaze narrowed on Ahmed. *So the rumors were true,* he thought.

"He doesn't want me and so he doesn't want you," Hessa hissed, nose to nose with her daughter.

The family froze in the entryway as understanding sluiced them like rainwater. Ahmed stood for a moment in the glare of their stares. He shifted the weekender bag into his opposite hand.

Saoud, the middle brother, stepped forward to question Ahmed, the baby of the family, but Hessa wasn't finished yet.

"Go," she screamed at her husband. "You'll never set foot in any house with me in it ever again." She collapsed onto the floor, her *abaya* billowing up around her like a mushroom, obscuring her face.

Saoud moved quickly to stand in front of his brother as his wife helped Hessa up. "Think of your daughter," she added pointedly. "The one that's still alive."

Abdulla brought Luluwa forward. Her face was tear-streaked and her body trembling so hard it was causing his hand to shake.

"Keep her, if you want," Ahmed said, his glance flickering over Luluwa's bent head. "My new wife will give me many sons." He sidestepped Mohammed and Saoud, continuing on down the stairs towards his car.

The look Hessa gave Luluwa was filled with loathing. She dissolved into another flood of tears.

The girl darted inside. Abdulla followed as his parents tried to deal with the aftermath of his uncle's leaving. His aunt looked as though she might faint. His cousins' faces were ashen. Mohammed and Saoud murmured in low voices about the best way to deal with their brother's child. She couldn't live in a house with boys; one of those boys, her cousins, might one day be her husband.

He followed Luluwa's wailings, sounds without any force, the bleating of a cat, like one of any number roaming the streets of the city. Without a male family member to look after her, she would be as abandoned as those animals. And, in the eyes of their society, as susceptible to straying. He found her on the sofa, typing away on her laptop, and hoped she wasn't posting their family's mess on the internet. Wedged next to her hip was an opaque paper bag stamped with their grandfather's name, the white tops of a few pill bottles visible.

Abdulla came and sat on the sofa next to her, unsure of what to do next.

He was assaulted by her screensaver, a photo of Fatima and Luluwa on the evening of the wedding reception. He hadn't yet arrived with the male relatives; the bride and the rest of the women were still celebrating without *hijab*. His wife's eyes stared back at him even as her sister's now poured tears that showed no sign of stopping.

With trembling hands Luluwa wrenched open the bag of medicine and dug around for pills. She let the laptop slip and he caught it before it hit the floor. As he righted it, the heading of the minimized Google tab caught his attention: *suicide*. For one moment he allowed himself to admit that the idea she was apparently contemplating had begun to dance at the edge of his own mind.

"Don't," he said. "What will we do if both of you are gone?"

He put the laptop aside and, as if calming a wild colt, reached out slowly, deliberately, to take the bottle from her shaking hands. With little effort he wrenched it from her, and with it any remaining shred of strength. She dissolved into incoherent sobs, a raging reminder of what it meant to be alive, to be the one left behind.

Abdulla folded her into his arms, this slip of a girl who used to hide his car keys so that her weekend visits with her sister and brother-in-law wouldn't have to end, this girl who had already lost so much, a sister and now a father and mother. Instead of shriveling into himself, as he had felt like doing from the moment he saw his family in mourning, Abdulla's heart went out to Luluwa. He murmured reassurances, trying to reverse the mirror of his own loss that he saw reflected in her eyes.

"We can do this," he said. "She would want us to."

She pulled away to look at him.

"Together," he said. From deep in his own grief he recognized the despair that would haunt him for years, and made a pledge to keep the decay he felt growing inside him from tainting someone so young. He would bear the guilt. It was his alone to bear.

He would speak to his father. If nothing else, perhaps Luluwa might gain a new brother, and he a little sister. Small comfort, but tied together in the knowledge of the loved one they had lost, a bond that might see them through what was to come.

79070516R00135

Made in the USA
Lexington, KY
17 January 2018